GOOD AS GOLD

Good as GOLD

SARINA BOWEN

Tuxbury Publishing LLC

PROLOGUE

TWENTY YEARS AGO

"Let's ride Devil's Dance next," Leila Giltmaker decides as they glide up the mountain on the chairlift. "The sun will have softened it up by now."

"Sure," Matteo agrees.

"Yup," Rory says.

"Yup?" Leila prods. "Rory, is that the proper way to address me today?"

"Yes, queen," he says sheepishly, while Matteo laughs.

On the way to the ski hill, Rory had lost a bet to Leila over which parking lots would be open today. Leila had been right, of course, and Rory had probably known it, but he'd stuck to his guns. He never liked to back down, even if it meant he'd have to do something ridiculous—like promising to call her "queen" all day.

There's a truthfulness to it anyway. Leila often calls the shots, and neither teenaged boy is too bothered by it. After all, she has good instincts. It was Leila who figured out that the waffle cart would give them a three-for-two deal at the end of the day, when the minimum-wage worker who manned the thing wanted to use up her batter and go home.

And it's Leila who has use of a car to drive their asses to the

1

mountain in the first place. Her family is more functional than either of theirs, by a factor of a million. The Giltmakers own several successful businesses in Colebury. Whereas Matteo and Rory are lucky to own second-hand snowboards and discounted ski passes.

So if Leila wants to pick the next ski run, that's cool. They're lucky to be spending their Saturday with the town's golden girl, and they both know it.

They're three in a row on the old triple chair—also Leila's choice—as opposed to the new high-speed quad. Sure, it's slower, and it makes a gear-grinding noise and smacks the backs of your knees as you sit down on it. But there's no line. And they don't need a fourth chair anyway. Three is the size of their little pack. They're the best snowboarders in town, and they spend every Saturday like this—gliding over the white terrain, the afternoon sunshine warming their black ski pants.

"Loser alert," Rory chuckles. "Two o'clock."

Sure enough, some guy in a full-body camo snowsuit is clenching his way across the slope below them. He's so nervous on his skis that he's dragging his poles behind him like brakes.

"Be nice," Leila chides. "Everybody starts somewhere."

But when the guy suddenly falls, both boys explode with laughter. Even Leila cracks a smile. She can't help it. The guy's spreadeagled on the snow like a bad cartoon and shaking snow out of his face.

"Tourists," Rory groans. "Can't run 'em over. Can't shoot 'em."

Leila knows that tourist dollars are the whole reason the mountain can afford to sell them fifteen-dollar student tickets. She doesn't point this out, though, because the old lift stops suddenly.

This happens whenever a kid falls down in the loading zone, and the lifty hits the red stop button. The whole contraption grinds to a sudden halt. But momentum makes their chair rock violently forward and then back again.

Leila feels her heart skip a beat as her snow pants slide an unwelcome inch toward the edge.

2

But Matteo's arm is already there, holding her firmly in place on the seat. "Going somewhere, Giltmaker?"

Her heart skips another beat, but it's different this time. "Nah," she says lightly. "I don't need a head start to beat you to the bottom."

"Ooh, fighting words."

The lift starts up again, and they glide forward. Matteo removes his arm, and Leila pretends not to miss it.

"We'll meet up at the half pipe?" she says as the chair arrives at the top.

"Of course," Matteo agrees. "Where else?"

She hops off the lift without another word. Thirty seconds later, she's speeding down the run, her long hair flying out from beneath the edge of her helmet.

At the top of the hill, Matteo takes an extra minute with his bindings, just so he can watch Leila ride. She catches a sweet little jump and grabs the board mid-flight like an X-gamer.

He laughs.

"What's so funny?" Rory asks, eyes following Leila as she disappears at the turn.

"Nothing. Ready?"

Rory doesn't move. He just frowns at Matteo. "You can't have her, you know."

"What?" He heard Rory just fine, and he knows exactly what he means. It's just that he's surprised to hear it said out loud.

"The Golden Girl will never go for you."

"Hey, no kidding." He understands it on a gut level—the same way he knows that a leaden sky over Vermont means that snow is coming.

But that's not the only thing he knows. "She'd never go for you either," he points out.

Rory snorts. "No kidding. But still—it's a deal, right? Neither one of us tries to get with her, and it doesn't get weird."

"Yeah, sure," Matteo agrees. He can't even picture either of them with Leila. She and her siblings win all the awards at school. Her family practically runs the town of Colebury. Their name literally means *gold maker*.

It isn't just family connections that set Leila apart, though. It's her *fire*. There are probably better words to describe it. But he doesn't know those words and wouldn't articulate them even if he did.

But it's Leila who pushed them both to compete in their first freestyle competition last month. Matteo won a bronze medal and an invitation to compete at the state level in March.

Leila won a silver in a slalom race, too. And now she's crafting a whole practice plan for both of them before the state competition.

Rory didn't win anything, and he's still salty about it. "We need a pact or something," he says. "Nobody dates Leila. It would wreck our whole vibe."

"True," he agrees. If his only two friends became a couple, he'd die. He really would.

"So it's a deal? You don't touch her. I don't either."

"Sure. Of course." Besides, as Rory already pointed out, she'd never go for the guy in the second-hand snow pants. The guy whose father is such a piece of work that he skips town for weeks at a time, forcing his mom to work two jobs and visit the food pantry.

Leila had been at his house once when the cops had called to say they had his dad in lockup. Matteo had wanted to die of embarrassment.

Making a pact with Rory is an easy decision. He'd never try anything with Leila. And this way, Rory won't either. He likes this plan.

So that's settled. "Let's go," he says. "Bet you can't get any air off that jump." He points at the spot Leila had soared from only a minute before.

"Bet I can."

And off they go.

CHAPTER 1
MATTEO
TWENTY YEARS LATER

APRIL

The speed limit on the narrow highway is fifty miles per hour, but I slow down as my rental car approaches Colebury. The sky is dark and cloudy, making the unlit road hard to see. And since I haven't been home in fourteen years, I'm not confident that I'll recognize the turnoff for my brother's bar.

I've almost reached the outskirts of town when my phone rings to the tune of "I Knew You Were Trouble." The rental car's screen says *Lissa calling*.

For a second, I consider declining the call. I only have two bars of service, and I'm in a hurry.

But I just can't do that. When a teenage girl who recently lost her dad calls, you answer. Day or night. Even if you're literally fourteen years late for a party.

I tap the screen. "Lissa? Can you hear me?"

"Omigod, Matteo. Where *are* you? I was going nuts! You didn't answer your phone. For *hours*."

Oh shit. "I was on a flight, honey. I didn't see that you called." The second I'd landed in Burlington, I'd high-tailed it to the rental counter.

"A *flight*?" she gasps. "God, I was *so* worried. When you didn't answer my calls, I went over to your place, and I banged on the door. I thought…" She hiccups. "After you canceled the last tours of the weekend… I had the *worst* idea." She lets out a sob.

Whoa. After a glance in the rear-view mirror, I step on the brake and pull over onto the shoulder. "Lissa, breathe. What is the matter? Did something happen?"

"No." She sniffles. "You left me a *note*, Matteo. It was kind of creepy."

"It was?" I'd written: *I'm sorry to miss our movie night. Love you lots.*

In what universe is that creepy? But then I'm struck with an awful idea. "Honey, are you saying you thought I might have…" I swallow. "…*killed* myself? Because that is *not* in the cards."

She lets out another sob.

Fucking hell. "Talk to me. Why would you think that?"

"You've been so depressed! And they tell us the signs at school. What to watch for."

I'm in way over my head right now. "Okay, listen up and listen good. I *promise* you that if I'm ever in a place that dark, I will do something smart about it. But I'm going to need you to promise me the same thing right now."

"Okay. I promise," she whimpers.

"Good." I scrub my forehead. "Look, I'm sorry to worry you. It's just that I decided last minute to take a trip."

"Where are you?"

"Vermont. My brother is getting married tomorrow. I wasn't going to come, but then I realized last night that I am a huge asshole…"

She lets out a watery laugh. "Not always, though."

"Thank you, I think. Anyway, I haven't visited my family in fourteen years. They probably hate me. They might not even let me in the door."

"That's not true!" she yelps. "Your sister loves you. Her kids are all over your refrigerator. And I met your mother once."

Those basic facts are true. When my sister had kids, I started talking to her regularly, and twice I've flown my mom out to visit. But I never once came home.

6

"Let's just say that it's not okay to be too busy to visit for more than a decade. So last night I got a wild hair and booked a flight. Then I started packing. My note to you was hasty, but I didn't mean to give you scary ideas." I'd slipped the note into their mail slot on my way out of town this morning, when Lissa was at school.

She snuffles. "Okay. I'm still mad you didn't explain. Mom is worried, too."

"Tell her I'm sorry. She's been on my case to go home, though. This is probably her fault, now that I think about it."

"Figures." Lissa giggles.

"Aw, don't tell her I said that." Poor Cara doesn't need another thing to worry about. It's been a devastating few months for all of us. In December, Cara's husband Sean—who was Lissa's dad, as well as my best friend and business partner—died in a snow-boarding accident.

None of us are over it. We'll never be over it. Four months later, I still see him every night in my dreams.

"I'm sorry I made you cry," I tell Sean's only child.

"Eh, crying is nothing anymore. It's like breathing."

I snort. Lissa always surprises me. I've known her for most of her life, and there has never been a single moment when she did what I expected her to. "Are you going to be okay?" I put my blinker on, look over my shoulder, and carefully pull back onto the highway toward Colebury.

"Yeah. Just don't *do* that again."

"Okay. From now on, with any travel arrangements I make, I'll text you the itinerary." Honestly, I'd do anything to make this child happy again.

It's partly my fault she lost her daddy.

"It's a wedding, huh? Do you have time to find a tux?"

"Heck no. I brought a jacket and a nice pair of khakis. This is Vermont. The dress code is dialed back a few notches."

"Which brother is this? Alec? The one who owns the bars?"

Lissa's memory is, as usual, bang on. "That's the guy. I'm on my way to one of his bars now. It's already ten o'clock here, and I didn't tell them I was coming, so I hope they're still there."

"You didn't tell them *at all*?" Lissa is incredulous. "You're going to make a big entrance? Way to bring the drama."

"Hey, it was last minute. But, yeah, they're going to give me a whole lot of shit when I finally show my face. Fourteen years is a long-ass time. Fourteen years ago, for example, you were still very attached to your pacifier."

"Sexy," she says.

I smile at the memory of a tiny little Lissa and her chubby-cheeked face.

"Why'd you stay away for so long?" she asks. "You weren't really too busy to go home. I've seen you spend entire weekends playing *Call of Duty*."

"I don't really know," I say with a laugh. If you want to hear the truth about yourself, ask a teenager.

"Was it because of a girl?"

Another bark of laughter.

"It was, wasn't it?" All of a sudden, her voice is bouncy and full of mischief. Like the old Lissa. "Who is this girl? Did she dump you?"

"Nobody dumped me." It comes out sounding defensive. "Good effort, Lissa. But you're not on the right track here."

And, yeah, I just lied to a child. Oops. There *had* been a girl, but she'd never been *my* girl. And that's just the way it is.

Still, it made coming home feel impossible. I didn't want to see the happy couple together.

"*Sure*," she says in a wizened, disbelieving tone.

"The GPS says I'm almost there, baby girl. Hope I can find this place. Wait—there it is."

I shouldn't have worried. The old mill building is brightly lit, and just a short distance from the road. This building had been abandoned when I was a teenager. I'd probably never looked twice at it.

"Well? First impressions?" Lissa demands.

"It's cool. More impressive than in the pictures I've seen on the family chat." The brick walls of the three-story renovated mill building rise handsomely against the nighttime sky. And the first-floor bar—the Gin Mill—is signed in cheerful neon and fronted by a crowded parking lot.

Nice work, Alec.

"Send me a selfie of your wedding outfit," she says. "I need to approve it."

"Sure, kid. Tell your mama hello for me."

"I will. Have fun, Matteo! Be safe, okay?"

That's something she always says to me now, and it breaks my heart a little to hear it. "Of course. Night, honey."

We disconnect as I pull into a parking space. There are actually *two* businesses sharing this lot—the bar, and a coffee shop called the Busy Bean. The coffee shop is my sister Zara's project. It's closed now, though, so I'll have to sample it tomorrow.

I climb out and lock the car. But then I stand there in the parking lot for another moment, just stretching my legs. And stalling. I don't know what kind of reception I'm about to receive.

Fourteen years is a long time. I've missed so much. I have a niece and a nephew I've met only on FaceTime. Three of my four siblings are entrepreneurs of businesses I haven't visited. And my youngest brother is a cop. I've never seen him in uniform.

When my mother asks me why I don't come home, I've never given her a good reason. I always tell her that it's hard work running a business. That the distance is too far. That I'm not good at taking time off.

Lies. I take plenty of time off. I just don't take it here.

I gulp down a breath of Vermont nighttime air. It smells like melting snow and pine trees. I wonder what life would have been like if I'd stayed here in Vermont. Would I co-own a bar with Alec? Or run a taxi service with my brother Damien?

The weird thing is that if you'd asked me four months ago who the most successful Rossi sibling was, I would have said me. I wouldn't even have hesitated. And on paper, it's probably true.

But Sean's death was a harsh dose of reality. Financial success feels pretty meaningless now. The truth is, I've missed my family.

I guess it's time to find out if they've missed me, too.

Walking toward the door, I hear music and laughter. I raise my eyes to the darkened upstairs windows. Alec shares one of those

9

apartments with his fiancé, May. And my youngest brother, Benito, just moved out of the other apartment and into a house he bought with the love of his life.

My family is killing it in all the ways that count, while I'm a goddamn wreck. But here goes nothing. I yank open the door, the way you pull off a Band-Aid.

After stepping inside, it only takes a couple moments to understand why the Gin Mill is a success. It's a big, friendly space. A sleek bar stretches along the lefthand wall, with a line three deep to reach the hardworking bartenders. To the right is a sea of high-top tables and a few booths. There's a jukebox against the far wall and a dartboard, too. Everywhere, people are talking and laughing, heads bent close, drinks in hand.

I left Vermont at eighteen, haven't been back to visit since I was twenty-two, but I've never felt like an outsider until right this second.

This ugly thought is broken when I spot my brother Damien. As soon as he catches me watching him, his eyes widen comically. I read "holy shit" on his lips as he passes through the crowd to greet me. "Matteoooo! I almost didn't recognize you. What's with the Jesus hair?" He waves a hand toward my head.

I run a self-conscious hand through my shoulder-length hair. "The women like it, and it saves money on haircuts."

He snorts. "Doesn't look like the money is a problem. Designer jeans, huh? You look like a tourist from Connecticut!"

My first thought is: *I am a tourist.*

My second thought is to slug him in the arm. "So the tourists from Connecticut have gotten better looking since I left?"

He laughs. "Let's get you a beer. Or is it champagne these days? What do expensive dudes with long hair drink?"

"Anything." I have never needed a drink more than I do right now.

"Hey, bartender!" Damien calls out, while I take in his buzz cut and the flannel shirt that is basically a uniform in Vermont. Damien is about fifteen months younger than I am. We're the eldest of the five Rossi kids. And I haven't been in the same room with him since he was a scrawny twenty-one-year-old.

"This stranger needs a beer," he says.

The bartender in question looks up. And, wow, it's my youngest brother, Benito. He was only eighteen last time I saw him. Now he's a strapping giant. Benito doesn't work here—he's the cop. But I guess he's filling in tonight so that my brother Alec can enjoy his own bachelor party.

Ben looks at me and lets out a hoot of laughter. "Who is this asshole crashing the party? Do we even know this guy?"

"Yeah, yeah. Very funny." I knew I'd take a beating. Hell, I deserve it.

Benito puts two fingers into his mouth and whistles. "Hey, Alec! I've got a new joke for you! Jesus walked into a bar…"

From the center of the crowd, my brother Alec—the guest of honor—whirls around to spot me. His eyes narrow. "I'm too young to meet Jesus!"

Everyone howls, and then I receive a series of back slaps and hugs while they talk over each other.

"Holy shit."

"I know, right?"

"Can't believe he made it."

Enough already. "But I said I'd try."

"Yeah, but we've heard that before," Alec says darkly. "At this point, we literally expect nothing."

"Ouch." I guess Alec is still angry. "Can I come to the wedding, though?"

"Yeah," he agrees. "Happy to have you." But his eyes don't look that happy.

"How about I buy a round?" I offer. "Can I crash on someone's couch tonight? Tomorrow I'll find an Airbnb or something."

"The first beer is on the house for designer Jesus," Benito says from behind the bar. "You look like Ralph Lauren in that suede jacket. Is ale okay?"

"Sure. Pour me something interesting." I ignore the dig about my clothes. I like nice things—it's not a crime.

He passes me a pint glass of a deep amber ale. "This is the original Goldenpour by our friends at Giltmaker. The foamies drive hundreds of miles for a pint."

I've read about this. After years of making beer as a passion project, Lyle Giltmaker hit the bigtime. "This beer won an award, yeah?"

"*All* the awards," Alec says. "It's like a fucking *cult*. There are lines down the block on tasting days at their brewery. Two pack maximum at the store—when they're not sold out."

"That's pretty impressive," I say, taking a sip. And the ale is terrific—really fruity and interesting. It's easy to see what the fuss is about.

"Hey, did you hear about the divorce?" Alec asks me.

"Saw it on social media," I say. Not like I could miss it. Lyle Giltmaker's wife made a big post when she left him.

After forty years of trying to make it big, the brewery is on top of the world. All that time I've been hoping that success would make it possible for Lyle to think about something other than beer. But apparently it doesn't work that way.

Guess the old man just learned that success isn't everything.

I feel for the guy.

My brother is still talking about beer tourists and cult brews. But every time he says "Giltmaker," I think of my old friend—Lyle's daughter, Leila. She used to be one of the most important people in my life.

I glance around the bar, checking for familiar faces. It's wild to see so many people from my past in one spot. But Leila's face is the one I'm really looking for.

I don't see her, and I'm both relieved and disappointed. Seeing everyone again is taking great reserves of emotional energy that I don't really have.

And Leila? Yeah. I might have to work up to that one.

"Want to play darts?" Alec asks me. "We're fixing to have a friendly tournament. Fifty dollar buy-in."

"Sounds like a shakedown," I point out. "But sure, dude. I will lose at darts in honor of your wedding."

"Don't they have darts in Colorado?" Alec asks, steering me toward the board.

"Yeah, but I haven't had time to play." He doesn't need to know that I spent much of the last four months lying on my bed in the dark, trying to understand how my best friend died, and wondering what I could have done about it.

I'll always wonder that.

I take another sip of excellent beer and follow my brothers toward the dartboard.

CHAPTER 2
LEILA

I have very mixed feelings as I enter the beautiful brick church in the center of Colebury. Of course I'm happy for May and Alec. But my own wedding happened inside these walls. And look how that turned out?

So pardon me if I have a whiff of PTSD whenever I hear a string quartet playing Pachelbel's Canon in D.

The ceremony will begin in just five minutes, but I still pause on the threshold of the sanctuary to straighten my spine and lift my chin. Then, with my shoulders back, I walk in alone.

Everybody knows by now. People have been whispering about it all over town. I can almost feel the eyeballs swiveling towards me.

She left him, they might be whispering. *He's devastated*.

I still feel guilty sometimes. And if I get my wish, the town will have plenty more to gossip about in the coming year.

But I'm ready for it. I'm braced. And I'm dressed to kill, in an eye-catching peach Boho dress with a chrysanthemum pattern and a triple-tiered skirt. The V-neck is provocative but stops short of scandalous. I've paired it with strappy heels, earrings strung with clusters of seed pearls, and a collection of thin, little, gold bangle bracelets. So let 'em stare.

And if my ex is in this church, let him stare, too.

"Bride, or groom?" the elderly usher asks as he hands me a wedding program.

"Mr. Vespucci," I whisper, scandalized. "It's a really small town. Are you seriously asking me to choose sides?"

"It's a tradition, Miss Giltmaker." He chuckles. "I don't make the rules."

I give him a wink and then take the program he's offering me. Then I proceed down the aisle.

The bride—May Shipley—is a lawyer, and an acquaintance of mine. Her family are lovely people. They grow apples and make award-winning cider from their picturesque orchard on a hilltop.

But I feel a stronger connection with the groom's family, so I slide into a pew on the right, amid the friends and extended family of the Rossi clan. Maybe it's because my father does business with the Rossis. Or maybe it's because I like a good underdog story.

The Rossis had it tough for years. Without her wayward husband's help, Maria Rossi raised five kids on nothing but hard work and sheer grit. She had four sons—all of them stupidly handsome—and a fun-loving, rule-breaking daughter.

These days, the Rossis are pillars of the community. Except Matteo, of course. My former best friend is the groom's brother. I say *former* because I haven't seen his face in fifteen years. He left home right after his high school graduation and barely ever came back.

Just like his father people whisper sometimes. But that's not really fair. At least, I hope it isn't. The Matteo I knew was serious about loyalty. He felt things deeply. He looked after the people who mattered to him.

Until he didn't anymore.

When I was a teen, I thought he was the most glamorous boy I knew. Maybe that says more about my teenage expectations than his sophistication. But he was always cool in a way that money can't buy, with his serious frown and his knowing gaze. He could build a fire with nothing but some scraps of wood and a piece of flint he carried in his pocket. He could find his way out of the woods by looking at the stars overhead. And he learned to land a

15

frontside alley-oop in the halfpipe before the rest of us had mastered it.

When he finally skipped town after my junior year of high school, I was so mad at him I cried. Although I thought he'd be back. He'd told me he would. There was even a moment there after he left when I thought he'd come back for *me*.

But clearly I was hallucinating. Because he eventually just dropped me as a friend. He stopped returning my calls. He faded from my life.

I'm still mad about it, if I'm honest. When I flip open the wedding program and skim the list of names of the wedding party, I'm not the least bit surprised to note that Matteo's is not there.

The last time I tried to contact him was about twelve years ago. I'd sent him a wedding invitation, but I didn't have the right Colorado address, and it was returned to sender.

Perhaps I could have asked his family to forward it, but Rory had told me to drop it. "He doesn't want anything to do with us," he'd said.

I hadn't questioned it, hadn't argued. That was on-brand for me at the time, unfortunately. There were so many things in my life I should have questioned—like my relationship to Rory, for example.

He loved me in his own way. Not that it was a good way. He *needed* me, though, and I fed on that. It was intoxicating to be so important to another human, I guess. And my family hated him, and it gave me a rebellious rush.

Those are all terrible reasons to marry someone, though.

Ask me how I know.

The string quartet changes their tune, breaking my reverie as a hush falls over the crowd. All eyes swivel toward the door, where the processional is beginning.

It's been a while since I've attended a wedding, and I'd forgotten the communal hush that falls over the crowd. The held-breath moment as we ready ourselves to witness something rare —big promises made. Lives merged.

The first one to walk down the aisle is the mother of the

bride. She's beaming. Next comes the flower girl. Nicole is a cute little redhead, almost four years old, who attends my preschool. She's the groom's niece. She stops in the middle of the aisle, plunges her hand into the basket of rose petals, and then hurls them onto the red rug before marching onward toward the front.

The whole church chuckles.

Alec, the groom, is next. He's a handsome, clean-cut guy, and when I catch sight of his smile, I feel a little thump of emotion in the center of my chest. Because his eyes are clear and bright, and his smile says he just won the lottery.

I honestly don't think anyone has ever looked at me like that. My husband sure didn't. In fact, Rory was high during our wedding ceremony all those years ago. Red eyes. Bleary expression. That was on-brand for him, too.

I'd been so ashamed, but I'd smiled through it. I'd known we weren't the perfect couple, but I'd gone through with the wedding, because I thought I could fix him. *Love will see us through*, and all that.

I'd like to revisit my twenty-two-year-old self and shake her. Fixer-uppers are fine for houses, but not for men.

The procession continues. There's Officer Benito Rossi, walking down the aisle with the bride's sister. And next comes Damien, the tallest, thinnest Rossi brother. On his arm is Lark, the bride's best friend.

My eyes move back one last time to the bride's sister-in-law, looking ravishing in a pink dress. And on her arm...

My blood suddenly stops circulating. The man accompanying her down the aisle isn't listed in the program. Nope. This man is a ghost—a specter my mind conjured and brought to life today.

He must be. How else would Julian Matteo Rossi be standing right there, only feet from where I sit. And not the scruffy, twenty-year-old version from my memories, either.

Nope. This model is the fully formed mid-thirties edition, with long hair and ridiculously broad shoulders. He comes equipped with smile lines and the deep tan of a man who spends a lot of time outdoors.

17

That swagger, though. Now that's familiar. And so is the flutter in my belly.

Hell.

Before I'm ready, Matteo passes me and I'm treated to a view of his equally illustrious backside. If you think about it, it's the view he's shown me way too often—the one I get when he's left me behind.

I guess I'm still salty about it. And if he knew he was coming to town for this wedding, he could have given me a head's up.

But—wait—maybe he called Rory instead. If that's the case, my ex probably gave him an earful about what a bitch I am. How I'd moved all my personal belongings out of our house while Rory was away on a guys' weekend, and then asked May to serve him with divorce papers the moment he got home.

It was a little cold, I'll admit. But you don't reason with Rory. If I'd sat him down for a big talk, he would have ended up stomping around, red-faced and yelling.

After that, the begging would start. And the promises. But I just couldn't take it anymore.

I close my eyes and take a deep breath. It's bad karma to think about your divorce during someone else's wedding. Just because I married the wrong man doesn't mean this happy couple is making the same mistake.

When I open my eyes again, the wedding party is assembled on the dais, and Father Peters asks everyone to rise.

As I stand, I am very careful not to stare at Matteo. Or wonder how long he's been in town and why he hasn't called me.

The first lovely strains of the Wedding March echo through the church, and May appears in an ivory wedding dress.

The guests make a happy noise—like a cross between a coo and a sigh. May is beaming as her elderly grandfather takes her arm. The two of them proceed toward the altar. Their progress is slow, but I've never seen anyone look so certain in her *life*. My friend is almost floating through the church, as if drawn toward her groom by a gravitational pull.

And—whoa—now I'm blinking through tears. Apparently, I'm

not entirely dead inside. There must be a little teaspoon of romance left somewhere in my body.

May climbs two carpeted stairs to reach her rightful place beside Alec. She passes her bouquet to her sister, and Alec takes both her hands in his.

My heart shimmies with joy. This unlikely surge of optimism is like a drug that I didn't even know I needed.

I let out a happy sigh and take my seat again with the rest of the congregation. "Dearly beloved…"

I make it, oh, ten seconds or so into the ceremony before my traitorous eyes wander from Father Peters and right over to Matteo.

Who's staring back at me.

When our gazes collide, his doesn't slide away the way I expect it to. If anything, it intensifies. I get lost in it for a long beat. His broody stare is a thing of beauty. The girls at our high school used to giggle about it.

And now it's directed at me? For a moment all I can do is stare back.

But then I remember I'm still mad at him, and I yank my attention back to the bride and groom.

Matteo has some explaining to do if he thinks he can just swoop into town without even a phone call.

CHAPTER 3
MATTEO

Weddings last forever.

At least it feels that way. After I spot Leila in the crowd, time slows down to a crawl, and it's a struggle not to stare at her. I can't stop cataloging all the things that are familiar—like her high cheekbones and thick brown hair with soft waves that tighten into curls when it rains.

The Golden Girl is still the most beautiful thing in the room.

Then my eyes dip to the low neckline of her dress, and I want to slap myself. Partly because she's married to the guy who used to be my other best friend. And partly because I packed those feelings away a long time ago.

Some things just weren't meant to be, no matter how badly your teenaged self craved them.

I made my choices. I left town, thinking I was the smart one. I craved success and validation. And it worked for a while. I had a big life, full of shiny new adventures. But look how that's turning out?

Rory was the smarter man all along. He stayed behind and married the best woman in Vermont.

It hurts me to think about it, so I try not to. The two of them as a couple will never make sense to me. Some of that is simple jealousy. I'll admit it.

Okay, a *lot* of it is jealousy. But still—I never considered myself good enough for Leila. My eyes find their way to her pretty face one more time. She's sitting perfectly still, her back straight, her eyes alight. There's just an energy to her that I've always been drawn to.

A decade and a half hasn't dimmed that. Nor my attraction to it.

It's going to be a long night.

————

My plan for after the wedding is to find Leila and to find the bar, not necessarily in that order.

I didn't count on photos. In fact, I had no earthly idea that agreeing to the last-minute request that I stand up for my brother in his wedding meant that I'd be posed in eighty-seven different shots afterward.

"Stop scowling," the bride says, poking me in the ribs. "Just two more, and then you can have some barbecue and a beer."

"Yes, ma'am."

"That's better. Where did Grandpa go?" she asks, looking around.

"He escaped after the first group shot," my brother tells her. "Sorry. He mumbled something about appetizers and hitched a ride down the hill."

"Smart man," I say under my breath.

"All right." May claps her hands. "I changed my mind. We're done here! Let's party."

A whoop goes up among the bridesmaids and groomsmen.

"See? I always knew you were cool," I mumble as I loosen my bowtie. And my brothers laugh.

She smacks my arm. "Interesting timing you've got, showing up in Vermont now."

I have no idea why people keep saying that to me.

But at least it's time for beer.

————

Alec's reception is at his *other* bar. Speakeasy is less than a quarter mile downriver from the Gin Mill, and it has an upstairs space that's meant for parties. There's a dance floor and a band on the second floor, and they're setting up a meal downstairs in the main bar and dining area.

"Goddamn, this place is cool," I say as I eye the converted mill with its brick walls, heavy wooden floors, and original beams. "Must have been a pricey renovation."

"You own, what, eight percent of this place?" Benito asks me. "Don't you get the quarterly updates?"

"Sure, but that doesn't mean I read them." My investment is small. "Looks like Alec is doing fine without any input from me."

"Uh-huh. Don't look now," Benito says. "But Leila Giltmaker is giving you the evil eye."

"Oh, where?" I lift my chin and look for her. "I owe both of them an apology."

"Both of them?" Benito asks.

"Yeah. Her and Rory. Where are they?"

"Huh," Benito says. Then he claps me on the shoulder. "This is going to be interesting."

Before I can ask why, Leila appears at my elbow. She holds out a hand, as if to shake. "Nice to meet you. I'm Leila, friend of the bride and ex-friend of one of the groom's brothers. The brother who disappeared and never came back and stopped replying to my texts right around the time that texts were invented."

"So it's going to be like that. All right." I shake her hand. "Nice to meet you, Leila Giltmaker. I'm Matteo."

"But we call him Designer Jesus," Benito says.

That's when I tug her forward and pull her into a hug. "Hi, honey. I'm *sorry*, okay? I'm a terrible person and a total idiot. I'm sorry I didn't call you or come home."

My apology is going well until I make a fatal error, which is to inhale. Her perfume smells like oranges and flowers, and the heat of her body against mine stirs a longing inside me that I haven't felt in a long time.

Stepping back, I take a look at her expression. Still grumpy. But maybe a little confused too. "Damn it all. I didn't expect you to actually apologize. If I stay mad now, I'm a bitch, right? Well played."

Benito laughs. "Infuriating, isn't he?"

I don't need his commentary, so I take Leila's hand and lead her onto the dance floor, where the four-piece band is playing their first slow song.

She doesn't immediately cooperate. She stares at me for another beat, before finally slipping a hand onto my shoulder. "You weren't even in the wedding program," she says. "Last minute addition?"

"Actually, yes." I sway to the music and smile at her. The song is "Perfect" by Ed Sheeran, and the band does it well. Good pick for a wedding, but I'm dying a little inside.

During high school, I never once asked Leila for a slow dance. I didn't think I could take three minutes in close contact like this—not without revealing how I felt about her.

And, yup. Torture. Her deep brown eyes at close range. The pretty dress. The soft lighting.

Then I realize that she's asked me a question, and I've forgotten to answer it. "I, uh, decided it was time to come home. Bought a last-minute ticket and showed up last night at the bachelor party."

"Oh." She gazes up at me, her expression a mix of surprise and confusion. "I see. Surprised they even recognized you."

"Yeah, yeah. You're not the only one to tell me I'm a dingus. You're not even the meanest. Maybe you should try harder. Just a suggestion."

Her mouth twitches again. But then she sighs. "I'm awfully mad at you."

"I imagine." I twirl her around in a circle. "You look amazing, though. This dress is fire." My gaze dips briefly to her cleavage, because I'm only human. "Guess I shouldn't say that. Rory will probably slug me. Where is he, anyway?" I drag my gaze away from temptation and scan the crowd.

No Rory. Huh. When I look back at Leila, she's narrowed her eyes at me. "He isn't here. I doubt he was invited."

"Oh." That's odd. "No plus-ones allowed?" That doesn't

sound like May and Alec at all. Unless the fire marshal gave this room a strict capacity.

Leila stares. "You really have been gone a while."

"Yeah, I think I just apologized for that. What's your point?"

"Matty, I *left* Rory. I didn't bring him to the wedding because we're no longer married."

"You…what?" I stammer. Because I could swear she just said they broke up.

"Our divorce was final a week ago. I'd assumed everybody knew that, since he had a drunken meltdown in the middle of the Gin Mill the night it was finalized. He sat at the bar and cried. Everybody is talking about it."

"*Oh,*" I say as my mind tries to come to grips with this news. So many things make more sense right now—like the way people keep asking me if I heard about the divorce and saying things like, *your timing is so interesting.*

But now I'm fucking up again, because "oh" is probably not the right response when your one-time best friend tells you she divorced your other one-time best friend. "I'm sorry to hear that," I try.

Leila's eyes flash. "So was Rory. But I just couldn't stay. You'll have to trust me on that."

"Oh, I'm sure. I meant—I'm sorry for your troubles."

Her expression softens by a few degrees. "Thank you."

"I had no idea," I blather. "None."

"I'm getting that." She gives me a hint of a smile.

"What did he do?" I demand. "Do you need me to kick his ass?"

I'd been joking. Mostly. But she gives her head a sharp shake. "There will be no ass-kicking. Just don't repeat whatever bullshit he says about me. I don't want to know."

"Deal. But I'm not a gossip, Leila. Whatever happened between you, it's none of my business."

Her eyes dip. "Thank you. I appreciate that."

"Hey. Chin up," I say, as if I have any right to give out pep talks while my own life is a dumpster fire. But I would do anything to cheer up Leila. "I heard there's going to be some excellent chow at this party."

I step a little closer, stop dancing, and just hug her again.

She freezes for a split second. Then sort of melts into my embrace. "I heard they also have liquor. And I don't even have to drive home."

I laugh into her hair, which smells amazing. "Why? Where are you staying?"

The song ends, unfortunately, and Leila takes a healthy step back. "I'm renting from your brother. Benito and Skye just bought a house."

"Oh. So it's *you*."

"What do you mean?"

I snort. "I thought I'd be able to crash at Benito's apartment, but I've been told I'll have to stay in a camper on my uncle's farm."

"Sorry." She smiles. "It's a really nice place, too. I signed a one-year lease."

"Well, good. I'm glad you had somewhere to go. And I won't be staying long, anyway."

"Oh." A flash of something like regret flashes through her eyes. "Just a quick vacation?"

"I'll be here a couple weeks. Figure it will take me that long to catch up with everybody."

"Yeah, I bet." She crosses her arms, and I absolutely do not notice that it enhances her cleavage even further. "You were away a *long* time. Like fifteen or sixteen years."

"Uh, yeah." It's actually fourteen, but I have my reasons for not correcting her. There's one trip home she can never know about.

"Who's the angriest at you?"

"I am!" my mother says, swooping in to wrap her arms around me. "It's me. I'm super mad." She starts kissing my cheek like a deranged person.

"Mom! Jesus."

Leila laughs.

"The meal is served, you two." Mom releases me. "Go downstairs and get yourselves a plate."

Now that's an idea I can get behind.

CHAPTER 4
LEILA

I can't decide how I feel about hanging out with Matteo again after all this time.

He steers me downstairs to the buffet, taking care to place himself behind me in line like a gentleman. We load our plates with ribs, brisket, and coleslaw. Mashed potatoes with garlic and chives. Homemade cornbread.

"What a spread," he says. "Let's find you a seat, and then I'll score us some drinks."

"Okay. Thanks."

He's making it very hard to stay angry at him. I'm a little annoyed at myself for that. Men have a habit of walking all over me, and I have a habit of forgiving them. It's kind of a pattern.

But you can't growl at a man who pulls out your chair at his family's table and asks very politely whether you'd prefer beer or cider. I choose the cider, and I wait patiently as his mother, two brothers, his sister, and various spouses gather around the table.

Matteo and his uncle Otto take the last two seats, and then we all dig in. Otto is the first to speak. "Matteo, I have a proposition for you. There's some work that needs doing around here this summer. Your family could use your help."

Zara—Matteo's sister—laughs. "Brace yourself, big brother. Fourteen years of odd jobs coming your way."

"The man owes us," Otto says, and he's not joking at all. "He's been off in Aspen, partying, getting soft, while the rest of us have been building something good in this town."

Whatever Matteo has been up to in Aspen, *getting soft* was not on the list. I can't help but notice how well the man fills out a dress shirt. And when we were dancing, I found that hard body *very* distracting. As usual.

Seeing him again is both wonderful and terrible. And so confusing.

Across the table from me, Zara rolls her eyes at her uncle, and I try to focus on the conversation. Otto is kind a of a hard-ass. He's one of my father's business partners, which tracks, because my father is also an unforgiving man.

Mrs. Rossi shakes her head at Otto. "You catch more flies with honey, Otto."

Matteo doesn't seem bothered by his uncle's words. He takes another bite of barbecue, chews slowly, and then responds. "I could stay a couple of weeks, I suppose. What do you need me to do?"

Otto doesn't get a chance to answer, because the bride and groom approach the table arm in arm, and we all turn to fuss over them. "How's the food?" May asks.

"Wonderful, honey," Mrs. Rossi says. "Can I make you a plate? You two should eat, too."

"We'll eat in a bit," Alec says. "We wanted to make the rounds first."

"This is a nice place, guys," Matteo says, indicating the room. "Well done."

"Glad you could drop by and see it for once," Alec says, his smile slipping off his face.

Uh-oh. I guess I'm not the only one who's still a little mad at Matteo.

"I'm glad I could come, too," Matteo says, not taking the bait. "If I'm still around after you two get back from your honeymoon, I'd love to hang out."

Alec scowls. "We'll see. But if you *really* want to make amends, you could do a few shifts behind the bar. The schedule is a night-mare while I'm away on our honeymoon."

"Sure," Matteo says immediately. "I'm in."

Alec blinks. "Huh. Okay. Damien is in charge while we're gone." He nods at their brother across the table. "Speak to him."

"I'll do that."

May pats her new husband's arm. "Come on. Unclench your teeth so we can say hello to the Nickels and Father Peters." She nods toward another table. "Then I want some brisket."

Alec's expression softens for his bride. "All right. Let's go."

They move on, and Matteo's sister pokes him in the ribs. "I have a job for you, too, big brother. Can I get in line?"

He hefts his pint glass. "Sure, lady. Take a number. Anyone else?"

The whole Rossi family starts talking at once. They're teasing Matteo and putting in requests. Benito wants his car washed. Damien asks for style tips. "Can I look like fancy Jesus, too?"

Matteo rolls his eyes, and I try not to laugh.

I've missed this. I've missed Matteo's brand of oldest-sibling exasperation. I've missed this rowdy family and the way they tease each other.

When I woke up today, I'd been dreading this wedding. I'm not used to being the black sheep—the ungrateful bitch who divorced Rory. That's what he wants all our friends to think of me.

Who knew Matteo would roll into town and replace me as everyone's favorite gossip nugget? They'll be talking about him for weeks, especially if he's pouring drinks behind his brother's bar.

I take another excellent bite of food and congratulate myself on my good fortune.

Life is always a little more exciting when Matteo is around. It's just true. And it will be tempting to park myself on a bar stool at the Gin Mill to watch him work. Just like the lust-filled teenager I used to be.

I'm too old to lust after Matteo. I have more pride than that now.

Probably.

I guess we'll find out.

CHAPTER 5
EIGHTEEN YEARS AGO
MATTEO IS 17

Matteo tries not to fidget as Lyle Giltmaker flips through the business plan he'd printed out today at the public library.

Mr. Giltmaker hasn't said anything yet, but Matteo is already sure that this was a stupid idea. Leila's father is never going to lend them the money they need to start their business.

But he let Rory talk him into this moment of humiliation anyway. "All the man can say is no."

That's true, although Rory is conspicuously absent. Rory'd had a reason for that, too. "He thinks I'm trash. You need to be the one to ask."

So it's Matteo who's sitting in Mr. Giltmaker's office, sweating through his shirt. Giltmaker Industries is housed in an old mill building. It's obvious that this spacious room has always been a rich man's office, with its floor-to-ceiling bookcases and its enormous walnut desk.

Matteo likes the space but finds it intimidating. Sitting behind the desk, Lyle frowns down at the pitch deck that Leila had helped him edit.

It's April, and graduation looms not even two months away. Matteo knows that he's not really college material, and he doesn't want to join the military like his younger brothers are planning to do.

His uncle Otto wants him to work on the farm, and that doesn't feel like quite the right fit, either.

Starting a business together was Rory's idea. "You have the smarts, and I have the charm. We'd be a good team. And if we own our own business, we won't have a boss riding our asses. We won't have to answer to nobody."

"*Anybody*," Leila had corrected him.

Rory had rolled his eyes. "All we need is enough money for a used van, and a set of tools."

The actual business idea had been Matteo's. It's right there on page one of the business plan Mr. Giltmaker is reviewing. *Boards and Blades: a mobile ski and snowboard sharpening service*. In a van, they could drive around to the luxury mountain homes that dot the area ski towns and sharpen skis for folks right there in their driveways.

Leila had squealed when he'd hit upon this idea. "Ooh! White-glove service," she'd said. "I like it."

Now Lyle sets the papers down and nails Matteo with a stare. "Not a bad idea, kid. And you seem motivated to succeed. But I can't just hand you five thousand dollars."

"I understand, sir," Matteo says. And he does. Who'd give *him* five large? When Lyle looks across the table, he probably sees a loser from the wrong side of town. One who sometimes catches himself staring at Leila's mouth, wondering what it would be like to kiss her.

"But here's what you do," Lyle says. "Go find a guy who has a business that's a little like yours. Maybe it's a ski shop in a wealthier town. Maybe it's a guy who works on high-end bikes. Find that guy and work for him for a season. Learn what he knows and which problems keep him up at night. Talk to his customers. Get some wisdom. Then find *another* guy and work for him, too. After that, you can come back here and ask me for *ten* grand, and I'll invest with you."

Matteo blinks. "Yeah, okay. I hear what you're saying. That's really good advice."

Lyle laughs suddenly. "Hell, if only my own kids could say that. Even once." He hands the proposal back to Matteo. "Save this and read it again after your first season of work. I bet you'll spot ten things that weren't quite right about this draft."

"Thank you. I'll do that." He rises to leave, feeling much better about the rejection than he'd expected to.

"Oh, and Matteo?" Lyle says before he reaches the door.

"Yes?"

"Find a better business partner than that Werner kid. Don't hitch your wagon to just anybody, yeah?"

"Uh, hmm," he says awkwardly. "Thanks again for, uh, reading this."

"My pleasure."

Matteo heads outside to where his friends are waiting in the gravel parking lot.

"Well?" Rory demands. "Did you do us proud?"

"Sort of," he says, collapsing onto the hood of Rory's beater. "He says we need more experience first."

"Fuck *that*," Rory sneers. "That's just a brush-off."

"Sorry," Leila says quietly, concern in her eyes.

"No, it's all good," Matteo says, sending her a quick smile. "What he said made sense."

Lots of sense, actually.

All the sense.

CHAPTER 6
LEILA

It's Friday night, and I'm lying on my couch reading a steamy book. That's what passes for excitement in my life these days.

Suddenly my phone pings with a text, and I put down my paperback to grab it.

As soon as I see the name, my heart deflates.

RORY

What size lightbulb fits above the mirror in the bathroom?

I roll my eyes, not that there's anyone here to see it. But I get these needy little queries from him all the time, and they make me feel surly.

On the one hand, it doesn't take much time to answer.

LEILA

40 watt, candelabra base.

But Rory's inability to behave like an adult was the core problem in our marriage. And, apparently, it's still my cross to bear.

I pick up my book again and try not to think about the other man who was supposed to call me this week. "I'd like to see you again before I go," Matteo had said after the wedding.

That had been six days ago, though, and there's been no word from him. As a matter of principle, I haven't gone into the Gin Mill to check up on him. Okay—I did *once*. Last night I ordered a pizza to go, and naturally looked around the place when I went in to pick it up. But Matteo wasn't there. His brother Damien was behind the bar with another one of the regular bartenders.

In my defense, I live over the bar. It's not like I drove out of my way to look for him. And in Matteo's defense, he has a big family. I keep reminding myself that he needs to prioritize them.

But there's no denying how hurt I'll feel if he disappears to Colorado again without calling me. We still need to catch up. I have questions. The night of the wedding, Matteo looked tired— all the way to the bone.

What's up with that?

When my phone finally rings, it startles me. I throw down my book and grab it, my tummy fluttering when I see Matteo's name on the screen. "Hello?"

"Hey, Leila. What are you up to?"

"Doing a little reading."

"You always were the smart one. Always reading."

Yeah, I guess that's true. Except back then, I was reading different material. These days I read only two kinds of books—the ones about how to get pregnant after your thirty-fifth birthday, and the ones like I'm reading tonight—a book about a billionaire who's secretly in love with the waitress at his favorite restaurant.

In fact, Matteo's call has come at a rather unfortunate moment. The billionaire and the waitress are just about to bone for the first time in the back of his limo.

"What's on your mind?" I ask.

A strange gurgle comes through the phone's speaker. "Okay," he says, "funny story. I'm at Zara's place. She and Dave went away for an overnight. They left me in charge."

"Wait. You're *babysitting*? Both kids?" I suddenly form a mental picture of Matteo holding a baby. And, sue me, he's shirt-less in this particular fantasy. If I ever saw that in real life, my ovaries might actually explode.

Before he can answer, I hear a baby's whimper. "Yeah," he says with a sigh. "And I did a fine job tucking in Nicole. She's asleep in her bed. But the baby is another story. Zara says he's usually asleep by eight, but…"

I glance at the clock. Nine thirty. "But?"

"But every time I put him down in the crib, he screams like he's on fire."

"Let me guess—when he cries, you pick him up again. And then the cycle repeats?"

"*Exactly*. Kid's lungs are great. I'm afraid he's going to wake his sister. Or the neighbors will call 911. Got any tips? This is kind of your area of expertise."

Blame my dead social life. Blame my steamy book. Or my baby fever. But I blurt, "You need some help?"

His voice is a sexy scrape. "You know I do. If you can get this kid to sleep, I'll call you queen for a week."

I snicker. "Fine. I can be there in five. No…ten."

"Bless you, your highness. You know where Zara's place is?"

"Actually, I do." Zara and Dave once held a party to raise funds for the preschool's scholarship program, so I've been to the house.

He sighs. "I keep forgetting that I'm the only asshole who doesn't know where the members of my family currently live. See you in ten? I can probably sing 'Itsy Bitsy Spider' a few more times before I drop dead of exhaustion."

"Hang in there. See you in a few."

We hang up, and I go racing for my closet. The truth is that I could probably get there in two minutes, but I'm too vain to hang out with Matteo in sweatpants and an old T-shirt printed with: *I can do anything. Except reach the top shelf. I can't do that*.

I exchange those clothes for a low-cut sweater, tight jeans, and little silver earrings with moonstones. Then I spend a couple minutes refreshing my makeup.

Let's not examine my motives. Nothing good will come of that.

Before heading out the door, I grab a bottle of wine and a bag of spicy cheese puffs. I climb in my car and make the short trip.

Zara and Dave's house is just up the hill and around the Colebury Green.

Matteo opens the door as I walk up the driveway. One of his strong arms is cradling Micah, who's ten months old.

Is there anything hotter than a big, strapping man holding a baby? No. Definitely not. As predicted, the sight causes my ovaries to dance a jig. I can't decide where to put my eyes. On the rugged man wearing a waffle-knit hoodie that stretches across his muscular chest? Or the snuggly baby in polar bear PJs?

"Look, buddy! Reinforcements," Matteo says as he ushers me inside.

"No progress, huh?" I toss my jacket onto a leather armchair in Zara's gorgeous living room.

Her husband is loaded, so they could probably live in a mansion. Instead, they've renovated their historic three-bedroom Tudor in the center of town. With its brick fireplace and antique wooden moldings, it's a lovely family home—the kind I'd hoped to live in at thirty-five.

"What am I doing wrong?" Matteo asks. "His diaper is dry. He refuses his bottle. I've tried everything. Well, everything except admitting defeat. My mom and my brothers are blowing up my phone asking me if I got the kids to sleep. I think they're taking bets."

I laugh, because it's so easy to picture his family doing that. "Hang on—don't you think that's a sign? I think they know something you don't. Maybe he doesn't like to go down for strangers."

"Maybe," he says with a handsome frown. "How should I know?"

"Let me have a chat with him. May I?" I hold out my arms.

"Be my guest. But, uh…" He gingerly extends the baby toward me. "I'm terrified of dropping him. He might be the first baby I ever held for longer than ten minutes."

Micah is a burly ten-month-old and not exactly fragile. But it's cute that Matteo is worried about him. "He can probably sense your unease." I take the warm, solid little guy into my arms, and he gazes up at me.

Wow. What a cutie. He has his daddy's dark red hair, and it's a little curly. He blinks up at me with sleepy brown eyes and a slightly put-out expression. Then he lifts both chubby fists and rubs his eyes.

"Somebody's overtired," I announce.

Matteo rolls his own set of handsome brown eyes. "Aren't we all. So why doesn't he just go to sleep?"

"Show me his room."

"Yes, queen."

He leads the way up the stairs. At the top, he enters a cute little nursery. There's a crib and a rocking chair made of blond wood, and a fuzzy rug covers the wood floor. A nightlight emits a warm glow on the windowsill.

I carry the baby in a slow lap around the room. "Okay, sir. I know you're disoriented. You're used to bedtime going a certain way. Mama isn't here, and that's a problem for you. This change in personnel was not pre-approved, right? And you would like a word with the manager."

Matteo snickers. Micah coos.

I begin to sway from foot to foot, and then I whisper, "The thing is? Everything is just fine. There's no reason to be afraid. Mama loves you. She's just out for the night with your daddy. He loves you, too."

With one hand, I begin to pat his back.

The little guy sighs. He rests his cheek against my shoulder. After a few minutes, he closes his eyes.

"You are magic," Matteo whispers.

"It's just confidence," I whisper back. "Want to finish the job? Just rock him in that chair and talk to him until he passes out. Then lay him down in the crib."

"Okay, sure." He sits down in the rocker and holds out his hands. "I need the bragging rights."

"Just tell him everything is all right. He'll believe you." I lean down and place him onto Matteo's chest. "When you think he's asleep, count to two hundred before you make the transfer."

"Yes, queen," he says softly. Then he winks.

At the door, I turn around for one more look. Matteo is rocking

SARINA BOWEN

slowly, his head tilted back, his body relaxed. He's rubbing the baby's back with a soft, circular stroke.

The sight gives me an honest-to-God ache behind my breastbone. I'm thirty-five years old, and this will never be my life.

That's on me. My own choices are to blame. I know this.

But it still hurts.

CHAPTER 7
MATTEO

"She's right, you know," I tell the baby after Leila leaves. "Everything is fine. Your mama will be back tomorrow, right after breakfast. If you sleep through the night, I'll let you watch some trash TV in the morning. I heard *Sesame Street* is your favorite."

Micah sighs again.

"Leila is pretty smart, yeah? I've always thought so. Shoulda called her an hour ago."

He'd been so fussy all evening. But the moment I'd handed him to Leila, the little guy had relaxed. Like, *finally, someone knows what she's doing.*

It just figures that the key to getting a baby to sleep is having the confidence that the baby will sleep. Life generally works that way.

And lately, confidence is in short supply. Micah probably understood this on a gut level—that his life was in the hands of someone who does not have his shit together.

But now his eyes are closed. Really closed. He's breathing slowly and deeply. I keep rocking for another few minutes. I don't want to fuck this up.

Besides, he's so cute like this. His round face is peaceful.

My mind wanders, and suddenly, I'm picturing Sean's face. That happens a lot lately—my dead friend pops into my thoughts, and I feel a little stab of pain.

Sean was a great dad. When Lissa was a baby, he held her all the time, often in a sling on his chest. He made it look easy, like so many other things. We even took her to the bar like that occasionally. We'd enjoy a quick pint while Lissa cooed at the women standing nearby.

I'm grateful Sean got those moments with her. But now he won't get to see her graduate from high school. Or meet her prom date. Or help her pick a college…

I swallow the lump in my throat and stand up slowly. Micah sleeps on.

Supporting his little body so he doesn't jostle, I carefully lay him down on his back in the crib.

I'm actually holding my breath as he adjusts his head on the sheet, screwing his eyes shut and wiggling his chubby arms into little goal posts.

But he doesn't wake up.

Stealthily, I pull my phone out of my pocket and take a dimly lit pic of the sleeping baby. Then I text it to the family chat.

MATTEO

Took me a while, but I got there.

By the time I turn off the lamp and tiptoe out of the room, my phone is already lighting up with congratulations.

DAMIEN

Wow, stud! So impressed.

ALEC

There's twenty bucks I'm never getting back. For sure I thought one of you would have to go over there and bail him out.

BENITO

We used to be impressed when Matteo seduced the girls. Now we're congratulating him on getting a baby to sleep. Is that progress? Or are we just not cool anymore?

ALEC

Speak for yourself. I'm the coolest.

When I get downstairs, I'm relieved to find that Leila is still here. In fact, she's in the kitchen opening a bottle of wine. "All good?" she asks.

"Yeah, thanks to you. Don't rat me out to my brothers, okay?" I show her the chat, and she laughs.

"I would never. Besides, you closed the deal."

"With coaching." I lean in and give her a one-armed hug. "Thanks. I needed that."

She turns to me with a warm smile. "Wine?"

"You think it's okay?" I glance toward the stairs. "I'm kind of on duty."

"Unless you've become a super lightweight in the past decade, I think a couple glasses are fine."

I take the glass she's poured me and thank her again. "Come and sit down with me. Didn't you also bring those spicy cheese puffs?"

"Of course. I'm still a big believer in snacks. Not everything has changed around here since you left."

I guess it hasn't, because I'm still wildly attracted to Leila. Maybe even more than I ever was before.

That's the real reason we can't get drunk together. I'll probably blurt it out, like an idiot. Even when I was a lovesick teenager, I'd managed not to do that.

It's kind of a miracle, really.

We go into my sister's generous living room and sit on the sofa. Leila kicks off her shoes and plunks down next to me.

"I thought you'd be out tonight," I tell her as she opens the cheese puffs and puts two napkins down on the coffee table. "Living the single girl's life."

She sniffs. "Like I'd even remember how that works. A lot of my friends are at home with their own children."

"Yeah? That's one thing I love about Aspen—there's always a party somewhere." Even if the partygoers are starting to look like kids to me.

"I can't even imagine." She eats a cheese puff and offers me the bag. "Can I ask you something?"

"Anything."

"What's wrong?"

A cheese puff stalls on its way to my mouth. "With me? Not a thing. Especially now that Sir Screams-a-lot is sleeping."

Leila tilts her head to the side, as if considering my answer. She sets her wine down on the coffee table and turns to me on the sofa, tucking her feet underneath her body, and the action is so familiar that I'm hit with a powerful wave of nostalgia.

"Try again," she says quietly. "I've known you a long time. And while I'm glad you found a reason to pop in for Alec's wedding, I can tell that something is going on with you. Do me the honor of not lying about it."

Shit. I guess Leila is still smarter than pretty much everyone else I know. I take a sip of wine to stall. "It has been a terrible year, and it's not that much fun to talk about."

"Oh, please. I recounted all my embarrassing troubles to *you* the other night. That was super fun."

I laugh. "Fair."

"So." She pats the sofa. "Spill the tea. What's got you looking so exhausted? Bad breakup?"

"Nah. It's actually worse. My business partner—and best friend—died in a snowboarding accident. And I was there to witness it."

She takes a sharp breath. "Oh honey, I'm *sorry*."

For some reason I shrug. As if that would make it less tragic. My throat is as dry as dust. There's a reason I keep this stuff to myself.

"How did it happen?"

Because we're both idiots. "We ride a lot of big-mountain terrain, yeah? A lot of it is pretty wooly. Sean was kinda famous in Aspen for riding stuff that other people feared. But…"

I stop and take a fortifying sip of wine. The thing is, picturing Sean on a mountaintop always used to make me smile. He had years of grand adventures and good times.

Until the day he didn't.

"He used to be the guy who'd poke you at the top of the run and ask, 'Think I should try that chute?' And I'd always give my honest opinion. Sometimes he listened, sometimes not. But he was just, like, *magic* on a snowboard. He could do things that other people only dream about." I shake my head. "And he had no ego, either. He didn't enter competitions. He just wanted to ride on powder under a blue sky and tell you stories in between runs."

"Sounds like a good friend," she whispers.

"The best. We worked for the same company. And then, a couple years in, he said, 'Let's start our own business. What do those guys have that we don't?' And I said, 'A helicopter that costs millions of dollars.'"

Leila laughs.

"But it turns out you can lease helicopters and you can hire pilots. Our big lucky break was buying a piece of land nobody wanted outside Aspen town limits. We needed a remote spot and approval for our helipads. That piece of land would probably cost two million now. But we had good timing and a dose of Sean's good luck."

I'm smiling now, even though I'm about to get to the depressing part. "Anyway—there was this particular peak we always liked to ride, but only on one side. The back of it was too hairy for paying guests. It had a mean chute right in front of a crevasse. It looked jumpable, but nobody had ever attempted it. The locals call it No Man's Run…" When I glance at Leila again, she looks scared. "You sure you want to hear this?"

She swallows hard. "Yeah."

I take a deep breath. "Last December, Sean heard that a crew of Canadians was going to film one of those guys taking first tracks on No Man's Run. So he said, 'I'll beat 'em to it. You can film it from the bird.'"

Leila watches me with deep, sad eyes.

My chest feels tight now. I put down my drink. "I could have told him no, but I didn't. He knew as much about safety as anyone, right? We'd just had a lot of snow, and of course he did some avalanche tests at the top. Those came out okay. But…" I take a deep breath. "I told him, 'I got a bad feeling about the snow pack. What if you let the kiddies have it?' And he just grinned and said, 'I got this, Matty. Make sure you get good video.'"

Leila puts her hands in front of her face. But then she takes them down. "He was a grown man, right? He made his own call?"

"Yeah. Forty years young. But I'd talked him out of some of his worst ideas before." I swallow hard. "Anyway, it looked good for a minute, there. The top part of his descent was textbook. He came through the chute, no problem. He made two nice crisp turns, and then he lined up for the jump. The crevasse was only about eight feet across, but…" My voice breaks on the last word.

I see it in my dreams every night. Sean approaches the rift. He bends his knees for the takeoff. And then the ground shifts beneath him. The moving snow pushes him right over the edge, and he vanishes, right before my eyes.

"He was just gone," I rasp, my voice stolen by emotion. "Fell eighty feet down. Took them three days to recover his body."

Leila lets out a heavy breath. "This was *not* your fault."

"Yeah, tell that to his sixteen-year-old daughter."

Her eyes grow wide. "Oh, *God*. Does she blame you?"

"Not really." I shake my head. "But she should. I was just hanging out above him in the helicopter, filming it and thinking —*This is going to look so badass on our website*."

Again, I try to clear my throat. But it will never be clear again.

"Matty," she says softly. "I'm sorry."

"Thank you. I'm sorry, too." That's the response I've honed over the last four months. Because I *am* sorry. Except there isn't a single fucking thing I can do about it now, except try not to run our company into the ground. "His wife and I still own the damn business. But we canceled most of our season after his death."

"Oh, Jesus," Leila whispers.

"Yeah. Helicopter leases aren't cheap, and now we have cash-flow problems. So if I look exhausted, now you know why."

She sets down her glass, rises up onto her knees and wraps her arms around me. "That's a lot."

I take a deep inhale, and the scent of her perfume socks me in the chest. My sleeping libido raises its head off the floor, perking up. She smells like flowers and feels like a goddess in my arms.

Fuck.

All too soon, she eases away and pours me another glug of wine. "Thank you for telling me."

"You're welcome." The weird thing is that I actually feel a little lighter. "Hey—want to watch *Meet the Parents*? For old time's sake?"

Her face breaks into a beautiful grin. "You know I do."

CHAPTER 8
EIGHTEEN YEARS AGO
LEILA IS 17. RORY AND MATTEO ARE 18.

Leila and Rory are at a bonfire.

It's October, and they're standing in a clearing in the woods that's this year's best party spot. The cops haven't discovered it yet, because the clearing isn't visible from the road. The fire is crackling, and the keg somebody paid their uncle to buy for them still has beer in it.

A stupid sophomore has sacrificed his truck's battery in order to play music from the stereo, and kids are dancing in the dying evening light.

Leila isn't enjoying herself, though. She's holding her red Solo cup listlessly and leaning against a hemlock tree. She's seventeen, and her senior year of high school has just begun.

It's her year to rule the school, but everything feels wrong, because Matteo left town last week. And Leila hadn't seen it coming.

Sure, he'd talked about going out west. She'd known he'd been serious, but she hadn't thought he'd leave *now*. The ink had barely dried on his high school diploma when he'd lit out of town.

"Hey."

She looks up to find Rory standing beside her. "Hey."

He crosses his arms. "I thought you liked this song."

"I do," she says, even though she hasn't registered what was playing.

46

"Then why are you making this face?" Rory makes an exaggerated hang-dog face.

Leila only shrugs. She doesn't want to explain herself.

"He'll be back," he says. "You know that, right?"

She blinks. "Sure. Of course."

"He won't last a month out there. Where's he going to live? He thinks he can get a job just like that." Rory snaps his fingers. "And a ski pass to Aspen. And an apartment to rent. Not likely. He'll be asking to borrow the money for a bus ticket home."

But Leila isn't so sure. Matteo is resourceful. And he's a hard worker who never complains. If anyone gives him a chance, he'll be employee of the month.

"Besides, we have plans for when he comes back. We'll get restaurant jobs and save up for our van."

Leila wonders why Rory hasn't already gotten that job and started saving. But she holds her tongue.

"Matteo needs us. He just doesn't realize it yet."

"Oh, for sure," she says. But then she thinks about it a beat longer. The thing about Matteo is he *doesn't* need them. He isn't like Rory, who constantly demands her attention. Matteo is more self-contained.

Now the three musketeers aren't three anymore, and her world suddenly feels smaller. Somehow, life just made more sense with Matteo around.

Strange, but true.

"Come on," Rory says, grabbing her free hand. "Drink that beer. Dance with me. You shouldn't mope. He isn't."

That is depressingly true.

Leila puts down her beer, which is tasteless, anyway. You can't grow up a Giltmaker and have any patience for cheap beer.

She follows him toward the fire.

Rory drops her hand and spins around. It's a dance move that's meant to make her laugh, and it works.

CHAPTER 9
LEILA

The TV is located in a den at the back of Zara and Dave's house. It's where Matteo will be sleeping tonight, and Zara has already turned the foldout couch into a bed for him. So we stretch out on it to watch our favorite movie from high school and finish the bottle of wine.

This is cozy.

Really cozy.

Even better—by the time Greg Focker gives the most awkward pre-dinner blessing in the history of time, Matteo is howling with laughter. When the credits roll, he turns his head and smiles at me. "Thank you." He reaches over and squeezes my arm. "I needed that so badly."

"I know you did. Why does your phone keep lighting up?" I ask.

"Does it?" He hauls himself up and grabs it off the end table. "It's just my idiot family. They're hazing me about getting the baby to sleep. Look."

He hands me the phone, and I see the photo he'd texted them of Micah asleep in the crib, followed by their jokes.

There are several new congratulatory texts, too:

DAMIEN

Dude, you slay!

BENITO

Good work, bro!

ALEC

I was sure you'd get a panicked call asking for help.

BENITO

Nah. He's smart enough to ask someone outside the family. We'd be too mean about it.

I snicker. But then I scroll down.

ZARA

Funny you should mention that, because look at this doorbell notification we got at dinner!

Cue a photo of me on the front porch, smiling at Matteo as he opens the door. "Oh boy. This is gonna be bad, yeah?"

"Nah." Matteo shrugs. "Those hooligans can think whatever they want about me. But that baby is asleep either way."

His family is having a field day with it.

DAMIEN

LOL! Busted.

BENITO

So resourceful! Asking the hot preschool teacher to bail your ass out. **Slow clap for big brother**

ZARA

I know, right? Leila is magic. Micah probably fell asleep the moment she stepped into the house.

"Wow, my reputation precedes me."

"Benito thinks you're hot, too." He gives me a playful nudge with his toe.

I laugh, but it makes me feel awkward to hear him tease me. It's the same as when we were in high school. I spent my entire junior year trying to impress him, but he remained the kind of guy friend who ruffled my hair and helped himself to my french

49

fries. And I had to watch him date every other girl in the entire school.

Now I'm stretched out on a bed with him, wishing I didn't have to go home.

"You staying?" he asks. Maybe Matteo can read my mind.

"You need me to?"

He shrugs. "I'll muddle through. But I like your company. And Zara says my niece thinks you're the most glamorous woman alive."

"Well, she's right," I tease. "I lead a very glamorous life making bread and playing circle games with four-year-olds."

"Aww." His grin turns sweet. "I never pictured you as a preschool teacher."

"Yeah, but what did we know about anything? I was sure all three of us would be snowboarding champions. That turned out about as well as my marriage."

He gets up off the bed. "You like the job, though? You like the kids?"

"Oh, I *love* the kids. In fact…" I stop myself just in time.

"In fact…?" he prompts, gathering up our wine glasses.

"Uh, never mind. It's kind of a long story."

Matteo puts the glasses right back down and sits on the edge of the bed. "I'm listening."

Gulp. I hadn't meant to share my big plan. Except with my mother. But Matteo's patient gaze is ready and waiting. "Pretty soon I'm going to try to have a child on my own."

His brown eyes widen. "Wow, really? How does that work, exactly?"

I laugh nervously. "With a sperm donor and a fertility special-ist. I've just started to do the research, but I'm not getting married again, and I'm running out of time."

He frowns. "You're not *old*, buddy."

"Actually, I am. Thirty-five is the cutoff point. Older than that, and you're referred to as a *geriatric pregnancy*."

"What the…? Really?" He looks alarmed.

"Yessir. But it only applies to women. Men can father babies forever."

He puts a comforting hand on my knee. "Wow, big news. So this is going to happen fast?"

I actually laugh. "Well, I'll try. The truth is that I waited too long to end my marriage."

"Did he not want kids?"

"Not really, no. We used to fight about it. He kept putting me off—saying next year would be better." I shrug, like the memory isn't killing me. "When I was getting really fed up, he eventually said, 'Fine, have a damn baby if you want one so bad.'"

Matteo's face falls.

"Yeah. And that's when I realized that having kids with him would be a mistake. So I dropped it. That was two years ago. It took me that long to get fed up enough to leave. But the minute I did, I started googling fertility clinics."

He whistles under his breath. "That's brave."

"Is it? Women raise kids alone all the time. And my mom will help out. She's desperate for grandkids."

"So was mine." He grins. "Luckily for the rest of us, Zara produced two. And she was alone at the beginning, right? I didn't mean that you couldn't handle it."

"I know," I say quickly. "But people will judge me. I'm not going to tell a soul until I'm sure it's happening."

"You just told me, though."

Yeah, I noticed that.

He nudges me playfully. "Good thing I'm a vault."

"Good thing."

He gets off the bed. "Let me find you a pair of Zara's sweatpants, and I'll give you my extra T-shirt."

"It's getting late. I bet the baby wakes up at six."

"*Six?*" Matteo shudders. "You'll help me with that, yeah? One of us can make the coffee. I don't think I can keep a baby alive without coffee."

"It's a deal," I promise him.

———

As I'd foretold, the baby wakes at dawn. I hear him cooing to himself over the baby monitor before I even open my eyes.

"Do-dle," he says. "Da-da-da-*dee.*"

I sit up. Beside me, Matteo is passed out on his stomach, the pillow curled under his face, the golden skin that covers his back muscles rippling...

Okay, not rippling. But now I know firsthand that the man is capable of ripples. When he took off his shirt last night, I almost swallowed my tongue.

"Doba doh," the baby says, so I turn the baby monitor off and hurry into the upstairs bathroom. By the time I emerge again, he's whimpering.

"Hey, fella," I say as I walk into his room. "Are you up?"

He babbles at me from the crib, where he's pulled himself up to stand, chubby hands clutching the wooden rail.

"What a big boy," I whisper, and he gives me a drooly smile.

When I lean over the crib, he raises his short arms trustingly. He's warm and heavy in my arms as I transport him to the changing table to switch out his diaper.

"You're so cheerful in the morning," I cluck. "What a great guy. I bet you could use a bottle, right?"

He babbles enthusiastically, his arms windmilling while I tape up the clean diaper and snap his PJs closed.

"Let's get to it, then." I heft him easily, taking care to hold the banister on my way downstairs.

In the kitchen, I find the bottle in the refrigerator with a sticky note. *Remove the top. Microwave for thirty seconds and then shake gently. Nipples are on the counter.*

I follow these instructions, noting that Zara uses glass baby bottles and natural rubber nipples exactly like the ones I've guiltily bookmarked on an all-natural baby store site.

That's putting the cart ahead of the horse. It will be a long time before I need to buy any of this stuff. But sometimes I can't help myself.

Micah grabs a handful of my hair and gives it a tug.

"You're being very patient," I say, kissing his fat little cheek. "Just twenty more seconds."

"Dodle-do," he says.

When the milk is warm, I screw on the nipple and carry him into the living room, where I settle myself into the corner of the couch.

This must be exactly what Zara does, too, because quickly Micah arranges himself in my arms and grabs for the bottle. And as soon as the nipple reaches its target, he begins to suck avidly.

Then he lets out a little sigh of contentment that makes my heart explode.

One time, when Rory and I were having yet another discussion about kids, he asked me point blank why I wanted a baby. "I know it's a thing that people want. But *why*? I'm not trying to be a dick. I just legit don't understand it."

It was harder to explain than I'd expected—especially since Rory isn't a fan of what he calls *woo-woo talk*.

The answer has something to do with the way I see life as a great circle. I was once a child like this, in my mother's arms. I don't remember it, but I know in my heart that it's true, and that it made me who I am.

We all leave this Earth. Before that happens, I need to do this for my own child. I want to hold her and feed her and tell her that she's loved.

I don't know why. I just do.

Meanwhile, Micah grips his bottle in two chunky little hands, and sucks gustily from the nipple. Like a little vacuum cleaner.

"Hey." Matteo stops in the doorway, his hair at seventy different angles, his eyes sleepy. And his abs are rippling *again*. "You could have poked me. Didn't mean to make you get up first."

"Don't worry about it." I make myself look away from all that golden skin. For years I didn't even glance at other men, because Rory was always so jealous.

But this is not the right moment to rediscover my libido. Just because I haven't had sex for a year doesn't mean my best friend wants me drooling on him.

He is, I guess, still one of my best friends—not an ex-friend. I don't need any more exes in my life. One is plenty.

"Just started the coffee pot." Matteo shuffles over to the sofa and leans over us. He brushes one big hand over the baby's feathery hair. "Good morning, fella. You must be a morning person. Want some coffee?"

"He's a little young for that." I give him a playful kick in his muscular calf.

"I meant you, goofus." He slides his palm over my hair, too. His hand is warm, and the sensation makes me want to close my eyes and lean into his touch. But he's already heading for the kitchen to see if the coffee is done.

I watch him go, and I'm definitely not focused on his firm backside, or the way his back muscles taper to a V at his hips.

Nope. Not me.

"Miss Leila!" an awed little voice says from the stairs. "You're here! In my *house!*" Nicole comes trotting down the staircase in pink pajamas. "Can we read a story?"

"Of course."

She bounds over to the bookshelf and chooses a collection of fairy tales. Then she climbs up onto the sofa beside me. "How 'bout *The Twelve Dancing Princesses*?"

"That's a fun one. Can you find the story by yourself?"

"Yup." She starts flipping pages.

Matteo returns with two coffee mugs just as Micah pops off the bottle and begins to wiggle. "Looks like you got your hands full, there. Let's do a trade." He sets both mugs down on the end table beside the sofa. Then he takes the baby from my arms.

And now I'm watching a ripped, shirtless man cuddle a baby. And my ovaries don't *actually* explode, but I'm certain they're whimpering a little.

"Do I have to burp him or something?" he asks.

"You could pat him on the back," I say, reaching for my coffee. "But at his age, he can probably get the job done by himself."

Matteo begins patting Micah's back, and the little guy lets rip with a tremendous belch almost immediately.

"Good man," Matteo says. "Taking care of business."

I sip my coffee, noting that there's a splash of milk in it, just the way I like it. Can't believe he remembered that.

"Found it!" Nicole announces. She snuggles close to me. "Once upon a time," she prompts.

Once upon a time there was a happy thirty-five-year-old woman who spent all her Saturday mornings just like this.

I clear my throat. "Once upon a time, there was a king with twelve daughters…"

It's hard to say which of those is the more outlandish fairy tale.

———

I leave Zara's house around nine thirty, looking a little disheveled in yesterday's clothes. And I'm pretty sure last night's makeup is still caked under my eyes.

I really want a second cup of coffee and a freshly baked treat from the Busy Bean. Living twenty paces from my favorite coffee shop is one perk of getting divorced. After I drive down the hill and park my car, I march into the Bean in spite of my flattened hair and odd fashion choices.

And the first person I see is my ex.

Fuck.

Rory is standing at the counter, waiting for his coffee. He's in his usual getup—jeans of questionable cleanliness and an old concert T-shirt.

I hesitate for a moment, wondering if I should just turn around and leave. But why should I let him chase me out of this place?

And anyway, it's too late now. He's turned to see me, and he's already studying me. "What's up with the outfit?"

Oh shit. I brace myself, because he's going to misinterpret the reason I look this way. "Nice greeting," I murmur, checking out the bakery display case, hoping he lets it go.

"No, really. Are those last night's clothes?"

Anger flares behind my breastbone. "You don't have any right to ask me that." It's true, but he won't like hearing it, and fear sparks along with my anger.

With a jerky motion, he grabs his coffee cup off the counter. "You little slut," he hisses under his breath. "Didn't take you long, did it?"

Oh no. "I was *babysitting*," I hiss. "Overnight. Not that it's any of your damn business."

He stomps out without another word, but I'm still mortified.

I shouldn't have explained myself. That's stooping to his level. But several people are staring now, and I lost my cool.

Audrey—Zara's business partner—clears her throat behind the counter. "You look like you could use a pretzel."

I take a deep breath and try not to cry. "You're right. I could."

CHAPTER 10
MATTEO

I'm on a mountaintop under a bright blue sky. The snow crunches under my feet.

Sean has a shovel in his hand. He plunges it into the snow-pack, then lifts the snow to check its density.

It's a standard test for avalanche risk. I squint to see the sample, but he chucks it before I can get a look. "Did you hear about the divorce?" he asks.

"Yeah. I heard about it."

"Interesting timing." He scoops another sample onto the shovel and holds it up.

"Can I see…"

He throws it down. And then the shovel, too. "Are you gonna tell her how you feel?"

"Why would I? Too late now."

Sean steps onto his snowboard.

"Hang on," I say. "Let's do another test."

"Tell her." He hops, starting his momentum toward the lip.

"Sean!" I yell. "WAIT."

He turns around to smile at me as a rooster crows nearby.

"WAIT!" I scream.

Then I spring up in bed, sweating and disoriented.

I'm in a trailer—my Uncle Otto's camper—where I'd taken a much-needed nap.

Or I'd tried to. The dreams just won't stop. I have them every night, pretty much.

Except for the other night on Zara and Dave's fold-out couch. I'd lain awake for a while, listening to Leila's breathing lengthen into sleep. Either she'd soothed me, or the baby didn't give me enough hours to dream awful things.

Once again, Otto's damn rooster is crowing at point-blank range, right outside the camper. It's his favorite hobby, and it woke me up at 4:45 this morning. *Er-ah-errr! Er-ah-errr!*

At least the rent is free.

I get up and take a quick shower in the trailer's tiny bathroom. Then I dress in good jeans and a crisp black shirt. Tonight I'm bartending at the Gin Mill with my sister, and my shift starts in an hour.

When I open the trailer door, the rooster is still standing there, giving me that creepy side-eye that chickens have perfected. Like he's considering attacking me, but he's still making up his mind.

"Go bother the hens," I tell him. "They like you more than I do."

He stares.

I head for my rental car, but before I get there, Otto opens the door to the main house. "Wait up," he says. "You gotta sign the paperwork."

"Oh, sure. Oops." I'd forgotten that he'd asked me to fill out a W9. "Is this really necessary?"

Otto scowls. "Your brother could lose his liquor license if his employees aren't documented correctly."

"Okay, fine." I don't need anyone blaming me for that. I climb the steps to Otto's farmhouse and go inside.

It's just like I remember—high ceilings, loveably creaky wood floors, and furniture that's faded but interesting.

I lived here for a brief time or two when I was a boy. My father had a bad habit of running out on my mother. If you added up all the places I lived during the first eighteen years of my life, the number is probably over a dozen.

Mom kept moving us into successively crappier accommodations. House to house, then to apartments. Then eventually the trailer park.

Otto offered to permanently move us all in—me and my four siblings, and Mom—but only if Mom agreed never to go back to my father.

She wouldn't agree to it, and at the time I didn't blame her. I still don't. Otto wanted to control her. And he wanted her to admit that she'd made foolish choices. It was a power struggle, and she wouldn't let him win.

All my siblings are younger than me, and some of them would have made a different choice. We were always crowded. Three kids to a room.

Everyone blames me for leaving Vermont. But they don't remember that I made their lives easier that way. My senior year, our trailer had bunk beds for me and Damien and a stow-away mattress on the floor for Alec.

Alec got a real bed when I left. But now he's pissed that I stayed gone. Where is the logic in that?

Otto sits me down at the big wooden dining table and passes me a set of papers. "We still have Sunday dinner here at least once a month. You'll come this week, yeah?"

"Sounds fun," I say, uncapping Otto's pen. I fill out my social security number and sign a liability waiver and an employee questionnaire. "Do I have any felony convictions? No."

"Good help is hard to find," Otto says. "Your brother had a guy stealing from him once."

"I know, Otto. I run a business, too."

"A *winter* business. You're done snowboarding for the season, right?"

My business actually operates at a low volume all year. In the summer we offer aerial tours and airport trips. But Otto doesn't want to hear it. "Yeah. So?" I shrug.

"Last summer I bought a beer wagon with Lyle Giltmaker. Plenty of demand for it, but I need a manager."

I shake my head. "That honestly sounds fun, but I have to earn some serious cash this summer. People are depending on me."

"You don't understand," he says. "The pay is great. Don't

underestimate the beer zealots. Those fuckers drive hundreds of miles to get a taste of the cult beers. It's a good business. But I gotta have a man I can trust. Alec is stretched too thin right now."

"I'll be back in Colorado in a few weeks."

"Just think about it," Otto presses as I sign the last form. "You could stay in the trailer for free. Rent out your place in Aspen. Sell beer all summer. Wear more of those tight shirts to maximize tips." He points at my chest, which is—admittedly—stretching the limits of a T-shirt that's a little on the small side. But Damien had told me that they wear black behind the bar, and this is my only black shirt.

I snort. "Now you're my pimp? I see how it is."

He doesn't even crack a smile. "Leila Giltmaker is working for her father this summer. Maybe that's a motivating factor."

"She is?"

He nods. "She needs extra cash, too. You're not the only one having a midlife crisis. Think about it."

"Okay, I'll think about it." I stand up from the table and push in my chair. "Later."

———

"Then he made a crack about this shirt being tight," I tell my sister as we cut limes to prep for the rush.

If there even *is* a Monday night rush. Tonight might be boring as shit. It's April, which is the quiet time in Vermont—between ski season and our beautiful summer weather.

"That is a boastful shirt if I ever saw one," she says. "Somebody goes to the gym. Otto had a point."

I let out a comical gasp. "Are you taking Otto's side? Who are you anymore?" Zara was a very rebellious teenager, and she and my uncle always locked horns.

"Hey, I'm always on your side. But I think you underestimate the earning power of that shirt in this bar. Once upon a time I had a whole closet full of low-cut tops. They're good for tips."

"It's not the same for guys." I snort.

She chuckles. "You'll see. You just won't care, because you've got heart eyes for Leila."

I don't dignify that with a response. Zara already gave me shit for Leila spending the night. She asked me point blank if we'd had wild monkey sex on her pull-out couch. And when I promised her we didn't, she looked disappointed.

My takeaway is that this town runs on cult beer and gossip.

And pizza. Thank God the Gin Mill's cook isn't also on his honeymoon, because I've already gobbled down a pie topped with pears and goat cheese. It was delicious.

My brother's bar probably prints money on the weekends.

Good for Alec. His life is on track.

That makes one of us.

──────

"Okay, remember when I worried that Monday night would be dull?" I complain to Zara as I reach over her head for another pint glass.

"Yup!" She's using one hand to pour gin over ice and the other to grab wedges of lime.

"Why didn't you warn me?" The bar is packed.

"What's the fun in that?" Then she points at my beer tap and shakes her head.

"Shit." The keg is kicked, and the beer is barely dribbling out into the glass.

"Swap it," she says. "I'll finish your order."

"Okay, sure." I'm definitely letting my little sister call the shots tonight. Before Zara had kids, and before she opened the Busy Bean, she used to work as an actual bartender. So she's faster at making the cocktails while I pull a million tap beers.

We've been buried under orders since six o'clock, with no end in sight. It's actually nice to slip into the narrow room behind the bar and change the keg in peace for a few minutes.

Alec better be having the time of his life in California. Because this is hard work.

The keg that I'm swapping out is for Goldenrod—the newest

cult beer made by Leila's father, Lyle Giltmaker. He hit it big a few years ago.

I just didn't realize how big until tonight. The Vermont beer scene is intense. One customer told me he drove up here from Arizona to visit three Vermont breweries. That sounds extreme to me.

Then again, I've been known to jump out of airplanes for fun. I guess we all have our hobbies.

As soon as the tap is changed, I head back behind the bar. Even though I could use a break, it's not fair to let my little sister handle the crowd by herself.

When I round the corner, I see a familiar face on the other side of the bar. My old friend Rory.

CHAPTER 11
MATTEO

Rory's dark eyes widen as I approach his barstool. "Fuck, no way," he says. "I saw you called me yesterday, but I had no idea you'd showed your ugly face in this town. And *workin'* too." He gives me his trademark cocky grin, but it looks a little tired.

"Yeah, yeah. I'm getting a lot of shit from a lot of people. Want a drink? Quick—before I get slammed."

"Course I do. How about a Goldenrod?"

I grab a pint glass and tease the fresh tap into service.

"There's a lot of foam on that. Amateur." Rory snorts.

"Yeah, so this one's on the house," I say, topping it up slowly and then placing it in front of Rory.

After that, I have a solid hour of hard labor. But it *is* a Monday night, and finally the place starts to quiet down.

Rory is a few beers in already. I pour a small drink for myself and lean against the bar to talk to him. "This job is exhausting," I complain. "Even when they tip well."

He grins. "Making big bucks? I'll bet the ladies like that long mane you got."

"I do okay."

He snorts. "I bet you do. You always pulled the hot chicks in high school, and I made do with your leftovers."

"That is *not* true." Rory was fearless with women when we were young. The pick-up lines that came out of his mouth? I'd always think, *That will never work*, and then ten minutes later he'd leave the party with the girl hanging on his arm.

"You know, it's interesting timing you coming back to town right now."

I'm getting tired of hearing that. And I don't like the unhappy gleam in my old friend's eye. "You mean because of you and Leila?"

"Well, duh." His expression grows even surlier. "You always had a thing for her."

"Sure, when we were kids. I don't deny it. But I had no idea you guys broke up. Saw her at Alec's wedding and the first thing I said was, 'Where's Rory?'"

He barks out a laugh. "Yeah? That musta gone over well."

"She looked at me like I'm the dumbest man alive." I shrug. "Then she told me it was over between you guys."

He shifts on his barstool. "Why *are* you here, then?"

"Because I'm having a rough year myself. Thought a trip home might put things in perspective."

This seems to appease him, and he sags, propping his chin in his hand. Rory looks thin, and the circles under his eyes are darker than mine. "Sorry to hear that."

"It's only April. This year better turn around, right?"

"Right." He raises his beer toward me, and I do the same. "Cheers."

I grab a cloth and wipe down the bar. "Where you working these days?"

"The job market is shit." He shakes his head. "I do some part time work here and there. Still trying to find the best fit."

"Uh-huh." It's an interesting take. I've seen a dozen Help Wanted signs in Colebury, and I've only been in town a few days.

"Might be desperate enough to try bartending, though. Maybe next door at Speakeasy. I hear they pay pretty good. But Lyle Giltmaker hates me, so I'm probably blackballed."

"Hmm." I don't mention that I'm a minority owner of Speakeasy. It's not my place to suggest they give Rory a job.

Honestly, I don't know why Rory would want to breathe the same air as his ex-father-in-law.

But it's none of my business.

"You remember those bonfires we used to have?" Rory asks. His voice has gone wistful. "Out in the woods. A keg of terrible beer—nothing like this fancy shit you have on tap."

"Sure I do." Nostalgia must be contagious, because I can suddenly picture it so clearly—Leila swinging her legs off the tailgate of her father's truck, impersonating a teacher.

Rory, drunk and doing handstands to impress the ladies.

Me, watching the firelight flicker across my friends' faces. "Those were some good times."

"They were," he agrees. "Our feet going numb in the snow. And the only music was from somebody's pickup truck. We'd always have to jump the battery afterwards." He laughs. "But it didn't matter, yeah? It was *enough*. We weren't always so fucking dissatisfied with our lives."

Actually, I was.

But now is not the time or place to say so. "They were simpler days," I say instead.

He pushes his glass toward me on the bar. "Can you spot me another? Money is a little tight."

"Just one," I say, reaching for his glass. Naturally Rory is drinking one of the more expensive beers in the whole joint. I take a ten out of the tip jar and toss it into the register before I pour him a beer.

"Oh, shit," he says in a dark voice. "Could this town be any fucking smaller?"

I lift my chin, checking the door. And there's Leila, her face alight with a smile. She's just walked in with Skye, my brother Benito's wife. Her eyes are shining with humor, and her cheeks are flushed.

She reminds me of a naughty angel, sent from heaven to make my heart beat a little faster.

Then I turn back and clock the anger on Rory's face. And I just know this is going to be bad. His lip has curled into a sneer, and his body is tense.

Fuck. Whatever Alec is paying me to tend bar tonight, it won't be enough if I have to throw my best friend out of the bar for harassing my *other* best friend.

"There are *two* bars on this road," Rory says. "They coulda picked the other one. Did she know you were working tonight?"

"Nah," I say immediately.

But Rory doesn't listen. "You guys were always panting for each other. She's probably here for you."

"*Listen.* Be mad at her if you want to. But don't make this about me."

He isn't listening. And now he's got the glassy stare of a guy who should have stopped drinking an hour ago. "Bitch thinks she's too good for me. I'm living in a house with no fucking plates in the cabinets. She took 'em all."

Yikes. The women haven't noticed either of us yet. They're facing the other way, eyeing the tables, looking for a place to sit. The only free one is a two-top on the far wall, and I'm privately imploring them to take it.

No dice. They turn toward the bar instead.

That's when the door opens once more to admit my brother Benito. The women wave him over, as if they were expecting him.

"Oh, Christ," my sister says under her breath. "Here we go."

Benito lifts his chin in greeting, and I give him a wave. Then I turn my gaze pointedly toward Rory.

My brother is a smart man, so he gets it. He steers Leila and Skye toward empty seats at the far end of the bar. Zara heads toward them immediately, saving me the awkwardness of ditching Rory to wait on his ex.

He glowers quietly for a few minutes while I pour an order for the server who's working the tables tonight.

"Aren't you gonna go say hello?" Rory sneers after a time. "She's single now."

"Easy, dude. I'll definitely say hello to her, but I'm busy here."

"Go on," he says. "Shoot your shot. You know you want to."

For fuck's sake. I lean on the bar and look him pointedly in the eyes. "I'm only saying this once. Maybe you two had a messy breakup, but I don't know the details, and I don't want to know. It never had a thing to do with me. Still doesn't."

"Clueless fucker," Rory mutters into his beer.

"Can you pour a Goldenrod for Ben?" Zara nudges me with her elbow. "And these margaritas are for the girls." She passes me two cocktails.

"Sure. Got it."

"Yeah, you do," Rory grumbles. "Get right on 'er."

Without further comment, I grab a glass and pour my brother's beer. Then I carry the drinks down the bar and deliver them. "Hey, ladies. Amateur bartender at your service."

My brother smirks. "Nice job tonight. I'll let Alec know you didn't burn the place down yet."

"Oh please. You're out with the ladies, and I'm back here serving beer to every thirsty tourist within five hundred miles."

Benito shrugs. "I've got overtime this week at work. Sorry."

"How convenient." I park my hip against the bar and take in Leila. She's wearing a black velvet shirt, tight jeans, and a lot of silver jewelry. And I am suddenly full of inappropriate thoughts.

Guess Rory knows a thing or two after all. Not that I'll admit it.

"Is there anything else I can get you guys? Food?"

"We ate already," Leila says. "I made dinner for Skye, and then Ben agreed to join us for another drink when he came to pick up Skye."

"Dinner, huh?" I'm just noticing that Leila and Skye both look a little tipsy. "Must have been some wine involved."

"That's what I was thinking," my brother says with a grin.

"There mighta' been," Skye says. Then she hiccups.

"Hey, barkeep!" yells Rory from down the bar. "My glass is empty." He sets it down with a thunk that betrays drunkenness.

"Shit," Leila hisses, looking down the bar. "Should I leave?"

"No way," I insist. "Enjoy your drink. I'll deal with him."

I make my way down the bar again, but my sister beats me to Rory. "You're cut off," she says firmly.

"No *way*, bitch. The minute *she* comes in here, you throw me out?" He bangs his glass on the bar again. "Matteo? A little service?"

For fuck's sake. I'm not about to let Rory call my sister a bitch and then hand him another free beer. Heads are turning all around the bar, and I know I need to choose my words carefully.

"Come outside," I say softly. "You got any smokes?"

He blinks. "Maybe."

"Let's go." I take off my apron. "I treated you to a drink, you can do me this small favor."

I'm expecting him to argue, but when I duck under the bar, he slides off the stool and walks with me toward the door.

We almost make it outside when he turns to Leila. "You took everything from me. Even the dining room table. But maybe you did me a favor, you know? You're a terrible lay."

I punch the door open and pull him through it. "That was unnecessary."

He leans against the brick exterior and stares up at the night sky. "Yeah, maybe."

"I can tell you're hurting. But when you have a tantrum like that, you only make yourself look bad."

"So?" he argues, patting his pockets. "She took everything, man. My car needs thousands in repairs. I eat dinner standing at the counter every night, like a loser. The place echoes." He produces a crumpled cigarette pack. "Only one left."

I quit smoking fifteen years ago, so I couldn't care less. "We'll share."

He lights up and offers me the ciggy. I take the world's smallest puff and struggle not to cough.

"Smooth moves." Rory laughs.

I just shrug. We stand there in the quiet while he smokes. He's going through a rough time, but he's not the only one. "Let me drive you home, okay? You live right up the hill, yeah?"

"Yeah." Defeated now, he leads me over to an old Dodge Charger.

"This car is actually cool. Can it be fixed up?"

"Maybe. It'd be expensive."

"I bet. Good bones, though."

"Let me start it," he says. "She's tricky."

I worry that this is a trick, and he'll drive off. But after he gets the engine running, he gets out of the driver's seat and puts himself on the passenger's side.

The drive to his house is just a few minutes. I'll have to walk back, and Zara might be annoyed with me for leaving her alone behind the bar, but it was worth it to prevent a scene or to make Benito handle Rory on his night off.

I start up the hill toward town while Rory smokes, his window open to the breeze. "I don't care about the fucking table," he says. "That wasn't really the point."

"Mmm," I say vaguely.

"She took my *pride*. I lived for that woman. She was the best thing that ever happened to me."

"That's hard," I say, hoping it sounds comforting. "But throwing tantrums in the bar isn't going to help you heal."

He swipes at his eyes, which are leaking. "I dream about her every night. Can't get her out of my head."

That's a topic I know plenty about. "We don't know what we have before it's gone, do we?"

Rory shakes his head, miserable.

And I know just how he feels.

CHAPTER 12
SEVENTEEN YEARS AGO
MATTEO IS 19, LEILA IS 18

On a March morning at dawn, Matteo finds himself behind the wheel of an ancient, rusting Volvo, driving slowly in the right lane to save gas. It's ninety-five miles from Aspen to Beaver Creek.

In exchange for a tank of gas, he's borrowed this shitty car from his new friend, Sean. He can't really afford to miss a day at work. He also can't afford the lift ticket he's going to have to buy when he gets there. He'll have to skip lunch in the overpriced cafe. He'll say he's not hungry.

Even so, he's been looking forward to this day trip all month. It's a struggle not to floor it just to get there five minutes earlier.

"Got a hot date?" Sean had asked when he'd handed over the keys.

"Not really," he'd said, deflecting the question. "It's just a friend from home."

It's not *just* any friend, though. It's Leila. She's on her annual spring break ski trip with her mother and her brothers. But this time—since it's Leila's last spring break before college—she begged for a trip to Colorado.

He can't *wait* to see her. He's actually early, arriving in the resort parking lot at eight a.m. He doesn't have any minutes left on his cheap cell phone plan, so he can't even let her know.

He buys his lift ticket and waits at their agreed-upon spot in front of the express lift, stomping his feet against the cold.

70

Suddenly she's right there—all bouncing hair and pink-cheeked smiles. "Omigod! Matty! This is so epic! We're going to ride all day! Just like old times." She sort of flings herself at him, and he catches her against his chest and takes a deep breath.

Citrussy shampoo. Cinnamon gum. All the good things in life, and so familiar he could cry. He's so homesick. These past four months have been the hardest of his life.

But he is determined not to let on. He smiles broadly and asks which lift they should ride first.

She grabs his arm and tugs. Just like old times. "My favorite run is called Cataract. You can see *everything* from the top!"

He follows her onto the lift, under a giant blue sky. Leila chatters to him about everything that's new in Vermont. "Rory is working in the Shipley's dairy barn three mornings a week. He hates the hours, though. He might learn to be a plumber."

"Really?" he tries and fails to picture that.

"Maybe." Leila shrugs. "That's this week's idea. He seems kind of restless, actually. But he's still talking about starting a business with you when you come back."

Matteo doesn't know how he feels about that. At the moment, starting a business feels impossible. Most things do.

"How's the new job?" Leila asks.

"Good," he says, and it isn't a lie. "I've only been there a month, but they run seven days a week, so they need all the days I can give them."

"I can't believe you get to snowboard for a *living*. That is wild."

"Until the snow melts," he reminds her. "Then I'll have to find something else to do." It's heavy on his mind.

"What's it like, though? How's the terrain?"

"Fantastic," he says. "I did ten thousand feet of vertical yesterday."

Leila makes a noise of disbelief, and her brown eyes sparkle. "Hot damn. I want your life."

She wouldn't, though, if she knew all the details. He's not about to admit that, not with the warm glow of her praise settling inside his chest.

Sure, his job is very cool. He works for Cat Tracks Tours—an Aspen company that runs private ski and snowboard excursions into the wilderness. Seven hundred dollars gets you a day of backcountry skiing on a snow cat—a heavyweight vehicle that's a cross between a tank and a tractor. It carries eight skiers and their gear uphill at four miles per hour.

Matteo is paid twenty dollars an hour—plus tips—to ski at the back of the customer groups to make sure they get down the terrain without getting lost or injured. If he's lucky, he'll be promoted to be a full-on guide next year. And if that goes well, he can start angling to work on helicopter tours, too.

But living on his own is so much harder than he'd expected. He's already on his third job, because the first two were unbearable. For the first few weeks he'd sharpened skis in a windowless room on the ski mountain. The pay was bad, and the manager was always yelling at him to work faster.

By the second week, he'd mentally torn up the business plan he'd shown Lyle Giltmaker. He wasn't going to spend the rest of his life waxing other people's skis. He'd traded up to a shift in an on-mountain cafeteria. It had been fun riding the chairlift to work and riding his board down afterwards. But the money was terrible, and everyone who worked there cared only about the next kegger and the cheapest weed.

Thank God for the snow cat gig. Now he's paid to be outside all day, and the owner of the company is an interesting man. He's figured out how to charge hundreds of dollars an hour for bringing tourists to land he *doesn't even own*. Best scam ever.

When the chairlift arrives at the summit, he follows Leila down an exhilarating run. Before Colorado, he hadn't known that a ski run could be so steep. Blankets of snow over endless terrain.

He lets Leila have first tracks, of course, just as if he were shepherding tourists at work. By now, he's an *excellent* snowboarder. Good thing, since it's really his only life skill.

Today it's all that matters, though. He and Leila are *flying*. Her cheeks are pink, and she can't stop smiling. So he doesn't either.

On the next lift, he tells her about the teenage boy he had to coax down the hill, turn by turn, after the poor kid had a panic attack at the top. He tells her about the oldest clients he's met so far. "Seventy-four years young and married for fifty years."

"Whoa!" She grips the safety bar and laughs. "I want to be those old people someday. Still having fun."

"Yeah, me too."

He doesn't tell her everything, though. Like how hungry he is sometimes on his strict twenty-dollars-a-day budget. Or the way his wallet was pickpocketed the only time he went to a party with the stoners.

How scary it is to suddenly have nothing, and no one.

He doesn't describe the icky bunkroom he calls home. Or the way that it always smells like feet. Those details feel unimportant today, anyway. There's only the mountain and the sound of Leila's laughter.

They ride for hours, until Leila claims to be dying of hunger. So they waste part of the last hour of the ski day sitting at a table in an on-mountain cafeteria, where Leila buys him a four-dollar cup of soup in spite of his claims that he isn't hungry.

He devours it, of course, while watching her dip Fritos into her chili.

"This is a perfect day, isn't it?" she says as they look out the window at the ski slope.

"Pretty much," he says. But that's an understatement. It's the best day *ever*. The sun is shining, and he has her all to himself.

Leila drops her plastic spoon into her empty chili bowl and says something startling. "Look, I don't have any right to ask. But you'll come back to Vermont someday, won't you?"

"Why? Is everything okay?"

"Well, yeah, but…" She props her head in her hand and studies him with big eyes. "I miss you. Kind of a lot."

His heart explodes.

"And so does Rory."

He deflates just as quickly.

"It's just not the same," she says, looking down at her empty bowl. "I know that's just life. I won't even be around next year."

"You'll be in Burlington," he clarifies, because she's going to college in the fall.

73

"Right." She shreds the wrapper from her straw into tiny pieces. "But I just… I can't stand the idea that we might not be close anymore. It just feels wrong. And I wondered if you felt that way, too."

When she lifts her vulnerable brown eyes to his, he almost can't breathe. "Absolutely," he says. "You're way too important to me."

Her face does something complicated. Her eyes warm to his, and he has to clamp his jaw shut to avoid saying anything even more revealing.

Her shy smile makes everything worth it. "Good," she says. "We're not done. We can't be."

"No," he agrees.

She pushes back from the table. "One more run. Let's make it a good one."

She chooses their last trail for its length, not its difficulty. It winds down the mountain, the low-slung sunshine blinding them from behind the evergreen trees. At the bottom, they carry their boards through the resort village at the mountain's base. It's the usual collection of bars, restaurants, and shops.

He can't suggest an après-ski drink, because his credit card might be declined, so they walk, Leila browsing various shop windows.

If it were up to him, the day would never end.

"That's pretty," she murmurs in front of a display of jewelry.

His eyes scan the display, and he knows immediately which item she's looking at. That's how well he knows her. There's a necklace—a silver chain, and a chunky silver snowflake pendant. But the details on it are done up in gold. It's pretty, and yet a little funky.

It's just *her*.

She tilts her head to try to see the price and then makes a face. "Four hundred bucks? Ouch."

Ouch, he privately agrees as she straightens and leads him toward the next window, which is full of colorful winter hats.

Still, he notes the name of the shop. *Alpine Arts*. It's way out of his price range.

But someday it won't be, he tells himself. If he works hard enough for a couple more years, he'll become the kind of guy who can afford gold jewelry for the golden girl.

That's when he'll be able to tell her how he feels.

But not until then.

CHAPTER 13
LEILA

You're a terrible lay.

I know they're the pathetic words of a man who can't think up a better insult.

Nonetheless, they land on me hard. I've never felt less sexy in my life than I feel tonight. I'm tired and tipsy. It's not easy being single at thirty-five in a small town and having your ex make a scene every week.

And Matteo *left* with him, which fills me with irrational despair. I know he was only trying to help. He walked Rory out for me and for the benefit of everyone else in the bar.

But there are a few things impeding my gratitude.

1: I'm drunk, which makes logic difficult.

B: I bet Rory sat there all night talking smack to Matteo about me.

The sight of them leaving together brought back every irrational high school emotion that I ever had. I feel excluded. Like I'm thirteen again and worried about shifting loyalties at the lunch table.

Emotions don't have to make sense. I pick up my third margarita and drink it down.

"Should I cut you off, too?" Zara asks gently from behind the bar.

"Probably," I say, careful to enunciate all the syllables. "Drinks are on me." I pull my credit card out of my pocket and slap it on the bar.

Zara doesn't pick up the card. "Benito already paid the tab."

"Fuck," I grumble. "I was trying to treat. You guys have been great to me. And pity is a bitch."

Skye just smiles. "But you made me dinner! And I had a great time tonight."

I suppose she has a point. I'd run into her today at the OB-GYN department at the hospital. I was there for an introductory exam with the fertility specialist and an eye-opening chat with the hospital's "financial coordinator."

Skye and I had hung out in the waiting room amid the outdated magazines, and she'd confessed two things to me: first, that she and Benito are about to start trying for a baby, and secondly that he had to work a stakeout tonight.

So I'd invited her over to dinner. I made my garlicky salmon Provençal. Skye brought a bottle of wine. "If I'm lucky, I'll have to give up wine pretty soon, so let's have some tonight," she'd said.

Except she isn't much of a drinker, so I may have had more than my share. I'd confessed to her that childlessness wasn't really okay with me, and that I'd asked the fertility specialist to take me through my options.

"Guess how much a vial of donor sperm costs?" I'd asked her. "Just guess."

"Um, five hundred dollars?"

"A thousand. And the doctor charges another two to four hundred for the job of delivering it."

She'd gasped. "I never realized how valuable Benito is. I better start treating him better."

We'd laughed and clinked our wine glasses together. But I'd felt an uncomfortable pang of jealousy. Skye and Benito are hope-lessly in love. They'd found each other again after a long separa-tion, and I can just tell they'll go the distance.

They'll have beautiful children too, of course. Probably by next year. She's only thirty, so she'll probably never even *meet* the fertility specialist.

Self-pity is ugly. I need to cut it out.

The door to the bar opens again. Matteo walks back in, and my heart gives a little spasm of joy.

Stupid heart.

"Did you drive his drunken ass home?" Benito asks.

"Sure did. Sorry, Zara!" he calls to his sister.

"We're almost done here." Zara shrugs. "Come back here and help me clean up. It's last call."

"Yes, ma'am." As he passes me, Matteo gives my elbow a casual squeeze. I meet his eye, and he winks as he walks on by. Behind the bar, he ties his apron and starts collecting dirty glassware and wiping down the surfaces.

That's what a real man does—quietly takes care of business. Rory was never that guy. Rory wanted a gold medal for taking out the garbage. He required constant external validation. He was so needy.

I'd known this when I married him, but I'd married him anyway.

Worse, I think I'd fed off his need. He made me feel powerful —like my opinion mattered.

Maybe that's why I put up with him for twelve wasted years.

Okay, that's harsh. Those years hadn't been all bad. In fact, Rory had been on a roll for the first few years of our marriage. He had a good job working for a snowboarding company. As a rep, he'd driven around New England to various ski mountains and let boarders demo the newest equipment.

It had been his dream job—hanging out with snowboard bros and getting paid to be the life of the party.

But then the company had tightened its belt, and let Rory go. He'd been indignant. He felt that life owed him a fun job. And when there were no more fun jobs to be had, he decided that he was meant to become an entrepreneur. He'd start his own company.

First, he wanted to be a fly-fishing guide, but hustling for customers was tough, and the work was too seasonal to be financially viable.

Then he went through a phase of selling nutritional supplements. We ended up with five hundred cans of some kind of powder in our basement before he realized it wasn't going to make him rich.

Then he decided to open his own niche snowboard manufacturing business. My father grudgingly invested ten thousand dollars. Not because I asked him to—Rory pitched him directly.

I could have predicted the outcome. It made for some very uncomfortable family holidays when my father would ask him for updates, and Rory didn't have much positive to say.

That's when Rory became really hard to live with. Failure wasn't a good look on him, and he took it out on everyone else, including me.

Especially me.

He took jobs and lost jobs and quit jobs at an age when all our friends seemed to be finding their footing in life.

When I questioned his logic, he accused me of looking down on him. And the truth is that I did. I wanted him to buck up and stick to a plan. I wanted to start a family. And he blamed me for pressuring him. He said I wasn't supportive.

Then, last fall, my mother and I took our annual shopping weekend in New York City, and she confessed to me that she was planning to leave my dad.

I was stunned. The timing seemed so strange. My father has never been more successful. He's on top of the world.

But my mother wasn't happy. Cognitively I knew this. They were always arguing. But I didn't imagine—after forty years—that she'd actually leave him. The audacity stunned me. I didn't think leaving a marriage was something you could do.

I'm not a quitter. It's just how I'm built.

But then—in the dressing room at Nordstrom's—she'd said something I couldn't forget. "Don't keep making a mistake, Leila, simply because you've invested a lot of time making it."

For a few weeks the idea had buzzed around me like a mosquito. I just couldn't shake it. Then Rory did something truly disrespectful to me. It hadn't been the first time. I'd been putting up with his bullshit for years.

And I just snapped. "Keep it up," I'd shrieked at him. "And we'll end up divorced."

I'd never uttered the D-word before. I'd shocked the both of us, but once the words had come crashing out of my mouth, I knew I'd changed everything.

I'd also known it was time.

He'd made the decision easier by totally flipping out and saying a whole lot of ugly things.

Now here I sit on a barstool, my drink reduced to ice cubes. My life badly in need of a do-over.

"Leila," Skye says gently. "Are you all right?"

"Yes!" It comes out a little slurred. "I'm fine."

"You're a better person than he is, and Rory can't take it," she says. "Everyone knows."

"I married him," I point out, articulating carefully. "That's on me."

"And then you divorced him." She pushes her barstool back and hops down. "Do you want us to walk you home?"

I blink. "Home is right upstairs. I'm good."

Benito gives my shoulder a squeeze. "Be well. And don't give that ass another thought."

"I won't," I lie.

The two lovebirds leave the bar. The place is really emptying out. Zara is counting the register and Matteo is cleaning up. He passes me a glass of ice water that I didn't ask for.

"Thanks. Appreciate it." I must look sloppy drunk.

My pride is so wounded at this point that it just doesn't matter. I sip my water slowly and watch the muscles in Matteo's arms flex as he scrubs out a sink.

Eventually, they begin to shut off the lights. Matteo comes around the bar and holds out his arm to me. "Come on, then. White-glove service upstairs."

"You don't have to walk me upstairs," I insist. But then I kind of miss the floor when I try to slide off the stool, and Matteo has to catch me.

And, *ohhhh*. As his arms close around me, I breathe in his scent. Like lime juice and heat. "That's just not fair. Who works a sweaty eight-hour shift and still smells so good?"

Zara laughs, and I realize I'd said that out loud. "Night, kids," she says. "Oh—Matteo, here." She offers him a thick envelope.

"Thanks." He grabs it and shoves it in his pocket. "Okay, Leila. Let's get you home." He uses the same patient voice he'd used with the baby the other night. "Let's put you to bed."

"Alone?" I clarify, just in case he means that in a fun way.

"Yep."

Zara cracks up.

Darn it.

He throws an arm around me and steers me out of the bar and over to the private entrance to the condos upstairs. "Can you open the door? Or tell me the code?"

My fingers feel thick and stumbly, so I recite the sequence of numbers. He opens the door and steers me inside. The ceilings in this old building are very tall, so when I look up the staircase, I sigh. "It's a *lot* of stairs."

"I noticed that," he says with a dry chuckle. "But here we go."

"Oh!" Suddenly, I'm lifted off the ground. It's a little shocking, but not unpleasant. I wrap my arms around his strong chest and lay my cheek against his shoulder. "You know, this shirt is really tight."

"So I've been told. Otto said it would be good for tips."

"I'd tip you," I agree in a low voice. "All night long."

He makes a strangled noise.

"Sorry." I must be heavy. Good thing I'm on the second floor.

He sets me down gently in front of the door. "Keys?"

I find them in my pocket and hand them over. He unlocks the door and escorts me inside. "Nice place," he says, eyeing the cheery brick walls, the beams on the ceiling, and the big old windows. "Wow."

It *is* a nice place. "My mom helped me furnish it. I left Rory everything, because he was so mad at me. The only thing I took was my grandma's china. And her dining table." I point toward the pine, gate-leg table against the wall. "It's been in my family for four generations. And Rory called me a thief for taking it."

He frowns. "Interesting."

"It's not even valuable, but I love it. My mother helped me with the rest." I've got a big, boho-style sofa with loosely draped slip-covers and a giant beaded ottoman. There's a console table against the far wall with a modest little TV, because I don't watch much TV.

"Let's sit," I suggest, shuffling toward the sofa. "My favorite thing to do is put my feet up and read. Or sometimes I just sit and think about how I spent all those prime childbearing years married to the wrong man."

Matteo laughs and sits down next to me. "You'll be okay, Leila. Tonight was just rough."

"It was. But I went to the doctor today. So now I know that a stranger's sperm is going to cost me a thousand dollars a pop."

"Come again?" he asks in a strangled voice.

"Exactly. Every time the sperm donor shakes hands with the milkman, it costs a grand. And I'll probably need five or six vials. If that fails, I'm looking at IVF for twelve thousand."

Matteo whistles. "What a racket."

I hiccup. "Yeah. Unless I find a donor privately. That's complicated. But I kind of hate having a kid with a stranger. They're supposed to screen them. But not everyone knows their medical history, you know?" I shiver. "So much trust to place in a sperm bank."

"Wild," he says. "Can I make you a cup of chamomile tea?"

"Oh!" I can hardly believe that he remembers that's my night-time drink. "That sounds so nice."

"And maybe some aspirin?" He gets off the couch. "Is it in the medicine cabinet?"

"Yeah," I say, sinking down into the sofa. I feel super drunk all of a sudden. I shouldn't let him take care of me, but it's so *nice*.

I actually nod off while he fusses in my kitchen, but I wake up enough to sip the tea and swallow the pills.

Then he sits down on the sofa right beside me. Close enough to touch. And I flop my heavy body onto his sturdier one. "Thank you," I whisper. "I'm kind of a mess."

"Just a little one," he says kindly, stroking my hair. "You'll be all right. You mind if I stay here with you? It's late."

"I don't mind." I take another sip of tea. "There's no bed in the second bedroom, though, so we'll have to share again. Not sure this couch is long enough for you."

He stands up and hauls me to my feet. "Let's find your pajamas."

"I threw them away. What's the point of being single if you can't sleep naked?"

Matteo swallows roughly. "Good point. I'll stay on the couch."

"Oh." Whoops. "I'll wear a big T-shirt. And then I can snuggle you. Nobody ever snuggles me anymore. It's been years since anyone snuggled me."

Matteo doesn't say anything about that. He walks me to my bedroom and finds me a big tee, and then leaves me alone in the bathroom so I can put it on.

When I emerge, the apartment is dark. He's saved me the trouble of turning all the lights out. I make it to the bed, where I climb under the covers and close my eyes.

Then I open them again. "Uh-oh."

"What?" he asks as he enters the room.

"I've got the spins."

"Need a bucket?"

I shake my head. "I'm not drunk enough to barf. I'm only drunk enough to act like a doofus and say stupid things."

Chuckling, he kicks off his jeans, and even in low light, I can see his abs as he gets into bed. "Like what stupid things?" he asks.

"You ripple," I complain. "It makes me thirsty."

"I *what?* Do you need a glass of water?"

"No, not like *that*." I sigh. Then I roll toward him. "Why didn't we ever hook up? When we were young and dumb. Why did I pick Rory?"

On the other side of the bed, he goes absolutely still. "That… I don't know, Leila. That was a long time ago."

It's not a very satisfying answer, and the tequila in my bloodstream just can't let it go. "Everything might have turned out different, if it was you," I whisper. "Everything! I wouldn't have married a man who resents me." Then I take a sharp breath. "Wait, that's selfish of me. You didn't want to be trapped here in Vermont. With me."

He sighs. "Let's not hold a competition for who made the stupidest choices, yeah? I'd be right beside you on the podium."

"Please. That's my trophy for sure," I grumble as the room does another loop. "I'm the dumb one. I married the wrong guy. And now I'm thirty-five, and I have to have babies with a test tube because there aren't any single men left who want to see me naked."

Matteo groans. "It's late, honey. Table this discussion? Tomorrow is another day. Another chance for me to be a better man. And for you to start over."

"Yeah." I sigh. "It's just that starting over is so scary. I really want a child. But I'm running out of time." I let out a dreamy sigh, picturing a baby in my arms.

I've done this often—imagining the warm, heavy bundle against my chest. The little chubby feet and starfish hands. Tonight, the baby of my daydreams has deep brown eyes. Just like…

"Ooh! You know what would be *amazing?*"

"Hmm?" he asks sleepily.

"You should be the father," I blurt. And as soon as the words are out, I realize how *perfect* this idea is. *Oh, wow.* I take a hot breath just imagining it. "You would make the most beautiful babies. They'd be so smart and so kind."

Matteo doesn't say anything, and for a moment, I fear that he's fallen asleep. But when I roll to face him, I find him staring at me, wide-eyed in the dark.

"What?" I demand. "It's a great idea. You know, if you're into it. You like sex, right?" And then I realize my mistake. "Or—wait —maybe you don't want sex with *me*. We could use a turkey baster. Problem solved."

Matteo opens his mouth. Then he closes it again. "*Leila,*" he says finally.

"What?" I'm wide awake now, still full of margaritas and excellent ideas. "I love this idea. I'm surprised I never had it before."

He pinches the space between his eyes. "Honey, nobody in their right mind wants me to be a father."

"That is *not* true," I insist. "Ask anyone. The women of Colebury would form a line."

He snorts. "Not the sober ones, honey. Let's try to get some sleep."

"I might be too drunk for that," I admit.

He chuckles and rolls onto his back. "Just try. Don't you have to work in the morning?"

"Oh shit. This might hurt."

He laughs again. "Night, buddy."

"Night," I whisper.

I close my eyes carefully, wishing the room would stop spinning.

And when it does, I dream of babies with dark-chocolate eyes.

CHAPTER 14
MATTEO

Leila's alarm goes off way too early. My eyes don't want to open.

"Ow," she says. Then I hear her fumble around for her phone, silencing it.

I drift off, but the damn alarm sounds again a little while later. From Leila's side of the bed comes a few whispered curses.

I lay still as she gets up and shuffles toward the bathroom. Poor girl is probably hungover. And unless I'm mistaken, she's due at the preschool in under an hour.

The shower comes on a couple minutes later, and I finally sit up. I'm groggy, and the room is in disarray.

Not as much disarray as my mind, though. Had Leila really asked me to...? Even privately, I almost can't finish the sentence. She'd asked me to... impregnate her.

Unbelievable.

I give my head a shake, and I look around for my clothes. I should get out of Leila's space so that she can get ready. And—bonus—I can hit up my sister's coffee shop, which is right across the parking lot.

After getting dressed, I trot down the stairs and cross the lot to the Busy Bean. It's already open for business, with a few early customers seated inside.

And even though she closed the Gin Mill last night, Zara is

behind the counter, using tongs to transfer a batch of steaming muffins onto a tray, and chatting with a customer.

I take a minute to look around at the baked goods inside the glass case and the comfortable but mismatched furniture in the spacious room.

My siblings are killing it. They must never sleep.

Finally, it's my turn to order, and I step up to the counter. "Hey, lady. Nice place you got here."

She looks up at me with a smirk. "I saw your car in the lot when I drove in this morning."

"So?" I shrug. "Had to make sure she was all right. She'll be feeling that hangover. Let me get her a cup of coffee to go—splash of milk—and whatever her favorite baked good is. Then double that order for me."

"Look who's a nice guy," she says, reaching for the paper cups. "So selfless. No ulterior motives at all."

I don't take the bait. "Do I get the sibling discount?"

"No such thing. I have four hungry brothers, and Audrey's family is similarly large. So everybody pays full price. Besides—I handed you a wad of cash last night. Five hundred bucks, I think."

I pat my pocket for the envelope. "Five *hundred*?" I pull it out and open the flap, fanning the twenties with my thumb. "This is too much. Don't give me your share." I set a twenty down on the counter.

"I didn't." She rings up my order. "That's your half, and we tipped out the dish washer, too. Alec's business is a cash cow, especially when Giltmaker has a brand-new product. That kind of business should last all summer."

"Five hundred," I repeat slowly. "On a Monday night."

"Could be seven hundred on the weekend, or six without that tight shirt you're wearing." She shakes out a bakery bag and puts a muffin inside for Leila. "The Jesus hair could go either way."

I roll my eyes.

She snickers. "Look, I know Otto wants you to stay for the summer. He has trouble getting good seasonal help. If cash is tight, you could make him a deal. Tell him you'll do some shifts, but only customer-facing work."

I do the math, picturing two or three thousand dollars a week of summer cash. I could lend all that money to my Aspen business and shore up our finances in the fall.

God, it's tempting.

Zara passes me a cup of coffee and a warm muffin on a plate. "This is carrot ginger."

"Sounds heavenly." I pick it up and take a bite. And then I groan, because it's delicious.

Just then the door flies open, and Zara and I both turn to see who it is.

Leila stands there with a wild look in her eye. She's dressed in a long skirt and a fuzzy purple sweater, her hair damp and curling around her face. "Morning," she says in a breathy, rushed voice. "Um, Matteo, I owe you an apology. But I'm running too late to do it justice. So…"

"Here." I take the bag that Zara has prepared for her, and I set it in her hands. "Coffee and a muffin. Take a breath, honey. We'll talk later."

She looks down into the bag, and then back up at me. Two spots of bright pink appear on her face—one on each cheek. "Wow. Thank you. And…I'm sorry. I was…wow." She swallows hard.

I step in and kiss her on the temple. "Go to work. Don't worry about a thing, okay?"

"Okay," she says breathily. "See you later?"

"Of course."

Leila leaves, and when I turn around, Zara is smirking at me again. "What was *that* about?"

"Nothing," I say quickly.

Zara looks skeptical. "Did that girl jump you last night? Is that why she's embarrassed?"

I shake my head. "Nah. She just said some amusing things."

"Pity." She looks disappointed. "What are you doing today, anyway?"

"Not sure. Do you know if Benito drives his own car to work?"

"Yep. He drives to the state police barracks and then switches vehicles. Why?"

"When I was asking the guys what I could do for them, he joked that I should wash his car." I shrug. "Thought it would be funny."

Zara's hands pause on the cups she's stacking. "Benny would say that's unnecessary, though."

"I know." I spread my hands in a gesture of humility. "But I don't feel right about staying away for so long, and I'll be back in Colorado before you know it. It's just a little thing."

She studies me, her expression serious. "We know your life is somewhere else. Benito doesn't need you to wash his car. He just needs you to answer our texts."

"I'll do that, too."

"Listen…" She grins. "If you really want to be a pal, you can pick up Nicole from nursery school at noon. Dave is golfing, so I was going to have to do it. But then my employees would have to cut their lunch breaks short."

"I'm free at noon. But is this nursery school…"

"Yep!" She grins. "Leila will be so happy to see you."

My eyes narrow at my sister. "Dave is golfing, huh. In April?"

"He's a big golfer," she says with a smile. "Very serious. What a huge favor you'd be doing us."

"Fine," I say with a grunt. "Sure."

"Tell Leila hi for me. I'll text you the address." She snickers. "Twelve sharp!" Then she heads back into the kitchen for another batch of muffins.

———

In the car on the way home, my phone rings.

It's Cara, so I answer immediately. "Hi, honey. Everything okay?" It's only six a.m. in Colorado.

"Everything is *fine*," Sean's wife says immediately. Maybe she's just like me now—certain that every phone call signifies a fresh disaster. "I was just up early and wondering how you're doing."

"Not bad. Sleeping in a trailer. Driving a rental car. Trying to make amends with my family."

"And how's that going?"

"Pretty good, actually. I worked a bartending shift last night. Later I'm picking up my niece from preschool."

"Pics, or it didn't happen." She giggles. "And what about the girl, Leila? Are you seeing her, too? Didn't you say she's a preschool teacher?"

It's a damn shame that women listen so well. "She's okay. I've seen her a couple times. She's going through a rough patch, too. She got, uh, divorced."

There's a silence, and for a second I think the call might have dropped. "*Divorced*. Wow. Interesting timing you have for visiting home."

"Can you not? It's just a coincidence. And try not to freak out when I ask you this question…"

"Ooh! Hit me."

"How do you think my place would do on Airbnb for the summer? I know you and Sean used to earn some coin that way."

"Interesting question," she says. "And we're sure this has nothing to do with Leila's divorce?"

I sigh. "Cara…"

"Yes, Matteo. You could make a mint on Airbnb. You'd need some good photos. But your place is great, and it's walking distance to everything. I'd probably ask five hundred a night, but then double that during the festivals. Or—another idea—I could ask my friend who works at the resort if they know of any VIPs who need a whole summer rental. You could ask twenty-five thousand for the season."

I whistle. "Would you ask her?"

"Of course."

"If this works, I could pay Lissa to go over there and box up all my clothes, clear out the toiletries, and so on."

"Sure, but let me clear out your stash first. Edibles. Condoms."

"Okay, oops."

She snickers. "The whole summer, though? We'll miss you."

"I'm sorry. This just seems like something I need to do."

Cara is quiet for a moment. "Is money really that tight? Could we lose the business?"

Hell. I don't want to lie to my old friend. She deserves the truth. "We won't lose everything. We have assets, but not enough cash. Making lease payments and payroll after Sean's death hurt us a lot without cash coming in. So if I can make fifty grand between the rental and the bartending, we start the new season in a good place."

"Okay." She sounds relieved. "We've had ups and downs before. I never realized we were one bad season away from trouble."

"But it wasn't an ordinary shitty season," I say gently. "It was the worst possible thing."

"Right." She clears her throat. "Thank you for dealing with this. I know you're making a sacrifice."

"It's fine," I insist. "I've needed to come home for years. I just didn't know it could be profitable, too."

"Let me call my friend. I'll do it today," Cara says.

"Thank you, honey. Love you."

"Love you, too, Matteo. I'll text you when I know something."

We say our goodbyes, and she hangs up. I drive another five miles out of town and pull into Otto's farm. When I get out of the car, the first thing I hear is that damn rooster.

Seems like he and I might get a chance to know each other a little better.

CHAPTER 15
FOURTEEN YEARS AGO
RORY AND MATTEO ARE 22, LEILA IS 21

Rory and Leila are supposed to be hanging the lights on the Christmas tree in the Giltmaker's family room. But instead of helping, Rory keeps putting his hands on her hips and kissing the back of her neck.

"Now is not the time," she whispers. "We're going to get caught."

"So?" he says, his hands lingering on her curves. He doesn't see the problem.

Leila is partly amused, partly annoyed. It's nice to be desired. Since they started up together, he wants her all the time.

But her parents don't like Rory, and she's trying to stay on their good side during Christmas break. It's just easier that way.

These days, her father doesn't like *anyone*. Not even Leila. Not since she had the audacity to change her major from business to human development. And now—just like he predicted—she's having trouble scaring up job prospects. Graduation is only a few months away, and she's been a ball of anxiety all semester.

She vented to Rory about it over Thanksgiving break, when he came to fetch her from Burlington. He listened, which was all she really needed him to do. And when she was done, he stunned her with a very ambitious kiss.

They ended up making out right there in his rusty Dodge.

She never saw this plot twist coming. For the last month,

Rory has been making weekend trips to Burlington, and the new thing between them has been a fun distraction at a fragile time.

Her family doesn't know. But they will if Rory keeps nuzzling her ear while she's trying to put lights on a Fraser fir. "Here," she says, pushing the string into his hands. "Loop this around back. This should be a five-minute job, and we've been here half an hour."

He gives her a smile that is not at all penitent, just as her phone beeps with a notification. The text is from her brother, who wants a ride to tonight's pond party.

"Not you," she grumbles, putting the phone away.

"What is it?" Rory asks.

"Nothing. I was hoping it was Matteo. He left me this weird message earlier—*I have a surprise for you.* But that's all he said. No explanation."

"Oh," Rory says, appearing on the other side of the tree again and handing her the string of lights. "I might know what that's about. He's coming to town for three days. I think."

Leila stares at him in shock. "Seriously? Why didn't he tell me?"

Rory shrugs and looks away. "I called him a few days ago, and he said his boss was goin' to a Vermont wedding and taking a private jet. He offered to give Matteo a lift."

"On a private *jet?*" Her eyebrows shoot up. "That's cool."

He shrugs again. "He wasn't sure it would work out. Maybe that's why he didn't tell you."

"Right," Leila breathes. But now her heart is thumping with excitement. *Matteo.* "When would he get here?"

"Dunno. I think tonight? I told him about the pond party. Said we were going."

"Why didn't you *tell* me this?" she demands.

Rory shoves his hands in his pockets and tries to think what to say. The reason is right in front of him—it's that look on her face. Unrestrained excitement. It makes him uneasy.

Everything about dating Leila makes him uneasy. He's nuts for her. Can't keep his hands off her. Can't believe his own luck. The first time he woke up next to her in her little room in Burlington he thought he might still be dreaming.

But he knows he's in over his head. She's not just any girl. And whatever fleeting impulse led her to get involved with him could evaporate at any moment.

The fear of screwing it up burns brightly inside him. Whenever he opens his mouth, the words coming out are never quite right. Not to mention that tomorrow is Christmas Eve, and he hasn't bought her a present yet. Nothing he can afford is anything she'd want. Even if he could figure out what that was.

It's fucking terrifying.

Naturally, Matteo picks right now to show his stupid face in Vermont.

"Did you tell him?" Leila asks softly. "About...?" She opens her mouth and closes it again, unwilling to give a name to whatever this is between them.

His heart drops another notch. "I didn't tell him nothing."

"But we'll have to."

The serious frown on her face makes him feel sick. As if it's a burden, not a joy, to tell their oldest friend that everything in Rory's life is suddenly a thousand times brighter than ever before.

"We could just...not," he suggests.

"But that will make it weird."

"You're making it weird right now," he says, and then smiles, hoping to joke his way out of this.

"No, I'm not." She folds her arms and stares him down with her trademark stubbornness. She presses her lips together, and he just wants to kiss her so bad it's hard to stand still.

"But why should *he* care what we do?" Rory asks. "When has he ever cared?"

"He cares," Leila insists. But then her eyes drop, because he has a point. Matteo has been home to Vermont exactly twice in the last four years.

Out of the corner of his eye, Rory sees a car stop outside at the curb. It's a taxi, and they're rare in Vermont. There's only one in Colebury.

Matteo's brother owns it.

Leila doesn't notice. She's facing Rory, and she's distracted by all the butterflies in her stomach. She's *elated* by the prospect of seeing Matteo. But that joy is a little confusing. The prospect of telling Matteo that she and Rory are a couple fills her with dread, and it's hard to say exactly why.

It's just awkward to talk about, she tells herself. *That's all.*

The other possibility is just too messy to allow herself to consider—that she's dating the wrong guy.

Rory steps forward and cups her face in his palm. "You're overthinking things again," he whispers. "You know I have to take serious measures when that happens."

She smiles, because he's right—she's *fantastic* at overthinking. And he's the opposite—all action, no regrets.

Be fearless, like Rory, she tells herself sometimes. And right now is one of those times. So when he leans in and kisses the corner of her mouth, it's not unwelcome.

The kiss escalates, as Rory's always do. It's hot and possessive.

Possessive is something Rory does well, she's discovered. It's nice to feel needed.

She wraps her arms around him, which means she doesn't notice the man standing outside in the snowy dark. The one who's staring up at the picture window.

———

Snow is falling on Matteo's hair and eyelashes while he looks up in horror. Pain blooms behind his breastbone as Rory lays another deep kiss on Leila.

He was so eager to see her, he couldn't wait another two hours for the pond party. He'd borrowed Damien's taxi and run right over here, her gift in his pocket.

But now he can't bring himself to ring the doorbell. Not with everything crumpling inside him. He's too hurt. And way too angry at himself for staying away too long.

For not realizing this would happen.

For thinking—even for a minute—that he had a chance with her.

95

He's completely forgotten to breathe, and when he finally remembers to gasp for air, that hurts, too.

Everything hurts. He turns away, but the image is burned in his mind, even as he climbs back into Damien's taxi and drives three blocks away.

Fuck the pond party. He'll go home to the crowded trailer and see his family.

First, he needs a minute to steady himself. Hell, more than a minute. If he returns immediately, everyone will ask what's wrong.

Just everything.

He pulls the little box out of his pocket and lifts off the lid. Inside, there's a classy, silver and gold snowflake pendant on a delicate silver chain. He'd returned to that jewelry shop almost three years later, and the design was still available.

It's a sign, he'd thought.

So stupid. She probably forgot all about it.

Just like she forgot about him.

The vise that's gripping his chest makes it hard to breathe. He closes the box, opens the glove compartment, and throws it inside. Literally throws it. Then he slams the compartment shut.

You can't have her, Rory had said once. It had been teenage smack talk, but he'd known in his bones that it was true.

Still is.

He pulls out his phone and opens his text thread with Sean, where there's a new message waiting.

> Hey dude. You make it okay? What's the boss's jet like?

> Bitchin.

> Guess what? I changed my mind. I'm in. When I get back, we'll start planning.

The dots pop up right away. Sean is typing.

> DUDE. STOKED!

Matteo hears those two words in Sean's voice, and he almost smiles.

Almost.

Sean wants to start their own backcountry tour company. It's super risky, and Matteo has been on the fence about it. So much could go wrong.

But now it doesn't matter. He literally has nothing else to lose.

CHAPTER 16
LEILA

There's a reason I don't usually drink. And that reason is four years old and refusing to share the gardening tools with the other children.

"Matthew," I say calmly. "All the children need tools. We are all friends here."

He stands there in his size-four jeans, hands gripping the tool caddy, and glares at me.

Across the yard, I can see my assistant squinting at us, trying to decide if she should intervene in this little standoff.

I give her a weak smile to show that everything is fine. But inside I'm saying a little prayer. *Dear God in heaven, I'll never drink again if you could just persuade him to share.*

Finally, just when I'm almost ready to kneel on the ground and beg, he drops the caddy into the dirt. "Okay. But the purple shovel is *mine.*"

I practically wilt with relief. My head is pounding, and my stomach is gurgling. If it weren't for the muffin and the coffee Matteo had given me, I might not have made it through the last four hours.

Until you've taught preschool hungover, you haven't lived.

Other children swarm, taking tools and spreading out around the garden. This preschool is special. We spend at least half our time outside, and the focus is collaborative, not academic. It's like an antidote to the modern world.

Yet the cost to send your child here from eight until noon each day is over ten thousand dollars for the school year. Which is not at all an antidote to the modern world.

The sun beats down on my back, and my head pounds guiltily. Waking up beside Matteo in bed again was an unwelcome surprise. That's twice in one week.

Yet no sex happened. Or will ever happen, especially after last night's embarrassments.

Honestly, it would be *less* embarrassing if I'd tried to kiss him. That probably happens to Matteo all the time. Instead, I'd asked him to *father my child*.

I let out a quiet groan just thinking about it.

"Miss Leila? Are you okay?" asks Gillian, a four-year-old with a shining dark bob.

"I'm doing quite well," I lie. "Are you?"

"My mama is here," she says with a smile.

I set down my tools and stand up to help Gillian find her backpack and greet her mother. It's pick-up time. The parents are streaming into the parking area now.

I've made it. Praise Jesus.

Oh wait—I've summoned him. It's not Jesus, exactly, but a hot guy with long hair and a body that probably makes women yell, *OH GOD.*

He is, unfortunately, the last man I want to see right now. Clearly, I owe Matteo an apology, but I'm not ready. I haven't rehearsed it eleventy-billion times in my head. I haven't found the right words to say—*I'm sorry I got drunk and flippantly asked you to father my child, even if that is my guiltiest desire.*

Nicole comes running out of the playhouse. "Uncle Matty! You came to get me?"

"Who else?" he asks. And when she grabs his hand, he hoists her up into the air and gives her a toss that makes her giggle.

My heart soars, and then plummets. This man has me tied in knots.

I march over to the picnic table, grab Nicole's things, and

bring them to Matteo. "If you guys aren't in a rush, I have something I'd like to say to you." I can't even look him in the eye, but it would be better to apologize now than to let my embarrassment fester.

"If Nicole is game, we'll wait." He crouches down to his niece's level. "Want to play a little longer?"

"'Course," she says, and runs off toward the playhouse.

"Guess we're staying," he says easily.

Oh boy. I hustle off to send the other children home. The parents are all right on time today, too. Those traitors. I'm going to have to give an unrehearsed apology.

When the play area is empty except for Nicole, I head over to the picnic table where Matteo is sitting in the sunshine, looking calm and thoughtful. And wildly attractive.

I sit across from him. "Thanks for waiting. I owe you an apology for last night."

He chuckles. "You really don't. I've had worse nights. It happens."

"Really? Lots of women get drunk and ask you to father their children? Wait—don't answer that. I can actually picture it."

He tips his head back and laughs. "Nah, but thanks for the ego boost."

"I'm never drinking tequila again."

"Good call." His smile is blinding. "Only a drunk person thinks I should be a father."

"Not true! I think you'd be perfect. That's why drunk Leila asked the question. My sin was assuming that it was a reasonable request. It's a huge deal, and I didn't mean to behave like it isn't."

He gives me a sideways glance. "Isn't that why most women would choose a sperm bank? Because they want an anonymous donor?"

"Do they?" I shrug. "Honestly, I'm kind of hung up on the anonymous part. It scares me. I'd rather my kid have half your genetic material than a stranger's. Because you're amazing."

He's staring at me now, and I realize I'm pedaling in the opposite direction that I meant to.

Shit.

"I'm not that amazing," he whispers. "Never have been. You can do better."

I sigh. "Look, I understand that you're not interested. And I will go to a sperm bank and never mention it to you again. But any kid would be lucky to be as strong and as kind as you are."

"So you're doing this?" he asks. "For sure?"

"Absolutely. If I can afford it in the fall. I'll need to work extra hours this summer to save up."

"I feel that." He shoves his hands into his pockets. "I might stick around Vermont and work for Otto and your dad."

My heart does a cartwheel. "Really?"

"Yeah. But only if I can rent out my condo in Aspen. It's in a very desirable building in the nicest part of town. That place has been a great investment. Hell, I could sell it and buy another place outside of town and solve all my cash issues at once. But I'd rather not uproot my life like that."

"Oh, wow." I picture him driving past my Colebury apartment all summer, and my belly shimmies.

Nicole jumps out of the playhouse, singing to herself. She grabs a child-sized broom and starts sweeping the doorstep.

Matteo watches her and smiles. "Just hypothetically," he says, "if you had a friend be your donor, would the child grow up knowing who the donor was?"

The question startles me. It almost sounds like he's considering my idea. "Well, yeah. At least when the child got older. Knowing your medical history is pretty important. It's one of the reasons that anonymous donors aren't my favorite idea. But knowing who that person is and having that man in your life aren't the same thing. The friend would set his own boundaries."

"Is that fair to a child, though?" he asks quietly. "Here's the name of your bio dad, but you can't call him except for medical information?"

I've thought long and hard about this already. "It's all about setting expectations. If I tell my child that I decided to raise her on my own, but conceived her with the help of a friend, that's a lot different than thinking, *Daddy rejected us*. She'll know it was a choice we made. Unless he wanted to be involved."

"You're brave to try to navigate all this. I can see why people go the anonymous route."

"Yeah, but anonymity is a fallacy. Those mail-in DNA tests that people use now have kind of blown up the whole concept. Anonymous donors can't count on staying that way anymore. It's just…really complicated. And yet there are still women like me who want a baby."

"Like I said, you're brave."

"Or desperate," I say, trying for a joke. "Sometimes that's the same thing."

But he doesn't smile. "Do you have any other friends earmarked for this honor?"

"Nope." I shake my head. "I don't know anyone else well enough to ask this huge favor. And it took me a lot of alcohol to ask you." I shrug. "And look how that turned out. I'm really sorry. Especially for making it weird by bringing up sex. I know you've never thought of me that way."

He laughs again. "It's cute that you think that."

I'm just processing that statement when he stands up suddenly. Nicole is running towards us. "Isn't it lunchtime yet?"

"Yeah, baby. I brought your car seat. You know how the seatbelt works?"

"A'course," she says, wrinkling her nose like that's a stupid question. "Let's go."

Matteo gives me an apologetic smile. "Do you have to teach an afternoon session, too?"

"Absolutely. But there's Advil for that."

He leans down, and gives me a kiss on the cheek. And I get goosebumps, just from that innocent touch. "Hang in there, Leila. Talk soon?"

I nod, speechless.

He goes, and not only am I treated to another view of his backside in a pair of faded jeans, but also of Nicole fitting her small hand into his.

My ovaries dance the mambo.

And then my head throbs.

It's just that kind of day.

CHAPTER 17
MATTEO

At the end of my unsettling week, I'm looking forward to Sunday dinner with my family. Luckily, the commute is a three-minute walk across my uncle's property.

I haven't attended one of these dinners since I was legal to drink. Aside from the bottle of wine I've brought, the traditions haven't changed. My mother has cooked herself into a frenzy in my uncle's kitchen. We try to help her prepare, but since she's fussy about her methods, she ends up shooing us away.

The guest list has slightly expanded to include my siblings' spouses. There's Skye, of course, and also Dave—Zara's husband—and their two children.

Alec and May aren't back from their honeymoon yet, so they're missing out on the pork roast, the eggplant lasagna, three different salads, and a giant homemade cheesecake.

Afterward, I'm feeling pretty fat and happy as we wash our way through a mountain of dishes.

"Want a beer?" Benito asks me when we're done.

"No thanks." My short-term job involves a lot of access to beer, and my liver could use a day off. "Let's go outside instead. You guys still throw around the football?"

Benito grins. "We usually just walk instead. Don't you remember how many times we ended up at urgent care after playing touch football?"

The man has a point. "Fine. Let's walk."

"Can we feed the chickens?" my niece pipes up.

"Sure, kid. Put on your shoes," I tell her.

We head outdoors, and it's just me, Benito, and Zara and the kids.

"Hold still," Zara says. Then she puts some kind of contraption over my head.

"What is this thing?"

"A baby carrier. Here. He's getting heavy for me." She lifts Micah's chubby body from Benito's hip and tucks him into the contraption. He's facing outward from my chest, and he seems to like it.

Fair enough.

Nicole scampers ahead of us as we walk between the pear trees. It's so early in the growing season that their leaves are the size of a fingernail. But I know from experience that this place will be lush and green within weeks.

"Catch any bad guys this week?" Zara asks her twin.

"Got a couple," Benito says. "But I'd rather hear about Matteo's week. How's Leila holding up? That's twice now that Rory has embarrassed her at the bar."

"She's all right, I guess. Although she says she's sworn off alcohol."

Benito grins. "I'd drink, too, if I had Rory for an ex."

"Yeah, well." I clear my throat. "That night I walked her upstairs, I ended up staying over. Just to make sure she was okay."

"*Really*," Ben says meaningfully. "How noble."

I give his shoulder a playful shove. "It wasn't like that. But she asked me something crazy."

"Was it—please rip off my clothes and do me?" Zara asks. "Because I think she's always wanted to ask you that."

"She has *not*. Obviously. Otherwise, that would have already happened. But you're not that far off."

Zara gives me a searching look. "What? I don't understand."

"This is in the vault," I say quietly. "Deep in the vault."

"Of course," my sister says. And Benito nods.

"She wants a child, and she's making plans to do that alone. That night when she got ripped, she asked me…" I clear my throat again. "To be the father."

"So I was *right*." Zara claps her hands together in delight. "Sort of."

"Are you going to do it?" Benito asks.

"*Heck* no." He must be joking. "I'm not the kind of guy who could knowingly get a woman pregnant and then leave town. That's what Dad did. And we hated him for it."

"Hmm," Zara says, and I'm sure she knows what I mean.

Our father was the worst—always leaving my mother to struggle alone. Always promising to do better and then repeating his mistakes.

I haven't seen him since I was eighteen years old, when he left for good. Later that year, I petitioned the state to change my name. I was born Julian Matteo DeSimone, Junior. As soon as I'd hit middle school, I'd shaken off my father's first name by asking people to call me Matteo.

Then, at eighteen, I asked the court to legally change my last name to Rossi—my mother's last name. My siblings liked this idea so much that they did the same thing the following year. They didn't even wait to turn eighteen—they asked my mother to sign off on it.

She did it, too. After all those years of putting up with his bull-shit, she'd finally realized she didn't have to anymore.

The whole lot of them seem much happier now. Not that I've been around much to see it.

"You're nothing like Dad," Zara says now.

"Thanks? I know that, though."

"Do you?" She shrugs. "The whole guilty routine you're doing this week says differently."

"Hey! Don't give him any grief for that," Benito argues. "My car is so shiny right now."

I'd finally snuck over to his place this morning and washed it while Benito and Skye were still asleep. I'd left a note on the windshield that said *you're welcome*.

"That was a joke," I point out. "Don't get used to it."

"The point is that you shouldn't feel guilty for living your life," Zara says. "And if Leila wants you to be her sperm donor, that's an honor. Say no if it makes you uncomfortable. But don't say no just because you think she doesn't know what she's doing."

"That would be *sexist*," my younger brother says gravely. Then he smirks, because sexism always sets Zara off, and Benito is a troublemaker.

Nicole comes trotting back to us. "Who wants to give me a piggyback ride!"

"Uncle Matteo does!" Benito says with a chuckle.

It's really no problem, so—mindful of the baby in front—I kneel down in the grass, and she climbs right up onto my back. We all resume walking toward the chicken coop.

"So what did you tell Leila?" Zara asks, pointing her phone at me to take a picture.

"I got her some Advil and a glass of water and told her it was time to sleep."

"No, *after*," Zara insists. "She said she wanted to apologize."

"Yeah, that was an awkward conversation. I told her there have to be better candidates for that job. She should really find some guy who went to Harvard or who plays the violin."

"But she asked *you*," Ben says. "Never tell a woman she doesn't know her own mind. They hate that."

"I see the rooster!" Nicole yells. "Can I give him some seeds?"

"Yeah, sure." I swing her to the ground and dig into my pocket. I've been keeping sunflower seeds handy, so I can lure the rooster back into his enclosure when I'm tired of hearing his crowing.

I kneel down on the ground and carefully parse some seeds into Nicole's small hand. "Give him those, and then I'll give you more for the hens."

She runs off again as I climb to my feet. The baby on my chest kicks happily. "So anyway, I told Leila that it was a wild idea to think of me as someone's daddy. Like, nobody could picture that, right?"

"Um…" my sister says. "I just watched you carry both my

children at the same time, and then provide Nicole with snacks for a bird. What do you think daddies look like, exactly?"

Benito snickers. "He even got Micah to go to sleep the other night. That's, like, next level."

"I'm so confused right now," I complain. "It sounds like you two actually think this isn't a dumb idea."

"It isn't—if both of you want it," Zara insists. "Tell me this—if you could snap your fingers and give Leila the life she desires, would you do it?"

"Of *course* I would. But it's more complicated than that."

"I know," my sister agrees. "It really is. But don't tell me you're not a good enough guy for the job. That's just not true."

"She's right," Benito says. "Leila should be so lucky."

Not sure I believe them. "It's not going to be me," I insist.

I just wish I could stop thinking about it.

CHAPTER 18
LEILA
MAY

Hangovers only last a day, but embarrassment lasts longer.

My week crawls by, and I avoid the bar downstairs at all costs. I don't even know if Matteo is working, but it's better to be safe than sorry.

My brother Nash surprises me by making a rare visit to town and invites me out to dinner. I'm pretty happy to say yes. I don't see him that often, and I like a free dinner as much as the next girl.

"Meet me at Speakeasy," he'd said. "Is eight o'clock too late?"

"If anything, it's too early."

"Why?" he'd asked.

"You'll see."

Sure enough, Speakeasy is jammed to the gills when we meet up at the front door. "Holy shit," Nash says, whistling under his breath as he peers through the front door at the line of people waiting for a table. "I guess all of Dad's projects are doing pretty well, yeah?"

"True story. We could ask them to bump us to the top of the list, but I'd feel like an asshole."

He laughs. "Got another idea?"

That's how we end up walking into the Gin Mill ten minutes later, even though I swore I'd steer clear of this place for a while.

Naturally, the man I'm avoiding is right there behind the bar, looking devastating in a tight-fitting henley, his hair pulled back into a man bun, his sleeves pushed up onto muscular forearms.

"Hey, isn't that Matteo?" my brother says. "What's he doing back in town?"

"Helping out while Alec is on his honeymoon," I say in a matter-of-fact tone. "And he'd probably ask the same question of you."

"I'm here for the usual reason," Nash says. "To get new ink."

"I figured." My brother values his favorite tattoo shop a lot more than he values his relationship with my father. Not that I blame him.

He pats his left shoulder. "If I say something annoying, don't slug me here."

"Noted."

"Do you mind eating at the bar?" he asks after scanning the room. "Looks like our best option."

I hold back my sigh. "No problem. There are two seats on the end."

"Let's grab 'em."

When I sit down in front of him, Matteo's eyes widen in surprise. "Hey, girly. Didn't expect to see you tonight." His eyes move to my brother, and he grins. "Or you. What's up, Nash?"

"Just passing through on my way to Montreal," my brother replies. "You?"

"Visiting the family." Matteo scoops ice into a glass and pours gin over it. "But I stayed away so long they put me to work."

"I see that." Nash chuckles.

"What can I pour for you guys? You having pizza, too? Kitchen closes in about forty-five minutes."

"We'll get our order in right away, then." Nash grabs a menu off the bar. "What's your favorite pie?"

"I like 'em all," Matteo says. "But tonight I put in a lot of orders for the one with serrano, feta, and onion jam. Sounds weird, but it's amazing. Then there's a Caesar salad pizza, which also sounds odd, but tastes great."

"One of each?" I say to my brother.

"Done," he says. "And I'd love a Goldenpour, please, because

God forbid, I sit in this town and order something from the competition."

Matteo laughs. "Couldn't have that, could we?"

But Nash is not really joking. My father is a very difficult man. He values loyalty above all other qualities in a person, and I don't think he'll ever forgive my brother for working for a competitor.

"Leila?" Matteo asks. "Want a margarita?" He gives me a wink.

"No thank you," I say, pushing the menu away. "Could I have a cranberry and soda?"

"Of course." He reaches for a glass.

"I decided I'm not drinking for a while."

"Interesting," my brother muses. "Any particular reason?"

I don't look at Matteo, but I can feel his smirk. "I live over a bar now, and it's a nice one. I don't want to feel like coming in here every night is hazardous to my health. So I'm laying off the sauce."

"Fair," Nash says, accepting his beer from Matteo. "Now tell me what else is going on in your life."

My face begins to burn as I imagine what he'd say if I answered him truthfully. "Not much," I say. "Let's talk about you instead."

———

Matteo didn't lie when he said that the new pizzas were fantastic. Who knew that Caesar salad belonged on top of a pizza? It clearly does.

And I'm strangely glad that I was forced to see Matteo again. That's the only way to make things normal between us again, right? Getting past my embarrassing question is the only way to go.

So after Nash leaves, I pull a book out of my bag and read at the bar. Matteo keeps my soda glass filled, and I enjoy a spicy novel with the pleasant hum of conversation around me.

This is better than sitting alone upstairs in the church-like quiet of my apartment, wondering why I married a man who didn't appreciate me enough to be a good husband.

Eventually the place quiets down. When I lift my head, I'm the last customer in the bar, and Matteo and another bartender are closing out the cash registers.

I close my book and drain my drink. "Don't I owe you for this last soda?"

"Nah. Nash closed out your tab ages ago. How are you two doing, anyway?" Matteo asks, bracing his hands on the bar.

This has the unfortunate effect of firming all the muscles in his upper body. I make sure to keep my eyes on his face while I answer the question. "I'm good. It was nice to catch up with Nash. He lives in Boston, and we don't see much of each other anymore."

"Huh. Does he know about your big plan?"

I pause a moment until the other bartender ducks under the bar and heads for the kitchen with the last batch of dirty glassware. "No," I tell Matteo. "Nash is bossy. Might try to talk me out of it. He might be my younger brother, but he doesn't understand his role."

"He doesn't bow down to the queen?" Matteo asks, grabbing a rag and wiping down the bar one last time.

"Exactly."

He laughs. "Okay, but when do you plan to tell your family?"

"My mother knows," I tell him. "But the rest? I guess when I can't hide it under a baggy shirt anymore."

He freezes mid-wipe. "That's sneaky. But sooner or later everyone will know. And they'll be nosy as fuck. This town…" He shakes his head.

"You're not wrong. And it's not like I'm immune to gossip. But this is too important to me. I'll handle it. Actually, I was working as the bartender at a faculty event in college…"

His chocolate-brown eyes lift, and he smiles. "I forgot you worked as a bartender in college. Why aren't you back here helping me?"

"Oh, please. I wrangled four-year-olds all day. But get this—on one of my shifts, I watched a male professor eye a female professor's belly, and then say, 'I didn't know you got married.'"

"Uh-oh." Matteo shakes his head. "Even I'm not dumb enough to say that."

"Right? And this woman gave him the sneer he deserved. She said, 'I thought you were so educated. It's actually possible to have a child without a husband.' And instead of laughing it off, he doubled down by asking her who the father was."

"Bruh." Matteo cringes. "*No*."

"I know. But all she said was, 'That's between my child and me. Someday you can ask her, and maybe she'll tell you.'"

"That's a badass response."

"I thought so too, and I never forgot it. Who knows? I might get to use that line myself someday soon."

He nods, thoughtful. "You've been thinking about this awhile, yeah?"

"I have."

He folds his arms across that impeccable chest. "My sister seems to think I should do this with you."

Wait, what? "You told your *sister*? There's another person I can never look in the eye again."

"Really?" He cocks his head. "I thought you really hoped I'd consider this."

"Um…" My mind whirls. Is he *actually* considering it? "I did. I do. So much that I couldn't ask you sober."

"I'm trying to give the idea its due, yeah? And I didn't think I could do that without a little confidential chat with Zara. She knows as much as anybody about having a baby alone."

"Of course she does." And of course he shouldn't have to consider something so important without a discussion with his family. "You're right. What did she say?"

He straightens the clean glassware on the shelf, a thoughtful expression on his face. "She said I should take it on faith that you knew what you were doing. And not to question the logic of using me, of all people."

"*Matteo*. The world needs more people like you. And Zara is right—if it's not you, it will be some other guy. A less wonderful guy."

His hands go still on the glassware. Then he slowly turns to face me, hands braced on the bar, a serious expression in his dark eyes. "Tell me exactly how this would go," he whispers. "How you'd time it. That kind of thing."

I blink. "Um…" I can't believe we're actually having this conversation. "In about eight days, the timing would be right. I'd use an ovulation kit to help me figure out the best possible day."

He nods once, encouraging me to go on. But I'm struggling, because I never rehearsed this conversation.

"I'd have some, um, papers for you to sign, explaining that the child would be entirely my responsibility, and that you were, um, *donating* at my specific request."

A smile slowly forms on his chiseled face. "Go on."

We're getting to the really tricky stuff. And *this* is why sober me would never have found a way to bring this up. "You would, um, have a routine test for…"

"STDs," he says. "Sure."

"Okay, yup, and…" I'm stammering now. "Uh, at my age, one time probably wouldn't be enough. So you'd be, um, signing up for a couple of months of this. And you'd have to abstain. Like, *really* abstain. Even from…" I cannot say the word *masturbation* in this bar. "They usually ask donors to, um, save it up for a couple days beforehand."

He drops his chin and laughs. "Okay. Yeah. That wouldn't have occurred to me."

My face is on fire now. "It's a lot to ask," I babble.

He stops laughing and looks down at me with a tenderness that takes my breath away. "But those details are small, aren't they? Compared with creating a whole new person. And being responsible for half their DNA."

"That's the easy part for me," I insist. "A kid could do so much worse than being half of you."

He drums his fingers against the bar. "Leila, I wish I were the guy you think I am."

Oh honey, you're everything. But somehow, he doesn't believe that. I swallow hard and hold his intense gaze.

He smiles, eventually. "You didn't quite give me *all* the details. Did you figure we'd do this the old-fashioned way? Or with a turkey baster? Because I have opinions."

Oh God. "Whatever, um, makes you the most comfortable. I don't have an opinion about that."

His eyebrows shoot upward. "Really? No opinion at all?"

"Um, no? I mean, I could make an argument either way."

Laughing, he shakes his head. "Really? Miss I-only-use-organic-lip-balm doesn't care? I would have thought the whole all-natural aspect of the DIY method was part of your calculus."

"Well…" I clear my throat. "Natural probably works best. It's just true. But I'd never want to make things awkward between us."

Matteo leans over, forearms on the bar, and gets close enough to me for a very private conversation. "You don't want to make things awkward."

I shake my head. "As much as I want a child, I wouldn't want to ruin our friendship."

"Huh. So let's talk this through. Behind door number one, we have old-fashioned sex. Everybody gets a little stress relief, and we make a baby the old-fashioned way."

He makes that sound so simple and breezy. But taking my clothes off with Matteo? I want to fan myself just thinking about it.

"Now, door number two is a situation where I come over to your place, and you hand me a paper cup. I go hide in your bathroom for twenty minutes with some porn on my phone and rub one out while you turn the TV up and pretend not to picture me doing it. Do I have that right?"

I nod, and my face is volcanic.

"Uh-huh," he says thoughtfully. "Then you go lie down in the bedroom with a cup of my still-warm spooge and try to get it all the way up where it counts. Then we order a pizza and repeat the whole process a couple hours later?"

I gulp.

"Sure, babe. That doesn't sound awkward at all." He tips his head back and laughs.

"Okay. Well." I eye the fire extinguisher behind the bar, wondering if we might need it for my face. "When you put it that way."

He laughs harder.

"I didn't know you were actually thinking about this."

"Can't seem to think about anything else." He shrugs. "The question is, though, whether I'm considering it because it's generous. Or because I want to bang you."

Oh my. His smile is full of heat, and I feel it everywhere. "Couldn't it be, um, both?"

His smile fades as he removes his apron. "I guess."

The other bartender emerges from the kitchen. "All set back here. Should I shut off the lights?"

"Sure thing!" Matteo calls.

I slide off the barstool, my heart pounding. Did we really just have that conversation?

Matteo ducks under the bar, keys in his hand. I head for the door like a zombie, my mind spinning with questions, and a few inappropriate images.

"Leila, honey? Isn't that your stuff?" He points at the bar, where I've left all my worldly possessions.

"Uh, yup." I hurry back and grab them. "Sorry."

"No problem," he says. But his smile knows all my secrets.

CHAPTER 19
MATTEO

I'm cutting limes behind the bar at the Gin Mill when Cara's text comes in.

> Buddy, I asked 50k and some fool said yes.

I read it twice before responding.

> Really??? FIFTY grand for three months?

She responds with a string of money emojis, and:

> Yup. May 15 to August 15. And with a 10k security deposit.

> Hope you're comfortable in that trailer because it looks like you're staying awhile.

I look up from my phone and let that sink in for a second. A whole summer in Vermont, serving beer. A year ago, I was planning a summer of travel and adventure, and now I'm a bartender.

But my family is here, and there are worse jobs. Besides, keeping busy is good for me right now. I can't spend the summer like I spent the spring—brooding on my sofa in Colorado.

So I write back to Cara.

Thank you, babe. Now we don't have to tap our
line of credit.

That's handy. But I hope you're not doing this
for me.

It's for me, too.

That's not even a lie. I want to do right by Cara and Lissa. And
I want to see a little more of my family.

And then there's Leila...

CARA

I'll send you some clothes. What else do you
need?

MATTEO

Not much. But some more clothes would be
nice.

Tight shirts, mostly.

CARA

No problem. We'll miss you!

MATTEO

I'll miss you guys, too!

I'm just about to shove my phone back into my pocket when I
see an email from the health clinic I visited in Burlington yesterday. I open it up and scan the results. As predicted, I'm healthy.
Without comment, I forward the email to Leila.

Unless she's gotten cold feet, I expect to hear from her in four
days or so with an urgent request for sex.

I can barely wrap my head around it, but I want to give Leila
her heart's desire.

It's an honor, my sister had said, and it resonated with me.

"Dude, on your phone behind the bar? Really?"

"Jesus." Startled, I drop my phone and glare at Alec, who's

picked this exact moment to arrive home from his honeymoon. "We're not even *open*. I just had to reply to a text!"

Alec laughs. "I'm *kidding*. You've been awesome. Connor tells me you're more useful than half the people who work here."

"Oh." My irritation falls away. "How was the honeymoon?"

"Didn't want to come back. Best two weeks ever." He strolls up to the bar, looking tan and relaxed. "What did I miss?"

"Not much. I did some babysitting. Poured about seven million beers. Ate a whole lot of those pizzas you make here. Woke up every morning at five, because Otto has a rooster who loves the sound of his own voice."

Alec laughs. "And my bars are both still standing?"

"I can only vouch for this one." I pat the bar top. "But I'm about to tell Otto that I can stay for the summer. He asked me to help manage a beer wagon that he and Lyle Giltmaker bought."

"Get out of here. Seriously?" He pulls out a barstool and sits down. "Don't tease me like this. They had so much trouble staffing that thing last summer, and of course Otto tried to make it my problem."

I shrug. "Someone wants to rent my Aspen condo for the season for fifty grand. I can stay at Otto's for free."

Alec slaps the bar. "This is the best news I've heard all day. Plus, I get a front row seat if you make an ass of yourself to Leila."

Oh God. I hate my siblings. "I'm not going to do that."

"Sure." He grins. "Of course not."

"She just got divorced."

"I noticed that." His grin expands.

There's no way in hell my family can know if I help Leila with her little project. I suppose Zara and Ben will wonder.

But I'm not admitting anything.

CHAPTER 20
LEILA

I'm sitting on my couch with a book when I happen to check my email. I find Matteo's message. No comment, just a battery of tests, all negative.

Holy…

Surprise makes me shoot to my feet. I can't believe he's going through with this. That's what this means, right?

I need to know. Matteo is probably downstairs tending bar—I think he was scheduled for tonight in case Alec's flight was late.

Then again, it's seven p.m., and the bar is probably three deep with thirsty patrons. I can't exactly have a private conversation with the man right now.

Does this mean he's all in? For real?

My heart has a serious case of the flutters, and my eyes feel damp. I can't believe he'd do this for me. It's too much to ask.

I pull out my phone with shaking hands.

> I got your email. But I don't want to jump to conclusions. Does this mean you've made up your mind?

While I wait for his reply, I pace around the apartment, trying to get used to the idea that this might really happen. I head down the hallway to the empty second bedroom and flip on the light.

It's a small room with windows facing the back of the building. I can picture a crib against the wall and a fuzzy rug covering the wood floor. A rocking chair just like Zara has. And a changing table on top of the dresser, where the drawers will be filled with little onesies and tiny socks.

I take a deep breath and try to breathe through my excitement. Then I flick off the light and leave the room. My bedroom is, of course, the only other room on this hallway. My eyes leap to the king-sized bed that's snugged against the brick wall.

A bed where Matteo might remove all my clothing.

The flutters in my stomach redouble.

Okay, don't panic. This will be fun. Matteo hinted that he was looking forward to it. So why am I so nervous all of a sudden?

Oh right—because I haven't gotten naked with anyone new since I was in college.

And Matteo is a lifelong friend. What if we have the most awkward sex in the history of sex?

I give a little shiver of horror, and then I hear my phone ping. I trot over to the sofa and pick it up.

MATTEO

I'm in. I want to do this for you.

Oh my heart. It's fluttering again.

In the interest of full disclosure, I also want to do you.

Now a different part of me flutters.

So when is it showtime?

I check the date, and do a little math.

LEILA:

Probably Saturday. Hopefully you're not planning a weekend away.

120

MATTEO

Saturday is the Vermont Taste Fest. I'll be taking the beer wagon on its maiden voyage. But that's over at six.

LEILA:

Okay, cool.

I slap my forehead. *Okay, cool?* I sound like we're planning a trip to the grocery store. Then again, I've never planned a meetup for sex before. With anyone. I don't know the rules.

If there's a special etiquette for arranging your own impregnation, none of the fertility books I'm reading have covered that yet.

My hands are sweating on my phone, and Matteo seems to be done with the conversation. I tuck my phone into my pocket and locate my wallet and keys. I've got to get out of this apartment for a little while. My nerves need exercise.

I head out—skipping the bar, where I'd probably just stare awkwardly at Matteo—and drive up the hill, through the cute center of town, and onto the commercial strip that follows. My destination is Walgreens. I have some business to take care of.

In the reproductive-health aisle, I take my time reading the packages for every brand of ovulation test. They all seem the same, and they all promise superior accuracy, so I choose a package of ten ovulation kits and also one pregnancy test.

Why not be prepared, right? Good vibes and all that.

In the front of the store, I add a pack of gum to my basket. Wait—I also need some breath mints. I haven't kissed anyone new since the Obama administration.

Hold on. Will there be kissing? I'd just assumed. But maybe that's too personal. How would I know how modern hookups work? But you never know…

I add an extra tin of breath mints to my basket, just in case.

I make my way to the self-checkout. "START SCANNING NOW!" the machine yells at me.

"Calm down," I whisper under my breath. I scan the mints and the gum and toss them into a bag. And then the ovulation kits…

"Leila?"

My chin snaps up. "Rory?" Holy cow. He's standing right in front of me. Practically in my face.

"Hey, uh, glad I caught you." He clears his throat. "I have a question. What is that special kind of soap the washer needs?"

"H-E!" I practically shout. "That stands for high efficiency." *Just please, please don't look at the last item in my basket.*

"Okay, uh, thanks." He gives me a quick, guilty smile. "Sorry to bother you. Exciting weekend, huh?"

Then it happens—his gaze drops to the basket, where a pregnancy test is the only item left.

"ARE YOU FINISHED SCANNING?" demands the checkout robot. "PRESS 'FINISH AND PAY,' OR PRESS 'NEED ASSISTANCE!'"

"Leila?" Rory gasps, his voice pure shock. "Are you…?"

"What? *No.* Hold on." I quickly scan the pregnancy test and throw it into my bag. Then, with a shaking hand, I pull out my credit card and finish the transaction.

Meanwhile, Rory's arms are crossed, and he's staring at me with the kind of mounting anger that suggests flames are about to erupt from all his facial orifices.

"PLEASE TAKE YOUR RECEIPT! THANK YOU AND GOODBYE!"

A receipt as long as highway 89 comes spooling out of the machine, and I grab it and head outside.

Rory follows me, and we barely clear the doors before he starts spitting questions at me. "Pregnant? Holy shit. Is it mine?"

"Shhh!" I demand. "God, no. If I were pregnant right now, that would be an immaculate conception."

He blinks. "Okay, yeah. But then what the fuck…?"

It's hard to speak through gritted teeth, but I manage it. "Sometimes women pick up things for their friends. Private things."

His face relaxes. "Oh. Shit. I just imagined…" He shakes his head.

"Well just *stop*," I insist. "Besides—you stonewalled me for *years* about having kids. And I respected that, until you made our

122

marriage impossible. That's when you gave up your right to inquire about my private life. So this will be the last time we ever have this conversation."

He rolls his eyes. "Yeah, 'cause it's such a good time."

"Whatever, Rory. Go roll your eyes at someone new. And if I'm ever lucky enough to move on with my life, you don't get to ask questions. You don't get to comment. Even if I leave the store with a carload of lube or condoms or Jack Daniel's or any goddamn thing! It's none of your business."

His face hardens. "Message received."

"Good. Now have a pleasant evening."

I turn around and storm off. After all this time, I finally learned how to make an exit.

Should have done it sooner.

CHAPTER 21
MATTEO

It's probably a blessing that I have to work today. Otherwise, I'd sit around all day fantasizing about upcoming events.

It's a warm Saturday, and I've already hauled my uncle's beer wagon behind his pickup truck to the fairgrounds in Tunbridge. Now I'm setting up under the hot sun.

The beer wagon is a jaunty metal trailer with a barrel-shaped roof. The exterior is painted a minty green, with stylish wooden panels and a narrow bar that folds down from the broad serving window. There's also a chalkboard where the menu and prices are meant to be posted.

The whole setup is really charming, and once again I have to marvel at my family's ingenuity. What better way to advertise craft beer than driving it all around New England to sell it at a premium?

I can already tell that it's going to be a busy day. The food festival doesn't start for another half hour, but the hordes are already queued up, buying tickets and gathering near the gate.

This is the only beer truck in the whole place, but there are at least two dozen food vendors, plus a homemade root beer guy, a maple soda guy, and a lemonade cart.

It's hot, too, so my line will be long. Otto swore he was sending out someone to help me, but so far, I don't see anyone else.

Setting up takes about a half hour. I've hooked the wagon to the power source and tested the taps. I've got three taps, each with different beers. The total number of kegs is four, although Otto provided me with only three hundred cups.

I've also got a few cases of bottles and cans of beer, an empty tip jar, and a hundred dollars in change.

And a tight T-shirt, because I'm here to make a profit. Although I'd better not be doing it alone, or Otto is going to get an earful.

Just when I'm starting to panic, I spot Lyle Giltmaker striding toward me. I haven't seen him since I was eighteen, but he has the same formidable set to his shoulders and the same scowl.

Well, this is awkward. I've just spent the first ten or so hours of the day trying not to think about the text Leila sent me this morning.

> Took an ovulation test this morning, and it showed me a smiley face. So unless you've changed your mind, tonight is the night.

After replying with a smiley face of my own, I've tried to put it out of my mind. But now I'm staring down her dad, who's reaching out to shake my hand.

"Hello, sir," I say as he approaches. "It's been a while."

We shake, and he squints up at me. "Did you swing by to ask me for a business loan?"

"What? No! I'm just helping out Otto."

He laughs suddenly. "*Joking*, kid. Jesus. Heard you own a heli-skiing business in fucking Aspen. Nice work."

"Thanks?" I'm so confused right now. "Do you happen to know who's coming to serve with me?"

"That would be me," he says grumpily. "The bartender we'd scheduled has a family emergency, and it was really too late to find anyone else."

"Uh, okay. Cool. Wasn't expecting it to be you."

"Me neither," he grumbles. "But you know how it is. These things happen when you run a business. Any other questions before this thing starts?"

"Well…" I try to pull my head back into the game. "Otto told me to price everything at ten bucks. But I think Goldenrod is going to sell out fast, so I'm going to raise the price." I open the metal door and hop down to the grass. With the side of my fist, I erase the 10 next to Goldenrod and replace it with 12.

"Making change will be messier," Lyle points out.

"I can count to eight," I insist. "Bigger problem—we don't even have enough cups to serve out these kegs."

"Well, *that* is a pain in the ass," he grumbles. "This crowd looks thirsty. I'm on it." He unlocks his phone and taps a number. "Leila. I'm up here in Tunbridge at the food fest, but Matteo says we don't have enough cups. Bring us a couple hundred?"

Uh-oh.

"You're trying to have a relaxing Saturday? Well, so was I. But we need cups, and you're the only member of this family within a hundred-mile radius that's speaking to me. So get in your car in ninety minutes and bring us some cups from the warehouse. You still want that summer job, right? Well, this is your first task."

You asshole. I manage not to say it aloud, but it's a close call. Lyle could have driven to the nearest country store and bought them out of cups.

But I don't get the chance to suggest it. He's already hung up, and now the festival gates are opening to the masses. A significant number of the ticket holders make a beeline toward our wagon.

Lyle and I climb inside the wagon and get to work.

Maybe he's a dick, but at least he's efficient. We pour beers. We pop the tops off bottles. We take cash and make change. We smile.

The beer flows out, and the money flows in. I have to empty the tip jar every twenty minutes. It's not lost on me that handing people eight dollars in change is better for the tip jar than handing them a ten.

Note to self—get a bigger tip jar.

I'm too busy to think about Leila or sex… At least until she shows up at the halfway mark, wearing a sundress and carrying a giant cardboard box full of cups.

Am I really taking that dress off her in a few hours? Unfuck-ingbelievable.

"Hey," she says, giving me a nervous smile as I hop out of the wagon to take the box. "I brought, uh…" She looks down at the box. "Cups."

Aw, Leila is nervous? I bite back a smile as I take the box. "Thank you, queen."

She smiles, then looks away.

"Leila, girl," her father says. "Could you help out in here so I can take a break?"

"S-sure," she stammers. "In a second!"

"And Matteo—change the Goldenrod tap?"

"Will do!" I call. I duck behind the trailer and drop the box to the ground, then reach into my back pocket for my pocketknife.

"Matteo?" Leila has followed me around to the back of the wagon. "Can I speak with you a sec?"

"Of course." I slice open the box. "What's on your mind?"

If she's about to call off our plans for later, I might just fall to my knees and weep.

CHAPTER 22
LEILA

Staring up at Matteo, I try to figure out what to say. I've spent the last few days imagining how tonight might unfold, and it's left me both jittery and turned on.

It doesn't help that Matteo's jeans fit his ass like a bumper sticker, and his tanned arms flex as he opens the box.

"Okay, look. If you think I'm wrecking everything, would you tell me?" I blurt. "We've known each other for over twenty years. That's a really long time. Two decades of, you know, not doing it. *It* meaning…" I gulp.

He stands up tall, his expressive eyebrows lifting. "Sex?"

"Well, yeah. I've just spent the last few days wondering if it would be *very* awkward. I don't want to torpedo our friendship."

"*Torpedo*. Interesting word choice."

I die inside.

He smirks, which shouldn't look sexy on a man, and yet somehow does on him. "Is that the only thing you're worried about?"

"Of course. Aren't you?"

"Fuck no."

"You're not? But what if it's awkward?"

"It won't be."

"Really? How do you know?"

He stares at me with knowing brown eyes while I wait for him to explain.

And he does—just not the way I'm expecting. Instead of using words, he puts his hands on my waist. My back hits the wagon, and his hot, bossy mouth takes mine in a sudden kiss.

Oh, I think as his hand strokes down my jaw, landing possessively at my neck. Then he changes his angle of attack and kisses me again as an urgent, hungry sound comes from his chest.

That sound vibrates wildly through all the cells of my body, and I feel myself soften everywhere that matters.

He kisses me again, with so much urgency that I forget myself and grip his hard body with both hands. Matteo's tongue strokes into my mouth. If heat had a taste, it would taste like Matteo's kiss. I feel seared from the inside.

Then, abruptly, it ends. He steps back, giving me a hot look. "That's how I know."

At that, he grabs two sleeves of cups from the box and disappears around the side of the wagon.

"Get that tap?" my father's voice asks.

"On it," he replies easily.

"We got a long line again," my father complains. "Where's Leila?"

"Just unpacking the cups," he says. "I'm sure she'll be here in a second."

Nope. I'm going to need a moment. I take several deep, calming breaths.

I'm only half as nervous, but I'm twice as eager, and there are still many hours to go.

I take another shaky breath, then I make myself duck around to the wagon's door and climb in.

———

The next couple of hours seem to last forever. Matteo and I work side by side, barely speaking, save for words like "two Goldenrods" and "two cups, please."

He's working as hard as a soldier in battle, and I can hardly keep up. My mind keeps straying to that kiss and wondering when I can get another one.

Luckily the beer runs out before the festival ends. "That was exhausting," my father complains as we begin to break down the wagon and pack the truck. "How about this—you two finish cleaning up, and you can split the tip jar."

"It's not really my money," I say quickly.

"Sure it is," Matteo insists as he faces a stack of bills. "You drove out here to bring us supplies and stayed to help. Lyle, here's your bank deposit. I'm changing out the tips for twenties, though, so I don't have to buy groceries with singles, like a stripper."

My father laughs as he takes the cash pouch. "All right. Good work today. Tomorrow I'll send Otto a bottle of scotch for convincing you to stick around this summer."

This summer. "The whole summer?" I squeak.

They both turn to look at me. "Yeah," my dad says, hitching up his pants. "He's going to run the wagon all over Vermont for us. It's good promo and very profitable, too."

"I was going to mention that," Matteo says, yanking the elastic out of his hair and sending dark waves tumbling to his shoulders. "Slipped my mind. Here's your split of the tip jar."

My mind is still stuck on having Matteo around all summer. I take the bills numbly, but then notice it's quite a stack. "Wait—how much did you just hand me?"

"Just over four hundred bucks," he says, untying his apron.

I look down at the wad of money. "*Really?*"

He shrugs. "People like to tip hardworking bartenders, almost as much as they like your family's beer."

"They even like to overpay for the mass-market crap in bottles," my dad says with a sniff.

"Spoken like a true beer snob," I mutter.

"You say that like it's an insult. Later, kids." My dad gives us a mock salute. "I'm going home to catch the hockey playoffs."

"Have a good evening," Matteo says cheerfully.

And just like that, we're alone.

All alone.

"You hungry?" Matteo asks.

"*Definitely*," I say in an overheated voice. And then I realize he meant for *food*.

"All right." His smile understands my mistake. "You mind stopping for takeout on the way home? I've got to drop off the wagon and Otto's truck. I can meet you at your place."

"Okay," I say, blushing furiously. "I can grab some food. What do you want?"

Instead of answering right away, he drags his gaze slowly down my body, and then up again. After a very thorough perusal, he meets my eyes. "Whatever you want. But pick something that can sit around a little while."

"Why?"

His shrug is nonchalant. "I might not let you eat it right away. Now let's move. Can't let that smiley face go to waste, yeah?" Then he winks. Like this is just a night of fun between friends.

Which it is, right? But it's also possibly changing the course of our friendship, and the course of our lives.

I take a deep breath and then turn to go before his smile engulfs me in flames.

———

Somehow I drive back to Colebury without crashing my car. I even manage to pick up food for two at my favorite noodle shop on the way.

At home, I set the food down on the counter, and then run to the bathroom to brush my teeth and splash water on my face. My hair is frizzy from the humid springtime air, but there's no helping that now.

I guess I'm ready. Last night I shaved and plucked and waxed every relevant inch of myself, feeling as foolish as a virgin on prom night. Going to bed with Matteo is a big deal, even if he won't admit it.

Back in the kitchen, I fill two glasses with ice and homemade lemonade. I'm taking the first gulp of mine when there's a knock on the door.

Breathe, I remind myself. Then I pop over to open the door.

He steps into the room and closes the door with a firm click. The look he gives me is molten.

Wow. Is it hot in here? "Lemonade?" I say, nipping back over to the kitchen area, where I've left our glasses. I'm trying for a breezy attitude. *See what a great hostess I am? I'm offering you a refreshing beverage before I remove your designer jeans.*

Matteo takes his glass and sips, watching me over the rim. I don't think I've fooled him. My heart is pounding so loudly I can practically hear it.

He sets down the glass and considers me. "You okay?"

"Yup," I say, bobbing my head like a frisky horse.

"All right." He circles the counter, stepping into my personal space. He takes my lemonade glass out of my hand and sets it down. Then he reaches up and cups my jaw in his hand.

His body radiates heat, and I feel an age-old pull that's achy and familiar. "It's just a *lot.* Big things. Big decisions. Big thoughts," I babble. "It's just so *big.*"

"That's what she said," he rumbles.

My eyes bulge. "Matteo!"

He smiles, and I relax just a touch. I don't even panic when he dips his head to kiss me. His mouth is both soft and firm. I get a whiff of lemonade, and also sunshine. My squirrel brain goes quiet for once, and my heart rate slows down as I lean into the kiss.

One of his broad hands lands at my back, pressing firmly between my shoulder blades, as if commanding me to be still.

I nearly go limp against his chest when he tilts his head and kisses me again. "That's better," he whispers between kisses. "Good girl."

I don't know why my knees go a little weak when he says that. Matteo catches me around the waist and leans me against the refrigerator. I grip his ribcage with both hands. He's so solid to the touch. Bulkier than my ex.

Lord help me, but I like it a lot.

Matteo breaks our kiss, and I let out a gasp of complaint. That kiss was basically holding me together. But now he lowers his mouth to my neck, and my body ripples with instant chills. I tip my head to the side to make room for the soft, wet kisses he's dropping onto my oversensitive skin.

"This dress," he rasps between kisses. He puts one of those big hands right on my breast and gives me a bossy squeeze. "Been wanting to rip it off you for hours."

Okay. Wow. I clench my thighs together at the idea of Matteo removing my dress. Hell, I can't even remember the last time I felt such hunger pointed in my direction. Maybe never. "There's a zipper," I volunteer.

He chuckles against my heated skin. "Good tip, honey. But I got this."

Indeed he does, because the same hand that squeezed my tit has now dipped beneath the hem of my dress. I actually whimper a little when it slides up the back of my thigh. His fingertips breech the elastic of my panties as he teases the swell of my ass, a naughty touch that makes me gasp again.

Matteo lowers his hot mouth onto mine and swallows my moan. This kiss isn't subtle, either. It's wet and hungry. I'm braced between his hard body and the refrigerator door as his tongue slides commandingly into my mouth.

But I don't feel trapped. I feel *held*. Like I don't have to think so hard for once, because Matteo has got this, and he's running the show.

And what a show it's going to be. Impossibly, his kiss deepens, and I flood with desire.

He must sense it, because he groans into my mouth. His roughened palm squeezes my ass, and I shamelessly hike a knee, wrapping my leg around his body. This draws him even closer, where I can fit myself against the hard ridge in his jeans.

Of all the hours we've spent together in our lives, not one of them felt like this. I've gone twenty years without knowing how he tastes (fabulous!) and without knowing the feel of his heated skin under my hands as I nudge his T-shirt up and out of the way, so I can handle more of him.

My exploration is cut off when he suddenly plucks me off the floor with one corded forearm under my ass.

I wrap my arms around him as he carries me out of the kitchen area and makes the turn down the hall toward my bedroom. A moment later I'm tossed gently onto the comforter. He leans down, his strong arms braced on the bed, and gazes at me with heavy-lidded eyes. "You ready?" he rasps.

"*Yes.*" It comes out as a whisper, even if it's true. My nipples are hard, and my panties are damp, and I don't know why we're still talking.

"Good," he growls. And then he pounces. There's no other word for it. His magic hands are everywhere, and his kiss is like fire. My nerves are gone. I'm too busy drinking down his kisses and tugging at his clothes. I hear the metallic *zzzz* of my zipper giving way as he relieves me of my dress. And then my bra. He curses under his breath as he flings it off the bed.

He dips his head down to kiss his way onto the swells of my breasts. I ought to feel very naked right now, but I'm too distracted by soft, hungry kisses and roughened hands caressing my skin. We both groan as one of my pebbled nipples slides against his tongue. I can't shut down my shiver.

As a teen I'd always wondered how it felt to be seduced by Matteo Rossi. And now I finally know.

It feels amazing.

I thread my fingers through his long hair and feel my thighs clench against too much nothingness.

Matteo takes his time. He leaves one breast, only to fall upon the other one. I give his hair an impatient tug.

"You need more?" he asks between twisting, licking kisses to my nipple.

"You know I do."

He chuckles, rising to kiss the sensitive place just beneath my ear. "Is this a good time to point out that you're the one who wanted to hand me a paper cup?"

"Don't gloat."

He laughs. And then he flattens me against the bed once again, his hard chest against my heavy breasts, and takes my mouth in an eager kiss.

My body softens instantly beneath his, welcoming the hard

ridge of his arousal between my legs. I lift my knees and pin him there, as if to show him how much better this could get.

"Patience," he says between kisses. "If this is my only night with you, it's gotta be a great one."

It already is, though. No one has ever worshipped me quite like this. For a moment, I feel sad about that. Years of inertia meant that I wasted so much time.

But then Matteo kisses his way down my body, and I forget all about my troubles. He hooks a thumb into the elastic at the hip of my string bikini underwear. But he doesn't remove them right away. Instead, he inches them down my body, centimeter by centimeter, kissing his way across my newly bared skin as he goes.

It's delicious agony. Every kiss brings his mouth closer to the target zone, but he's taking his sweet time to get there.

Oh my. I haven't been teased like this before. Not this decade, anyway. And certainly, I haven't had a man's mouth anywhere near my—

The panties are yanked away.

Oh, wow.

Mmm.

CHAPTER 23
MATTEO

Leila moans as I pleasure her, and I'm basically shaking with arousal myself.

Turning her on is just as overwhelming as I'd known it would be. No—*more*. Because I hadn't anticipated this feeling of reverence.

It's not just sex. I'm changing lives, maybe. Leila's. A baby's. Even my own.

I kick off my jeans and briefs.

"Yes," she whimpers. "Please." Her fingers tighten in my hair. She's begging now.

But I'm a bastard about it. I won't be rushed. This may be our only time together, so I slow things down with a too-gentle kiss to her tummy. And another to the crease of her thigh.

She trembles with need. I crawl up her body, kissing the flutter of her pulse at her throat. She tugs my chest down onto hers. And then she sighs my name, like a prayer across her lips. "*Matteo*."

I'm a strong man. But not strong enough to hold out against that. I do the only thing I can, which is to lift her knee and slot myself into place at her entrance.

Hovering over her, our eyes lock. The night holds its breath. Her lips part again, and she arches her back in anticipation.

And then I do it. I slide myself home. And *fuuuck*... I thought I was prepared for this, but nope. Her body's heated clench is a revelation. The silent "oh" of pleasure on her lips makes me want to weep.

Lust swamps me, but I make myself wait. Another moment of stillness brings me closer to this brand-new place we've arrived.

"*Matteo*," she whispers again, her hands gripping my shoulders, her eyes wide with wonder.

"*Queen.*"

Her eyes dilate with anticipation, and then I finally begin to move. Slowly, I brace my hands on the mattress, and begin a dance as old as time.

But it feels sharp and new. Every breath we share is electric. Every little gasp she makes gives me chills.

"Kiss me," she breathes, and I'm struck with wonder all over again. *Kissing Leila*. My sixteen-year-old self wanted nothing more. My thirty-six-year-old self can't even believe his luck. I groan into her mouth.

Her arms snake around my neck, and the sweet slide of her tongue against mine is almost more than I can take. My control slips, and I can't go slow any longer. I snap my hips forward as she moans.

We were made for this. The thought licks through me like a fire in a dry thicket. There's no denying the way her body tightens around my cock and the way her knees clench my hips. Like we're two halves of a whole.

I can feel it building inside me—the tension and the heat. I bear down and bite my lip against the need to come. It's all for her. But I'll cling to this moment for one more selfish breath.

Until Leila suddenly gasps in my arms, and then gasps again. Her body pulses around me, and I can't wait any longer. With one more urgent push, I let go, and the relief is swift and so pure that I have to bury my face in Leila's neck and groan.

"Oh, fuck," she whispers, clutching me to her chest. "Oh wow," she pants.

I roll us both to the side and fit my mouth to hers. Our kisses are sloppy and exhausted and wildly intimate. My heart is still beating like a sprinter's, because I'm still inside her, and I haven't come down from the high.

I never want to, either.

Gradually, Leila's grip on my body relaxes. I reluctantly disengage, and she rolls onto her back.

I'm not ready to stop touching her. Her skin is so soft. My hand finds its way to her flat stomach. I spread my fingers, trying to imagine a baby bump here. One that I made.

The idea isn't nearly as terrifying as it used to be. Although I'm aware that the endorphins in my system are singing like a choir.

But I really want this to work. "What do we do next?" I whisper. "You should probably lie still for a little while, yeah?"

She turns her chin to take me in and gives me a shy smile. "Some people think it helps, but nobody knows for sure."

I let my hand go heavy on her belly. "Then you stay right here."

"You must be hungry, though. I'm a terrible hostess."

I raise an eyebrow at that. "Actually, I disagree."

She laughs.

"The food is right in the kitchen, yeah? How about I make you a plate?" I punctuate this thought with a kiss to her neck.

Wait, is that allowed now that we're done?

"That would be nice." She runs a lazy hand down my chest, and it feels fantastic. So I guess the little bubble we're in tonight hasn't burst yet. Though I'm afraid that the moment I get out of this bed, it will.

Not bothering with clothes, I reluctantly rise and pad into her kitchen. I unpack the food. It's from Pim's Noodle Shop, which is unfamiliar to me. It smells amazing. There's a big portion of pad Thai and a green curry with rice.

I put each of our plates in the microwave for thirty seconds, and I refresh Leila's lemonade glass before carrying her dinner into the bedroom.

When I arrive, Leila clutches the sheet to her chest and sits up against the headboard.

Oh man. The sight of her looking rumpled and well fucked

makes my cock stir. "Thank you," she says, her voice husky. And I can't help but notice the trip her gaze takes down my body and back up again.

"I parked behind the building," I say suddenly.

"Mmm?" she drags her eyes off my body.

"My rental car. I hid it. So I can spend the night, and nobody will really notice."

"Oh." Her cheeks pink up. "Good idea. Aren't you eating, too?"

I go back to the kitchen for my own plate, and together we have dinner in bed.

She gives me a sideways glance, and I can tell she's over-thinking things again.

"What?" I demand. "I can hear your gears turning from here."

She smiles and shakes her head. "This is nice. I mean, eating takeout together."

"Well, yeah. We've done that before. It's just that we're not usually naked."

She bites her lip and then changes the topic. "What's the restaurant scene like in Aspen? I bet it's better than here."

"Well, sure. But they're feeding literally the richest, pickiest people in the world. I've had some amazing meals. Lots of food I can't even pronounce. But the downside is you don't even want to try to eat out in Aspen on a big holiday weekend. There are weeks when the town is so overrun with tourists that it's better just staying home."

"Ah." She tucks a noodle into her mouth and licks her lips.

My tired dick twitches again.

"The locals party on Sunday nights and Monday nights. Even after Sean settled down with Cara, that was still our time to eat out or hit the bars."

"Fascinating." She smiles. "Tell me the truth—it's fun to spot celebrities, right?"

"I guess? They're just people, though. Once I was finishing up at a urinal when this guy unzips next to me. And I'm, like, that's the cop on CSI."

She laughs. "And what's the town like?"

"Beautiful. Little old buildings, just like in a cowboy movie, with the mountains shooting up right at the end of the street. But the younger people who work in town can't afford to live nearby anymore. Sean and Cara bought a little house seven years ago, and I was worried that they overpaid. But that place is worth two million now."

"That's got to ease her mind," Leila says.

"Yeah, but she's got a mortgage, and her daughter needs to stay in the school district another year. She can't sell…" These are things I worry about in the darkest part of the night. "They had a life insurance policy, but it was small, because we're expensive to insure."

"Oh." Leila's eyes widen. "I suppose you would be."

And now she looks troubled, so I change the subject. "Want to watch a movie?"

"Of course I do."

———

"Hey, Matteo?"

I turn to look at Sean. "Yeah?"

We're on top of a mountain peak, but I can't tell which one. It's unfamiliar, and very, *very* tall.

"Lissa's birthday is coming up fast." Sean leans over and checks the binding on his snowboard.

"What? Not until November, yeah?"

He stands up. "Don't forget to make a restaurant reservation, though. You know how it gets."

"Hang on," I say, inching toward the lip of the peak. When I look down the mountain, it's so steep and rocky that I can't even see the bottom. "Dude, I don't even see a line here. What's your plan?"

"She likes surf and turf for special occasions," he says. "The Catch, or maybe 316, if you can get in." He hops his board toward the lip.

"Wait, Sean," I say. I look down again, and the view suddenly gives me vertigo. "That's like a fifty-foot drop. There's nowhere to land."

He gives me a big, bright smile. Then he leaps over the edge.

CHAPTER 24
LEILA

This isn't the first night I've spent in a bed with Matteo, but it's the first one where I've slept so lightly. I keep opening my eyes to marvel at the sight of Matteo sleeping next to me.

Naked.

So when he suddenly jerks in his sleep, my eyes fly open.

He sits up very quickly, dropping his head into his hands for a gasping breath.

"Matty," I whisper. "What's wrong?"

He doesn't answer right away, and when he does, "Sorry," is all he says. Then he lies back down again, and I realize it's the only answer I'm getting.

Outside, it's still pitch dark, but there are no sounds from the bar's parking lot. So it's probably between two and four a.m.

We should both be sleeping, but I roll toward him instead, placing a hand on his chest. He covers it with his own, his heart thudding eagerly beneath my fingertips.

Slowly, I stroke my thumb across his pec, with the impish thought that he might be ticklish.

When he moves, though, it isn't to get away from me. Instead, he rolls onto my naked body in one smooth maneuver. He stares down at me, his dark eyes shining in the near blackness of my room.

"Are you okay?" I whisper.

Once again, he's not in the mood to answer questions. He sinks his hips purposefully onto mine and kisses me. Hard. And then he does it again. And when I part my lips and lick his lower lip, he actually growls.

After that, he kisses me like he's on fire, and I'm the only source of water. I'm a hundred percent onboard with this, caressing his skin everywhere I can reach, while our feet tangle beneath the sheet.

When he shifts his hips, his shaft thickens against my thigh, and I spread my legs, the invitation unmistakable.

He makes a low sound of satisfaction and shifts again, lining himself up. But he doesn't penetrate me yet. He makes me wait for it. He sucks on my tongue, and then drops his mouth to place hot, wet kisses on my neck, while I shiver and squirm.

The thick head of his cock is *right there*. I bear down on the tip, trying to fill myself if he won't do it for me.

"Fuck," he grunts. And then he's filling me in one fast slide.

I arch my back and moan. I'd had no idea what this would be like. I thought the sex would be two friends fumbling sweetly together. I thought we'd end up laughing.

Nope. We're like wild animals—hips pumping, hearts pounding. The rest of the world sleeps, but we can't get enough.

He pins my hands in place on the mattress and pushes his tongue into my mouth again. The tension in my core ratchets higher. I'm desperate to find my peak, and I'm also desperate not to.

It's like I'm living someone else's life right now. I'm a naked Cinderella, borrowing Prince Charming for a few dances before the sun comes up to take him away again.

Somewhere in the back of my mind, I know this can't last. But I push all reasonable thoughts aside, and I enjoy it while I can.

———

I'm dozing again in the shallow waters of sleep when I feel Matteo stir beside me. I open my eyes to see gray morning light pushing into the room. Then I close them again.

He makes a trip into my bathroom, and I hear the shower running.

I doze a little longer. If his plan is to sneak out early, I'll let him go without a fuss. Maybe that's the only way to do this—to pretend that the night wasn't as shockingly intimate as I found it to be.

After his shower, I hear the telltale sounds of a man getting dressed as quietly as he can. I brace myself to hear the click of the door as he leaves.

But he comes back to the bedroom and sits beside me on the bed. He smooths the hair from my face, and I open my eyes to his serious gaze.

He licks his lower lip. "You okay?"

"Totally." My voice is hoarse from disuse. "You?"

A flash of a smile. "Never better." He plays with my hair a moment before speaking again. "So you'll tell me if it worked, yeah? Or if we need to try again?"

"Of course. It's a waiting game now. I'll take the vitamins, stay off the alcohol, and then I'll either get my period or not. Even if I don't, you won't see me celebrating. So many early pregnancies don't make it."

He nods. "I'll be thinking about you. Hope you get everything you want."

I gaze up into his chocolate eyes and swallow hard. "Thank you."

His gaze sweeps my face, lingering on my lips. I hold my breath, hoping for one last kiss. Instead, he leans down and presses a kiss to my forehead. Then he stands up and exits the room.

The door clicks loudly as he leaves, just as I knew it would.

CHAPTER 25
MATTEO

I feel strangely raw as I exit Leila's building into the cool spring morning. My car is waiting for me by the dumpsters, and I make a mental note to call the rental company today and negotiate a better long-term rate.

There are a million things I need to do today, but I know I'm going to spend most of my hours preoccupied with thoughts of Leila. I'll be wondering if she'll get pregnant. And how she's feeling about it.

She wanted a sperm donor, and I delivered. But it feels like I left a piece of my soul up on the second floor.

Still worth it, though, if she gets what she wants.

As I pull around the building, an employee of my sister's coffee shop steps outside to flip the sign to OPEN. So instead of turning onto the highway, I choose a parking spot and get out of the car again.

Coffee will make everything better. I head inside to order an espresso and one of those hot pretzels they sell.

The person behind the counter is Zara, and the first question she asks me isn't "Can I take your order?" It's "What are you doing at this end of town so early?"

"Do you ask all your customers that?" I scan the case to see if there are any offerings I haven't tried yet.

"It depends on if I happened to see their cars parked by the dumpsters when I came in this morning."

Well, shit. I was happy to ask Zara's opinion when I was sure she'd tell me Leila's plan was crazy. But now that I've agreed to help Leila, I have a few regrets about having told Zara. "Here's the deal," I say quietly. "We can't talk about it. There's no telling what will come of it."

She pulls a face. "I suppose you have a point. Okay. I won't tell."

"Not a *soul*."

"Not even Benito?"

I shake my head.

"Fine." She shrugs. "You want the pretzel or the bagel? There's smoked salmon today and chive cream cheese."

"The pretzel."

"You want a sassy four-year-old, too?" she says, tapping on the register screen. "Cute but argues with everything I say. Fifty percent off today."

I snort. "Is this your way of asking me to babysit again?"

"Nope. Just venting."

"Can I have a double espresso, too?"

"Oh, I assumed. You can swipe your card." She moves over to the espresso machine to make my coffee. "So I don't get any details at all?"

"Nope," I say firmly. "Not sure what there even is to say."

She pops out from behind the machine to give me a disbelieving stare. "Seriously? After twenty years of pining, you finally—"

"*Zara.*"

She sighs. "You are no fun at all."

I believe her. One hundred percent.

———

Leila doesn't ping me that night or the next day, so I shoot her a text.

How are you doing? Feeling upbeat?

I'm good! You?

Of course. Want to hang out this week? My
weekend is spoken for, though.

Maybe!

That's all I get. A "maybe."

It's hard not to think about her, though, and my thoughts still
feel raw—as if our night together exposed all the hungriest parts
of me. The desperate parts. My nightmares, too.

People say that getting naked with friends is dangerous, and
now I know it's true. I've never felt more naked in my life.

My family keeps me busy with their various jobs and errands,
but I find myself looking for Leila everywhere. At the coffee shop.
At the gas station.

Then, one night when I'm tending bar with Alec, a group of
women enter the bar and I catch a glimpse of wavy hair. My attention snaps onto her as she chats with Skye and May and a couple
other women I don't recognize.

"Girls' night, huh?" Alec says when they approach the bar.
He's already reaching for a few glasses. "What'll it be, ladies?"

"Tonic and lime," May says, because she doesn't drink.

"I'll have the same," Leila says. Her eyes flit in my direction,
and she gives me a quick, private smile.

"Hold up—you're going to make me order a margarita alone?"
one of the other women protests.

"Yeah, sorry," Leila says with a shrug. "New policy of mine—
when you live over a bar, you can't drink there every night."

"Hey dude. Excuse me?" One of the beer tourists at my end of
the bar is waving his credit card at me. "Those women are pretty,
but I'm trying to cash out here."

Fine. I'll take this impatient turd's money, because that's my
job. And I'll even make the kind of small talk that is good for tips.

147

He doesn't look like he'll appreciate my tight T-shirt, but you never know.

By the time I'm done, Leila and her friends are gathered around a table at the far end of the room.

Figures.

"You looking for someone?" my brother asks me. Then he snickers.

"Shut it," I grumble.

"How's it going there? Any new and exciting developments?"

You have no idea. I shake my head. "It's not like that."

"But you wish it was," he counters.

"I wish a lot of things. You want me to change the Long Trail tap?"

He falls for my change of topic. "Sure. Thanks."

When I return, Rory's waiting for me on a barstool, and I groan inside.

It must show on my face, because he holds up both hands in submission. "Hey, I won't say a word to her. Promise."

"Better mean that." I toss a coaster down on the bar. "What are you drinking? No freebies tonight, because Alec is back to watch my every move."

Rory shakes his head. "I'm not staying. I just came in to ask you a favor."

Uh oh. "How can I help you?"

"That beer truck your uncle has you working on? He said you're doing a wedding next weekend. He also said the pay is five hundred bucks, but the tips will be shitty because it's an open bar."

Fuck. I don't really want to work a shift with Rory. And that's a tough realization. A better friend than me would be hanging out with him, making sure he's on the mend from his divorce.

But me? I feel guilty just seeing his face.

"...Otto said I gotta ask you before he'll hire me. He says you're in charge."

"Me?" Goddamn it.

Rory nods. "You're the manager. You make the call."

Thanks, Otto. Thanks a crap ton. "You sure you want to pour beer for six hours straight? It'll be hot, and we've got to wear a dress shirt, and it's an hour away. And we don't get to drink anything on shift."

"Yeah, no problem." He nods vigorously.

"Okay," I say, giving in. Otto and Lyle are still having trouble staffing their various businesses, and I don't want to do the wedding alone. "Sure. Let's give it a whirl."

Eight hours in a beer truck with Rory. How bad could it be?

———

Pretty bad, as it turns out. But not for the reasons I'd imagined.

Rory turns up dressed in black jeans and a white dress shirt, which is more or less appropriate. This is Vermont, and the wedding reception is set up in tents on the grassy slope of a flower farm. The bride and groom are wearing formal attire and Birkenstocks on their feet.

That's how Vermont rolls.

Rory is uncomplaining during the setup, and a hard worker once we get into the thick of things, which is immediately. The pace of work reaches a frenzy at about nine p.m. "I thought we were busy before," he says, as the makeshift dance floor shakes with the DJ's bass. "But this is crazy."

He's not wrong. We've served an unholy amount of beer at this wedding, while the guy serving wine at the other truck across the way looks bored.

"Look how happy they are," he says when we finally get a lull. "That guy looks like he won the fucking lottery." He nods toward the bride and groom, who are slow dancing together.

"He's just looking forward to the honeymoon," I say lightly.

"Nah. He's happy because he hasn't fucked it all up yet," Rory says. "She still thinks he hung the moon. I was that guy once. When I still had my corporate job? Leila didn't think I was a loser."

I cast around for a suitable change of subject and come up dry. But I *really* don't want to talk about Leila.

"She can't stand the sight of me now," he says darkly. "Hon-

149

estly can't believe we lasted as long as we did. I was never good enough for her."

My gaze shifts toward the dance floor, and I find myself hoping that another dozen partygoers will suddenly get thirsty.

But no such luck.

"You know why I kissed Leila the first time?" he asks.

No, I really don't. "Why does anyone kiss anyone?"

Rory snorts. "It was a little more complicated than that. It was her senior year in college. Didn't seem like you were ever gonna start a business with me. And Leila was gonna have to get a job somewhere and leave me behind, too."

I sigh.

"I had nothing to lose, so I just went for it one night. Planted one right on her. She didn't stop me, you know? So I did it again the following week. Then I fucked her, and she liked it."

My stomach bottoms out. I don't want to hear this.

"Couldn't believe my luck. For a while, whenever we were together, I thought it would be the last time. But somehow, we were an honest-to-God couple. And I thought—at least that asshole Matteo will never have this."

"*Rory.* Jesus."

He shrugs. "Just being honest. I'm not proud of it. I loved her, but I knew she was too good for me. And when people started to ask if we were going to get married, I braced myself and bought a ring. Never been more fucking terrified in my life. She said yes, but I was still scared, yeah? Had to get high to make it through the ceremony. I knew I was in over my head."

Listening to this story makes me feel sick for a dozen reasons. I feel guilty about sleeping with Leila while Rory is basically mourning her.

Maybe I *shouldn't* feel guilty, but I still do.

And I also feel jealous of Rory for everything they shared.

God, I don't want to have these thoughts.

A man wanders up to the window for a beer, and I've never been so happy to see anyone in my life. I pour his drink carefully, with as much attention as I'd give to defusing a bomb. Anything to shut Rory up.

But when the man leaves, Rory starts talking again. "When things finally started to go downhill, I was almost relieved. It made more sense, you know? I knew I was on borrowed time."

"Rory." I sigh. "They have therapists for this."

He shrugs. "Story's almost over. I was a dick to her. I got defensive. Didn't make an effort. Felt like she should just love me anyway—like we promised. Till death do us part, you know?"

Ouch. "That's rough, man. Marriage is hard. Probably why I've never been brave enough to try it."

Rory shakes his head. "You probably look at me and think—*I never would have fucked that up, you dumbass.* Best girl in the world and look what happened."

"Don't put words in my mouth," I insist. "Fucked up some stuff this year myself."

"Then you know," Rory says.

"I'm afraid I do."

———

The night finally ends, and we ride home along a sleepy highway in silence. When I drop him off, Rory asks me if I can hire him again, and I guiltily say yes before the truck door slams.

In the morning, I wake up to more signs of summer in the orchard. The trees are bursting with pear blossoms and happy bees.

As the season progresses, I've begun to feel weirdly settled.

I've learned how to sleep through the rooster's noise. I still hear him at dawn, but now I roll over and go back to sleep. And when I lie in my trailer at night, I'm serenaded by the frogs and the owls. With the windows open, the sound of nature is surprisingly loud.

The only thing that keeps me awake is that Leila is still avoiding me. It's been a couple of weeks now. Maybe I'm not the only one with an intimacy hangover. But I don't know what to do about it.

Then one Sunday night—after another long weekend of

pouring beers in the beer wagon—Alec calls me from the bar. "Hey, dude. You busy?"

"Why?" I ask warily. "This was my night off."

He chuckles. "Calm down. I'm not asking you to work. But there's a certain friend of yours sitting at the bar lookin' sad."

"Hell, is it Rory?"

"No way. I wouldn't bother you about that. It's Leila. She just looks like she could use a friend."

"Oh." I rub my forehead, wondering what she'd think if I turned up to talk to her. Then I have an unsettling thought. "Hey, Alec, what's she drinking?"

"Gin and tonic. She's only on her second, so this isn't an intervention."

"Cool. Thanks, man." I'm already on my feet. "I think I'm in the mood to have a drink myself."

He laughs. "I bet."

CHAPTER 26
LEILA

I turn another page, but the billionaire in my latest book is getting on my last nerve. He's obviously lusting after the spunky female yacht captain, but he refuses to admit it.

Just bang her already, dude. I need the distraction.

He hems and haws for another two pages, before he finally pushes her up against a cabinet of life preservers and kisses the hell out of her.

Thank you, sir. Much appreciated.

Someone sits down on the barstool beside me. In my peripheral vision, I can feel him checking me out. But nope. I'm only interested in fictional men tonight, and it took hours for this book to get spicy, so I turn the page and ignore him.

The billionaire slips his hand into the heroine's panties. "You're so wet for me," he says, and I almost roll my eyes. *That's because you dragged this out for fifty extra pages.*

In the next paragraph, a deckhand interrupts them with an emergency. Something about a broken rudder.

"No fucking *way*," I grumble. I'm too hormonal right now for this kind of interruption.

I slap the book down on the bar in disgust and drain my drink.

"Everything okay over here?" the man beside me asks.

I startle when I realize it's Matteo. He's sipping a pint of beer and watching me with amused brown eyes.

"Hi," I squeak. I'm suddenly grateful that I put on a cute top and some mascara before I came down here. "Didn't realize it was you! I was just…" My eyes flip to the closed book on the bar, and I'm also grateful that discreet covers are a thing now. Because Matteo doesn't need to know how dirty my taste in reading has gotten since the night we spent together.

"You've been avoiding me," he says calmly. "So I came to see why."

"Oh." *Busted*. "I'm sorry. I thought you were probably busy catching up with your family."

"Too busy for you?" His brown eyes wander my face. "When has that ever happened?"

Seriously? "Oh, I don't know. The last decade and a half?"

His face falls, and I feel swamped with guilt. He doesn't deserve any pushback from me. At all. "I'm sorry. I don't know what's wrong with me. I just…" My eyes flicker onto his sad ones. "I have been avoiding you just a wee little bit."

The corners of his mouth twitch. "I see. Am I allowed to ask why?"

My cheeks pick that moment to heat. "You're doing me this, uh, big favor…" It's not easy to discuss this in a bar, damn it.

"How big?" Matteo asks, his eyebrows knitting together. "Would you say this big?" He holds his hands about eight inches apart.

"Matteo."

He grins. "Sorry. Couldn't resist. You were saying?"

Well, great. Now I'm thinking about his dick. Which is not small. I sigh. "I just didn't know how to navigate it, okay? I didn't want to hang on you. I didn't want to be that super-needy friend. Not when you were already, uh, so generous with me."

"Aw, buddy. You're not even my neediest friend. Don't stay away, okay? You'll make me think I did something wrong."

"Wrong? Not a chance." But now I feel like the worst friend in the world. It's hard to explain how totally stupid I've been. "I thought I'd have some, um, exciting news to share with you soon. I was hoping, anyway. But…" I swallow hard and try to figure out how to put this in a crowded bar.

But Matteo already knows. He looks pointedly at my empty cocktail glass. "You're having some gin, huh?"

"Yeah." My voice sounds defeated. "All of a sudden, tonight became the perfect moment for it."

"I see. I'm so sorry, sweetheart."

His soft words go *straight* to my tear ducts. "It's okay," I say, willing myself not to cry.

Like I said, I'm feeling really hormonal. My period showed up today—one whole day late. That's not even unusual for me. But still, I had one glorious day of imagining I was pregnant.

Okay, fifteen glorious days. I know better than to count unhatched chickens, but I did it anyway.

Even that metaphor hits too close to home today. Shit.

My eyes water.

"Oh, *honey*," Matteo says. And then he leans over and folds me into a hard hug. "I'm really sorry."

I inhale the woodsy scent of him and shamelessly lean into his hard body. But it actually makes the weepy feelings worse.

"Swear to God I tried," he whispers. "Put my whole back into it."

This makes me laugh, because I was there. And yup. Ten out of ten, the man did try. I pull myself back from the brink, grabbing a cocktail napkin to dab at my eyes. "It's not you, goofball."

He gives me a hot smile. Or just a smile, I suppose, except that all of his are hot. "I'm still sorry."

"It's fine," I insist. "It's totally normal, too. That's the dumb thing. You're supposed to try for a whole *year* before you even start to worry. But I just had this stupid idea…" Lord, this is embarrassing. "It's dumb. But I thought maybe after the year I just had, that the universe would toss me a softball."

He squeezes my shoulder, and it feels so good. "I get it. I really do. Does this mean you'll want to try again?" He winks.

My face heats, of course. Even though I'm sad, and I have cramps, I still get a flutter just thinking about it. "Well, yeah. If you're up for it."

He raises a single dark eyebrow. His brothers have been

SARINA BOWEN

calling him Designer Jesus, but I think he looks more like Heath Ledger at his hottest.

And when I realize what I said, my face goes from hot to sizzling. *Up for it*. Oof. "I didn't mean it like that."

"I know." He flashes me an evil grin. "But it still won't be a problem. So… Two weeks from now?" He pulls out his phone.

"*Approximately.*"

"Leaving myself a reminder." He taps something into his calendar.

"Jeez. What are you putting in there? I'm still keeping this quiet."

He shows me his phone. It says: SHOOTING RANGE.

I laugh.

He smiles. Then he elbows me in a friendly way. "Buy you another drink? Want to split a pizza?"

"Yes!" I feel a hundred percent better, and he's only been sitting here ten minutes. "Can I pick the toppings?"

"Yes, queen. Always."

———

I order us the pie with sausage and olives. It's delicious. Midway through the first piece, Matteo turns to me again. "I'm only here for the summer. So let's hang out, yeah? While we still have the chance."

"You're right," I agree. "I apologize."

"It'll be just like old times," he says.

Except he's wrong. In those old times, I didn't know how his kisses taste. I didn't know how smooth his skin is. And I didn't know the deep growl he makes when he comes.

So, yup, my mind keeps wandering to inappropriate places while we talk.

I knew this would happen. That's why I haven't called him to hang out. And I've rarely come into the bar, just in case he was working.

I honestly thought I'd get pregnant on the first try. My mother got pregnant effortlessly. That's the word she used. "All three times, too!"

Foolishly, I'd assumed it would work the same way for me. I'd still be in lust with Matteo, but the job would already be done. I could focus on getting over those feelings. Now, as soon as I stop feeling crampy and awful, I'm probably going to fantasize about round two.

We end up outside on the deck together, leaning against the railing, watching the river roll by in the moonlight. It would be more romantic than my sad little heart can handle, except we're also arguing about which Phish song is the best one.

I'm team "Reba," and I will die on this hill. He's spinning some bullshit story about "Fluffhead" having the best composition in modern music.

But then his phone rings, and the ringtone… "Is that a *Taylor Swift song?*" I hoot. "Who *are* you?"

"Sorry," he says. "I have to take this." He swipes to answer the call. "Hey, girl. Everything okay?" And whatever the woman on the other end says, it makes him smile.

My stomach dives right off a cliff. I don't know why I'm so surprised that there's a woman calling Matteo. Or that he looks so happy about it.

"That's cool," he says. "Why are there no pictures of you in this dress on my phone yet?"

My mood plummets another thousand yards.

Of *course* there are women in his life. Maybe they're not exclusive—otherwise, he wouldn't have signed up for my little project.

So why can't I breathe?

"What does your mom think of the dress?" he asks the woman on the phone.

Okay, that's a weird question.

"Uh-huh," he says with a grin that makes me feel melty inside. "You think maybe if she's paying for it, she might get a say? Oh— I see. Yeah, I owe you a hundred bucks. But I thought you wanted a check? You told me you were *so over Venmo*. Your words. And you called me a geezer for suggesting PayPal."

And suddenly my chest loosens, because I think I know who he's talking to—the teenage daughter of his friend.

"Yeah, I'll send you the cash before I go to bed, okay? But don't go behind your mom's back. That's not cool. Okay. Good girl. Love you too!"

He hangs up, still smiling. "Sorry. I always take Lissa's calls. That kid has had a rough year."

"I know. I'm sorry," I say. What I really mean is—*I'm sorry I was briefly jealous of a grieving teenager.*

He shakes his head, his smile falling away. "I'd do anything for that kid. I feel so damn bad."

And now I just want to hug him.

Get a grip, Giltmaker. He's not really yours.

But every time he smiles, I wonder what that might be like.

CHAPTER 27
MATTEO
JUNE

Spring tilts into summer, and things really heat up.

I don't mean the weather, either. I mean me.

It was my idea to hang out with Leila, right? I enjoy every minute we've spent together, but my attraction to her is out of control.

No matter what we're doing—watching a movie, playing bocci on the riverbank, having dinner together—my thoughts invariably turn to sex.

You can't really blame me, seeing as my services are going to be needed again soon. In the next few days, Leila is going to get another smiley face when she takes the test.

So I've got a smiley face, too. Right inside my pants.

Making things even harder—literally—we often see each other at work. Her school year has ended, so she's working for her father's brewing operation and is often on duty at the warehouse when I pick up kegs and other supplies.

I feel like a pot that's been left to simmer on the back burner until you need it. My whole body is at a low boil whenever I think about her. And even sometimes when I'm not.

It's like being seventeen again, but I'm legal to drink, and I don't have acne.

On Saturday, I roll up to the loading dock of the Giltmaker Brewery to pick up the beer for another party. Every time I arrive here, I marvel at how different this place looks. When I was a teenager, Lyle ran two or three businesses out of the old mill. But it still felt like a small operation.

Those other businesses are long gone. Now the big brick building contains only the rapidly expanding brewery, including Lyle's office, a retail counter and a busy warehouse.

But that means traffic six days a week. I actually have to wait my turn behind a delivery truck before I can pick up my beer.

Tonight's event is in Woodstock, and Rory is going to work with me again. But I push that thought out of my mind as Leila appears in the loading dock door in denim shorts and a top that draws the eye to her cleavage.

My eyes, anyway. It's probably just an ordinary neckline. But I'm a drooling dog who's hungry for his next meal.

"Hey Matteo!" she calls. "I'm ready for you."

"If only," I mutter under my breath.

Leila means the beer, of course. She's got four icy kegs and a couple of coolers full of cans and bottles. "The bride made a lot of requests," she says. "Including NA beer for the non-drinkers. So make sure you keep track of those."

"Yes, queen."

I lean over the coolers and take a look. The NA beer is a product that Alec developed in cooperation with Lyle Giltmaker. In addition to all their other efforts, they're trying to take over the market for beer drinkers who avoid alcohol.

Between Alec, Lyle, Zara, and Otto, they have an entire beverage empire.

My job is just to tote the beer around and serve it, and tonight that feels like plenty. I heft the first cooler and walk it to the wagon. Leila puts a keg onto a dolly and joins me.

She peers tentatively inside the wagon. "Is he here with you?" she asks in a low voice.

She means Rory, and I shake my head. "Nope. Picking him up in half an hour. Didn't think it made sense to bring him here."

"Thank you." Leila visibly relaxes, which is why I'd made that plan. "So…" She looks down at her shoes. "Do you have any plans for tomorrow night?"

My body tightens immediately. "You tell me. Do I?"

She blushes. "Tomorrow is probably a smiley-face day."

"Thank fuck. I'm dying here."

She laughs and claps a hand over her mouth.

"Hey, you *told* me to save it up for you. So I am. Not sure why that's funny."

"I'm not laughing at you," she hoots. "Just wasn't sure you still wanted to be on this tilt-a-whirl ride with me."

Hmm. I slide open the beer wagon's door and tug the keg inside. "Come here a second?"

"Why?" She climbs into the wagon.

I put my hands on either side of her face, and tilt her chin up so she's looking right at me. "Listen…"

Her lips part temptingly. "I'm listening."

"I know this a big deal to you. I'm not gonna back out just because it didn't work the first time."

She blinks up at me. "You're only here for another couple months, though. It might not be enough time. And I never meant to drag you into my little pity spiral."

"There're perks, though."

She gives me a shy, flirty smile, and that's when my control snaps. Two seconds later I have my tongue inside her mouth. Leila doesn't miss a beat. Her fingers are already laced through my hair.

We kiss like long-lost lovers, and she feels like heaven pressed up against my body.

Annnd it's official—this is the worst idea I've ever had, because I'm not allowed to touch her until tomorrow night.

At the earliest.

"Fuck," I say, pulling back.

She lets out a shuddery breath. "We can't. Not yet."

"Yeah, yeah. Just know that I'll be watching for your text. I have to work another event tomorrow night. A private party down in Putney. Ends after ten, so I probably won't get back until late. That a problem?"

She scrubs a hand across her forehead. "No, nope. That's probably going to be good timing."

"So how about this—wait for me in my trailer? That way you can sleep if you want to. And I won't have to drop off the wagon on my way to find you."

"S-sure," she stammers. "I could do that."

I take a deep breath and try to cool down. But the way Leila is looking at me right now doesn't help at all. Even in the dim light, I can see the flutter of her pulse in her throat. I just want to kiss her there while I fuck her. "When I'm driving home tomorrow night, I'm gonna picture you waiting in my bed. Naked."

She gulps.

"I leave the trailer unlocked. Come over whenever you're ready."

"Okay," she breathes. Pretty sure she's feeling just as ready as I am.

"Bring your toothbrush. I'll make sure I've got some food for breakfast. We'll need a couple rounds to make sure we've been *very* thorough."

Leila lets out a gusty breath. "Got it. I'll be ready."

"Got extra ice packs in the warehouse?"

She blinks. "Why? The coolers are full."

"I need some in my briefs." I pinch her arm.

She cracks up. "I'll put them in your order for tomorrow."

"Good girl. Now let's do this." I point at the keg. "This beer isn't going to load itself, missy."

She gives me an eye roll and hops out of the wagon.

———

I never claimed to be a smart man. A wiser man would have told Leila to wait in a potato sack. Or maybe a hazmat suit.

For all of Saturday night and Sunday, I keep flashing back to the kiss in the beer wagon, and my trousers feel uncomfortably tight.

God, her mouth. I need more. By Sunday night, I feel like I'm dying, and the party I'm serving seems to last forever. It's a golf banquet and heavy on the speeches.

If a man can stay semi erect during an awards ceremony for

golf, you know he's hard up. The only saving grace is that tonight I'm working alone. There are only sixty party guests and they're mostly retirees, so I made the right call when'd I'd decided to keep the whole service fee to myself.

Rory isn't here, which is a blessing, because I'm not capable of small talk tonight. And if I think too much about him, I'll start feeling guilty again. I didn't agree to help Leila as some kind of revenge plot against him.

At least I hope I didn't.

I serve another beer and hold back my sigh. The minutes tick by. Even geezers like to party. They don't clear out until eleven, and the drive is two hours.

In the truck, I put on a playlist to stay awake, but I don't really need it. I picture Leila sleeping alone in my bed, the sheet pulled up over her breasts. Her eyes closed. Head thrown back on my pillow.

When she dreams at night, I wonder what she sees. Maybe she sees herself rocking the child I'm going to put inside her.

It's a clear night, and I press the accelerator down another degree. Pedal to the metal, I can't believe I'm racing home to a woman who needs my seed to have a child. Hell, a year ago I'd have laughed in the face of whoever suggested I'd do this.

But it's Leila who needs me, so I'm there, no question. As I cross the county line, my body already aches for her, and by the time I pull the wagon into Otto's gravel drive, I'm made of heat.

It doesn't matter that it's one in the morning. All my senses are on fire as I climb out of the truck and walk across the farmland toward my trailer.

The night is quiet, except for the distant sound of bullfrogs in the pond, and the trailer is dark. The creak of the door breaks the silence, and I lock the door behind me. There's just enough moonlight to illuminate her sleeping form on the bed.

She doesn't stir. I toe off my shoes and remove my clothes.

Naked, I approach the bed. It's just as I'd imagined. The curve of her cheekbone against the pillow. Her generous chest lifting the sheet on each steady breath.

My cock swells as I watch her sleep. There's something primal about standing over her, ready to serve myself to her, like a stud horse.

Just here to do my job, ma'am.

I kneel at the side of the bed, my knees on the floor, and I slide the sheet off her breasts. And I lean right over and suck one of her nipples into my mouth.

She stirs, inhaling deeply, but I don't budge. Going about my work, I suck her tit, gently biting the nipple as her hand fumbles into my hair.

I switch breasts, licking everything in my path. She moans quietly, her body shifting, making space for me on the bed.

Rising from the floor, I give the sheet a tug and fling it off the bed. She's spread out beneath me, her skin dark against the moonlit glow of the white sheet, her legs splayed open.

My cock swells again. I'm painfully hard in the best possible way. I've never felt as alive as I do right now, bending over the bed, dropping my hungry mouth right to the center of her.

"Oh," she gasps, spreading her legs even wider. "*Mmm.*"

With a sigh of happiness, I flatten my tongue against her clit. Her legs tremble and then relax as her fingers rake into my hair.

She tastes like sex, and the scent makes me throb. But I take my time warming her up, kissing her thighs, her pussy, everything I can reach until she's gripping the edges of the mattress, her hips undulating beneath my mouth. She tugs on my hair, urgently now.

I lift my gaze, and find her watching me in the dark, her eyes heavy-lidded, her breasts bouncing softly as she moves her hips.

Goddamn. She's so sexy I want to weep. So I army-crawl up her body and kiss her once, hard, and then look her in the eyes. "You good?"

She nods, then lifts her hips in invitation.

"Glad to hear it," I say. "Because I'm in the mood to fuck like a beast."

"Matteo," she breathes.

Wasting no more time, I notch my cock against her and slide inside. But for all my tough talk, our joining is a shock to my system. I brace my elbows on the bed and gaze down at her while I remember to breathe.

"I missed you," I say, apropos of nothing.

And I don't mean on the long drive home from Putney.

I mean all these years.

CHAPTER 28
LEILA

Matteo has always been rather intense. I've always liked that about him. Even at fifteen, he was a serious person.

Tonight, though, that intensity is dialed up to eleven. When I pull him down to kiss me, it's electric. Ten minutes ago, I was asleep, and now I'm on the cusp of a climax.

I've started having feelings about Matteo that are entirely inappropriate to this situation. But I guess I'll worry about that later. Right now, I can only lift my hips to meet each rhythmic thrust. I can only enjoy it.

Abruptly, he makes a guttural sound, then pulls out.

I'm ready to stage a protest. But he's grasping my hips and flipping me like a pancake. I inhale sharply as he pulls me onto my hands and knees. And then I exhale with relief as he pushes inside again.

Okay. Wow. Two iron hands hold my hips right where he needs me as he starts to thrust again.

The pace he sets is aggressive. I try to keep up at first, but he holds me still, one hand planted in the center of my back, my forehead sinking onto the sheet.

"Stay there. Good girl," he rasps, and the praise has the strangest effect on me. I feel myself surrendering in a new way, my overstimulated breasts melting toward the mattress, my hips canted back for his pleasure.

Letting someone else take over is new for me. My life usually doesn't work this way—the moment I stop paying attention is usually the moment everything goes wrong.

But not tonight. Something in Matteo's firm touch tells me it's okay to just give in. I spread my hands against the paneled wall and ride his thrusts as if they were waves on the ocean.

"Leila," he rasps, and the sound causes my body to tighten deliciously around him. "Fuck." He reaches around to cup the place where we're joined, and the sudden stimulation makes me gasp and shiver.

He slows his pace, and I feel *everything*. Every tremor and slide. Every breath on my neck. And then the pulse and heat as he spills inside me, cursing wickedly as he comes.

Fireworks go off behind my eyelids as I follow him to climax. He strokes me and whispers into my ear as I shimmy and buck against his unyielding body.

By the time I remember how to slow my breathing, we're sinking together toward the sheets. He rolls me onto his chest, and I can hear the thudding of his heart beneath my ear.

We spread out this way together, the sheets thrown everywhere, our sweat cooling as we come down from the high. And I can't say a word of what I'm really thinking.

You amaze me.

Why did we never do this before?

Even if I don't get pregnant, you are still *just what I needed.*

None of that is anything he wants to hear, so I gently stroke his chest instead.

He sighs weightily. Eventually, he leans down and plucks the sheet off the floor and arranges it on top of us.

"Rest now," he whispers, stroking my hair. "Gotta have you ready for round two."

"Yessir." I kiss his chest, and then marvel for a moment that I am allowed to do that.

His hand lands in my hair, holding my lips to his skin. "You kill me. You know that?"

I'm not sure how to answer. So I just spread my body against his, like a lazy cat.

He rolls, making himself the big spoon. And then his hand comes to rest on my tummy. "Here," he whispers, his hand tightening on my midriff. "We're going to put a baby *right* here. Maybe we already have."

My heart threatens to explode.

It will be a miracle if I can fall asleep. Ever again.

CHAPTER 29
MATTEO

Time passes. Summer advances. The air is warm, and the June bugs resume their yearly dance of bonking themselves against the window screens at night.

And in between jobs and family dinners and movie nights—and lustful thoughts about Leila—I'm busy planning the upcoming snowboarding season.

Usually, I look forward to it. But this year it just feels wrong.

"Monday the sixth of July will be our launch date," Cara says into my earbuds.

"The sixth," I repeat, scribbling it onto the notebook in my lap. I'm sitting in a rocker on Otto's front porch, a cold soda beside me. "You'll make a graphic? And send the link to the email list?"

"Of course," she says. Cara does almost all of our marketing and admin. "But you still need to tell me if you want to open the calendar with half the usual capacity. Or if you're confident that you can hire another guide during the preseason, then I'll put up the usual number of slots."

"Right," I say, because I've been thinking about it for a few days already. "When do I have to decide?"

"Soon," she says. "I thought you were going to call Arnie and feel him out about a permanent job."

"I did. He didn't sound ready to commit. But there are some other guys I can call."

169

"And women," Cara points out.

"And women," I repeat. "You want the job? We can hire someone for the office instead."

"No way. It's a critical moment for the business, and it wouldn't feel right to turn over the office to a newcomer right now."

"Yeah. True." We fall silent for a moment, and I hope she's not too worried. "We'll get through this season. It's not gonna be easy, but we can do it."

"We can," she says softly. "If the situation was reversed, this is what he'd do."

I picture Sean's fierce smile, and I know she's right. That man was strong. "Put up the full calendar," I decide. "I'll interview people in August and September. We've got plenty of time to find the right employees."

"If you're sure."

"I'm sure." We need the cashflow. Running at half capacity isn't an option, since we are leasing a hundred percent of a very expensive helicopter. "What's that website we use for job postings?"

"Let me handle it. Just email me a complete job description."

"Will do."

After we hang up, I try to scratch out a job description on my notebook. *Heli-skiing guide. Big mountain experience necessary. Avalanche training. CPR certification…*

I set down my pen and try to picture myself driving to work this winter, parking my car behind the hangar next to some stranger's car. Knowing Sean's beat-up Jeep won't be there in the lot.

We won't be slurping coffee together at dawn, waiting for our first customers of the day to show up. They'll look either pumped up or nervous. Or a combination of both.

Colorado will go on. The snow on the peaks will be as untracked and beautiful as ever. But Sean won't be there to see it, or to swap war stories at the bar after work, either.

I fucking dread the coming winter. But it's coming for me

anyway. I'll show up and give it all I can. Because Sean would do the same for me.

Closing the notebook, I pull out my phone. He's still in my contacts. I tap his number and listen to it ring.

After a moment, his voicemail message kicks in. "Yo, you've reached Sean."

I stop breathing.

"If you're looking for wisdom, you've got the wrong number. If you're looking to book a ride with me, you can do that on heli hops dot com. If you're looking to buy me a drink, text me instead! Love you. Later."

I put the phone away and lift my face to the sky. The frogs are singing and the stars are shining, like everything is just fine.

It isn't. And I don't know if it ever will be.

———

At least I'm busy. The beer wagon is in great demand. Otto keeps shooting me texts, asking if he can add dates to my schedule. And I keep saying yes, because the money is great.

I keep hiring Rory, too. That's working out better than I'd expected.

"When I was young, I honestly thought I was above this kind of work," he says one hot June Saturday when we're sweating in the wagon at a music festival. "I had a lot of big ideas, and I thought they made me a genius."

"Tell me about it," I say as I pour my hundredth beer that hour.

"But *your* company didn't go out of business," he points out.

"Not yet. And I am grateful. But being in charge is exhausting." That's a big understatement, but I am not about to discuss Sean's death while we try to serve all fifty people in line.

"No kidding. Which is why bartending is kinda nice. Just happy to be making money right now," he says. "One day at a time."

"Right," I agree. "Sometimes that's the best you can do."

Rory hands a beer to another thirsty client. "Another couple months like this, and I won't have to take money from Leila anymore."

My hands freeze on the stack of cups. "Say what?"

Rory gives me a guilty sideways glance. "I get alimony."

"Alimony?" I echo. "*Why?*"

"Just assumed she told you." He gives a guilty shrug. "I get a thousand dollars a month from her—but only for a year. To help me get on my feet."

I fish a bottle out of the cooler, sell it to the customer, and then turn back to Rory.

"Dude, hear this—Leila doesn't complain about you to me. I wouldn't want her to. I don't have big opinions about your marriage. It's not my place."

"Yeah." He sighs. "Thanks."

"But since you brought it up, I don't know why an able-bodied man would take money from his ex. Sometimes the pride hurts worse than the bank account."

"I guess," he grumbles. "But when she left me, I could barely get out of bed for a month. So depressed. I'm pulling it together now."

"Yeah, you are," I say. And now I feel like a shit for lecturing him at all. As if I didn't fuck up my own finances by being depressed.

Losing Leila could bring a man to his knees. I guess I'm not surprised it happened to him.

And one thing's for sure—if Leila gets pregnant, I won't be bragging about it to anyone. Rory wouldn't be able to take it.

"The Goldenrod tap is kicked," he says. "You want me to change it?"

"I got it, man. Thanks," I tell him. "You keep doing what you're doing."

———

The jobs keep coming. I'm sitting outside the trailer, drinking coffee and keeping an eye on that evil rooster when yet another text from Otto comes in.

> Can you handle one more? Next Saturday night.
> Good pay because a party planner fucked up,
> and they're desperate.

Scanning the details, I mull it over for about five seconds. But then I reply: *I'll **do** it*. More money is more money. Plus, it's a week away.

I should offer it to Rory, except he and I are working together the evening before. That's a lot of togetherness in the wagon. This is another wedding. Those make him broody.

And I'm the boss, right? On a whim, I dial Leila. "Want to make five hundred bucks at a wedding?" I ask her. "It's next Saturday night."

"Oh, I really do," she says. "Where is it?"

"Down in Norwich. About an hour's drive."

"No problem. Just don't tell my dad, because he asked me to increase my warehouse hours, and I said no."

"You slacker. I won't say a word."

Leila chuckles. "Hey, Matteo? There's something I need to tell you. I'm not pregnant."

Everything inside me sags. "Really? Shit." Then I realize that's not a proper response. "I mean—I'm sorry. Are you all right?"

"I am," she says convincingly. "It wasn't as big a surprise this time. I'm in a good place."

"Okay," I whisper. "I'm still sorry."

"Don't be sorry. It will happen for me or not, you know? I have to make my peace with it. So I'm just going to sit here, treat myself to some chocolate, and not worry too much."

I swallow hard. "You need anything? More chocolate?"

"Probably not a great idea," she says, and there's humor in her voice. "But I appreciate the offer. I'll see you Saturday night, okay?"

"Actually—what are you doing tonight?" I ask.

"Sitting on my couch with the bottle of Advil nearby. Why?"

"I'm in the mood to cook, and I can't do that in a trailer. Can I make you dinner?"

She's so quiet for a second that I wonder if she's going to turn me down. "Wait, you *cook?*"

"Yeah, sure. Doesn't everyone?"

"No sir," she says. "And I will eat anything you make me. But I swear I'm okay—you don't have to do this."

"I know that, honey. I'm shamelessly using you for your kitchen. Steak and loaded baked potatoes okay? I'll be there at six."

We hang up, and I sip my coffee in the sunshine.

The sadness I feel makes no sense. I'm not the one who wants to raise a baby. This is Leila's project.

But I really care about her. More than she can know. Somehow, it's gotten a lot easier to picture her holding a child who has Rossi-brown eyes. I feel ready for that to happen.

But maybe it never will.

CHAPTER 30
LEILA

Sure, sex is nice. But have you ever watched a hot guy make homemade blue cheese dressing in your kitchen, while you sit like a lump on a stool sipping red wine?

If I didn't have cramps, I'd probably get turned on watching him operate my salad spinner.

The more time I spend with Matteo, the harder I struggle not to compare him to Rory. My ex didn't cook. At all. He had no interest in it. That man would have eaten the same fast-food hamburgers every night of his life if I'd let him. We were so mismatched it isn't even funny.

"I've been thinking," Matteo says as he checks the baked potatoes in the oven. "In two weeks, I'll still be here for round three. And maybe round four after that. But come August, I'm heading back to Colorado."

"That's right," I agree, careful to keep my voice pleasant. "I've done that math, too. It's okay. Either it happens or it doesn't."

He straightens up and gives me a look that knows exactly how much this matters to me. "Do you ever call in sick at school?"

"Rarely. Why?"

He picks up my pepper grinder and seasons the steaks. "There's a daily flight from Burlington to Denver. You could make a couple strategic visits to Colorado. Just saying."

There goes that heart flutter again. "Like, a cross-continental booty call?"

"Exactly like that." He wiggles his bushy eyebrows. "Or, if that doesn't work, we could skip a couple months until I could get away in late November, or early December at the latest. But that's my last window for leaving Colorado until late spring."

He says this matter-of-factly. As if he wasn't offering to make a continued sacrifice on my behalf. "Wow, I really appreciate it. And I will think about this. But at some point, this project is going to cramp your style."

I can't help but wonder how he'll feel about forgoing casual sex in Colorado while he's trying to get me pregnant. It probably hasn't even occurred to him.

He leans on the counter and looks me right in the eyes. "Maybe let me worry about that, okay?"

There's a lump in my throat now that red wine can't fix. "I don't deserve you," I admit.

"That is *not* true," he argues immediately. "And it never will be."

I'm not so sure, though. When dinner is served, it's *delicious*.

———

Here's the thing about summer in Vermont—it's hard to be too sad when the sky is blue, the air is sweet, and you're about to make five hundred bucks pouring beer at a wedding.

Also, parties are fun. I'm wearing a sexy yellow sundress with spaghetti straps and a short, flirty skirt. I've tamed my hair into an up-do, and I'm wearing my favorite fresh-water pearl earrings.

I'm in a good place, and I'm looking forward to this job—both the view and the paycheck. And by "view" I mean the sight of Matteo loading the cold beer into the wagon as I park outside the warehouse. He's wearing a crisp dress shirt and khaki pants that fit as if they were molded to his hunky body.

When I step out of the car, he turns to smile at me. His smile fades, as he takes a moment to look me up and down. Then he gives me a gruff hello before pointedly picking up a keg and walking away.

"Hey!" I cry, hopping off the loading dock and following him to the wagon's entrance. "What's up with you? Something wrong?"

"That dress," he rumbles.

"What are you talking about?" I'm dressed at least as nicely as he is. "This dress happens to be perfect. It says *wedding,* but it also says *outdoor work on a warm day.* And these shoes—" I point down at my strappy sandals. "—can slay all day."

"I know," he grunts. "You are goddamn edible in that dress and those shoes. And I'm gonna spend the next six hours droolin'."

Oh. "Well, that's your problem, not mine."

"I got that." He leaves the wagon to grab another keg, and I take a look at the inventory in the coolers.

"Hey look!" I bend over to pull a bottle out of the cooler, and he groans. "What now?" I demand. But then I realize that I might have given him a view of my tiny underwear. *Oops.* I stand up again. "Look—this is my brother's beer." I hold up the bottle. "The client must have requested it. Otherwise, my father would never have stocked it."

"Really?" He frowns at the bottle. "Your brother is—what—the COO of that company? Isn't Daddy impressed?"

I snort. "Not hardly. My father calls him a sellout. To his face."

"Rough." Matteo shakes his head. "I always thought your dad was kind of abrasive. Usually not to me, though."

"He likes you." I shrug. "You're part of a rare club. I'm also a member. But Nash is not."

"Well, that's weird."

"It's unhealthy." I snap the cooler closed. "The only reason that Nash and I get along is because I acknowledge that I know I've had it easy with Dad."

"What did Nash ever do to him, anyway?"

"He left to work for a soulless brewing conglomerate." I tug the cooler toward the hand truck, but Matteo just picks it up and carries it to the wagon.

I watch his muscles flex, and I'm not even sorry.

Not that I'd admit it, but he's right—spending time together is a little more fraught than I'd expected it to be. Although I've been faking it pretty well these past couple weeks. We hang out sometimes, and I can usually manage to string sentences together without thinking about sex.

Mostly. But not always.

It's a quiet drive down to Norwich in Otto's truck. I play some old music to amuse Matteo—the stuff we listened to in high school.

"Green Day makes me feel like a rebellious teen again." He chuckles, his fingers drumming on the steering wheel. "Still popular with the snowboard jockeys, too. I hear these tunes a lot in Colorado."

As we get deeper into the playlist, I hear Kelly Clarkson's "Since U Been Gone." And "We Belong Together," by Mariah Carey.

Something strange comes over me as I listen to the lyrics. I have a sudden, crystalline memory of listening to these songs, lying on my bed… thinking about Matteo.

Okay, wow. I'd forgotten how *visceral* my feelings for Matteo had been back then—the gut punch of missing him so fiercely that I cried along to love songs. And that teenage, hormone-fueled certainty that I'd lost something precious.

"What?" Matteo says.

I realize I've been staring at him and jerk my chin away. "Nothing," I mumble. "Just thinking about high school."

He turns his attention back to the road, but my heart is pounding away. It's been a long time since senior year. I'd long ago forced those feelings down, locking them away somewhere they couldn't hurt me. This summer has broken that lock.

At seventeen, I'd ached for Matteo in that hot, pure way reserved only for teenagers. And all for a boy who'd never so much as kissed me.

I shiver, even though I'm not cold. I sneak another glance at Matteo, and it sears me to the core. *I'm falling for him.* Or maybe I fell already—eighteen years ago.

It's going to be ugly when he leaves again. I can already tell. No wonder I practically melt every time he smiles at me. I've been here before. I'm making all my teenage mistakes for a second time.

"Almost there," he says, slowing down to take the highway exit. He's holding the steering wheel at ten and two—a safe driver and a good man. A great friend.

That's what we're supposed to be. Friends with a fun, once-a-month naked hobby.

Another song comes on. It's "She Will Be Loved" by Maroon 5. My chest starts to ache right in time with the music.

Ow.

My heart is about to crack in half when Matteo abruptly punches the *off* button on the stereo. Silence descends in the truck's cab. "Sorry." He clears his throat. "Need to find this place. Can you look for Hopson Road?"

"Of course."

———

Once the wedding reception gets underway, there's little time for sentimental yearning.

Mostly. Every time Matteo laughs, I feel it all over my body. And he's so close that I can smell his spicy aftershave. I'd like to bury my face in his neck, but instead I'm counting the remaining cups, hoping there are enough.

These wedding guests can *drink*. As the sky goes dark, we're already on our third keg of Goldenpour. The tipsier they get, the more the bridesmaids flirt with Matteo.

"So where do you live?" asks a particularly pretty one. She's leaning casually against the bar.

And by "casually" I mean she's hoisted her breasts onto the serving shelf, and she's practically drooling on him.

"Colorado," he says with a shrug. "Just visiting for a while."

Her face falls.

"Looks like they're cutting the cake," he says, pointing toward the wedding tent. "Do they need you guys over there?"

"Oh. Whoopsy!" The bridesmaid whirls and trots off toward the tent as quickly as a girl can run in satin heels, and I hear Matteo chuckle.

And good riddance to you.

"Check out that cake," he says. "Fancy."

It's three layers, decorated with lifelike roses. "That really is beautiful. This whole wedding is first rate."

We watch the bride and groom cut their first slice. The groom takes a bit and jams it onto the bride's lips, while onlookers laugh.

"I don't get that custom," Matteo says. "Why make a mess with the most expensive cake of your life, in front of everyone you know?"

"No idea," I agree. I hadn't let Rory do that to me at our wedding, thank God.

I almost say—*you can skip it at your wedding.* But the thought stops me cold. *Matteo's wedding.* That's a thing that could happen someday. Just because he hasn't met The One, doesn't mean he never will.

Hell, he could meet her any minute now. Maybe he climbs aboard his first Colorado ski tour of next season and—*bam*—there she is. The woman of his dreams.

How I hate that idea. Which makes me a terrible friend.

"Hey, want some cupcakes?" I look up to see that the bridesmaid is already back and carrying a cupcake in each hand. "I forgot my beer, so I brought you a treat."

"Thanks! We love cupcakes," Matteo says easily. "I set your beer aside for you." He hands her a cup of Goldenpour.

"You're the *best.*" She puts a hair toss into the word, and I feel grumpy again.

Get over yourself, Giltmaker.

I'm almost thankful when another rush of drinkers arrives at the counter, thirsty for a beverage to go with their cake.

———

"Thank Christ," Matteo says when the band finally stops playing. "Let's pack up and get out of here."

We get to work cleaning up, and when we're finally on the road, it's already past midnight.

"Play some more tunes?" Matteo suggests from the driver's seat.

"Of course." I dig out my phone and press Play.

Matteo laughs when Train starts singing "Drops of Jupiter." "Okay, not sure this song aged very well."

"Oh please," I argue. "This song probably thinks the same about you."

"What?" He laughs. "I'm aging like a stud."

That's alarmingly true. "Just be kind to our high school jams. Didn't it take this band a decade to get their first hit? They just never gave up. I saw it on MTV."

Matteo cracks another grin. "Sure, girl. MTV, huh? So you're not old at all."

"You shut up."

He laughs. And then, to my surprise, he pulls off the road at a spot overlooking the Connecticut River.

"Why'd you stop?" I ask.

"Because cupcakes." He unbuckles his seatbelt and gets out of the truck. "I forgot I'd put them in the empty cooler."

"Oh damn. I want one."

He grins at me before disappearing for a moment.

By the time he reappears, my mouth is watering. "What kind do you think they are?"

He shrugs. "The kind that are about to disappear. Here."

I take the cake and carefully pick the wrapper off. The first bite makes me moan. "Ooooh lemon! And buttercream."

Matteo gives me a frown. "Cut that out."

"What?"

"That noise you just made is illegal in seven states." He runs a hand through his long hair, gives me an arch look, and then bites into his cupcake.

Then *he* moans, and the sound makes my hormones pop and fizz.

God, I've got to rein it in. I take another bite of cupcake.

SARINA BOWEN

There's so much frosting, that a large blob of buttercream ends up on my thumb.

I almost lick it off. Almost. But something makes me hesitate. And then my evil brain asks a crucial question—how would buttercream look in Matteo's mustache?

I lean toward him, aiming that blob of frosting for his upper lip. As a woman with two younger siblings, I've always known that hesitation is the death of an attack.

But it's a miscalculation, because Matteo has *four* younger siblings. He's seen it all before.

He catches my wrist in one of his big hands. And then? The remaining quarter cupcake from his *other* hand is smushed firmly onto my mouth.

All over my mouth.

Suddenly, the truck echoes with two competing sounds—my shriek of dismay and his laughter.

Indignant, I tongue the bulk of the cupcake from my face and into my mouth, because that's the easiest solution. "You ass."

He just laughs and refuses to let go of my wrist. I have to set the remains of my cupcake in the cupholder and use my free hand to scrape the rest of the mess from my skin.

Matteo watches this with amusement. Then he lifts my trapped hand to his mouth and sucks the buttercream off my thumb.

Deeply.

With his tongue.

I gasp, the sound making it abundantly clear how I feel about this sudden reacquaintance with his tongue and its capabilities.

Our eyes lock. Before I can form a thought, Matteo is leaning across the bench seat to capture my mouth with his.

Oh boy. His kiss is like one of those sentimental songs on my playlist—familiar and exciting at the same time. I sink into the rhythm without missing a beat.

When he pulls back, it's only to whisper against my mouth, "Don't know what tastes better. You, or the buttercream."

And then? That skillful tongue handily removes the rest of the frosting from my lips.

By the time he's done, my hands are clenched on his biceps, and my nipples are urgent peaks inside my bra. As if he can sense my need, he cups my breast, his thumb grazing my nipple.

I whimper. Today is not a smiley-face day, and we both know it.

This was never part of the plan, but I don't think I care. It's after midnight on a dark Vermont road. I'm alone with this man I've always wanted, even when I was too young and dumb to understand it.

Fuck it.

My hand ventures down his chest and lands on the fly of his trousers. Boldly, I pop the button.

Matteo inhales sharply. The sound goes straight to my nipples, but also to my ego. The fact that I can surprise him is like gasoline on my personal fire.

That's why I plunge my hand into his boxer briefs and pull out his thickening cock. And that's why I lean right over and suck the head into my mouth.

He lets fly with a string of curses, and it brings me so much joy. I have never felt as sexy as I do right now.

Matteo grips my hair and groans deeply. He's hard and heavy on my tongue, and I'm slightly frustrated by the lack of maneuverable space between his tight belly and the steering wheel. But I make up for it in enthusiasm. If I'm careful, I can take more of him into my mouth, and he helps me out by lifting his powerful hips off the seat.

Who knew this could be so wildly erotic? Giving head was something I've only done out of a sense of obligation, as a prelude to the fun part.

But now it *is* the fun part. Every time Matteo makes another broken sound, I feel a rush of heat between my legs. Knowing I have the power to thrill him is so exciting.

Suddenly he lifts me off his body, and the truck's seat goes sliding back.

"Panties off," he growls. "Get over here."

As I sit up, he's already shoving his trousers and underwear down and reclining the seat.

My body temperature shoots up as I fumble under the skirt of my dress.

"Right now, sweetheart," he says. "Come finish what you started."

"*You* started it," I argue as I kick off my shoes and underwear. It's awkward business trying to spin around and maneuver toward his side of the seat.

He solves this problem by hauling me onto his body. The moment I land on his thighs, his tongue is in my mouth, and his hands are unzipping my dress.

"You don't have to do that," I say between kisses as he unclips my bra.

"The fuck I don't. Need to play with your tits while you ride me."

Whoosh. That's the sound of flames licking my body. I'm basically naked, making out in a truck, his erection trapped between my legs. His hands are everywhere at once—cupping my ass, stroking my nipples, tugging on my hair.

We're *shameless*. I'm burning up in the best possible way. Impatient, too. I lever my body off his lap. "Do it," I gasp.

"Do what?" he taunts me. "Ask nice."

I growl impatiently. "Give it to me so I can ride you."

"Yes, queen," he whispers as the thick head of him lines up right where I want it.

Before he can change his mind, I sink down on his cock with a happy moan, filling myself.

"Damn." He tips his head against the headrest, his chest muscles flexing. "I will never get used to the feel of you. So good."

I'm too busy to reply. I rise and then sink deliciously down again. This wins me an appreciative groan. So I do it again. And again. Slowly, though. Just finding my rhythm.

Matteo has his own ideas. His big hands grip my waist. Then he braces his feet against the floor and pumps his hips.

It's... wow.

"Wow," I pant, and then kiss him. Hard.

Just wow.

———

Afterward, I lie against his chest, my eyes screwed shut, so I don't have to face the aftermath.

I'm trying very hard not to think about the line we just crossed.

"You know," he says after a long silence. "I've come around on the whole cake smash thing."

I laugh and then bury my face against his neck. "We probably shouldn't have done this." I can't believe I'm naked in his uncle's truck, still straddling Matteo.

His hands go still on my body. "Why not? Serious question."

"Public indecency, for starters. But also, it's just… not part of our plan."

He lifts my chin so he can study me with those bottomless brown eyes. "Tell me something—is anything in your life going to plan? Because mine isn't."

"Well, no."

His smile is a little wry. "I realize you only need me two days a month, Leila. But I'm still attracted to you on the other twenty-eight. In case that's not obvious."

There's that flutter in my tummy again. I lean into his hand. "You're a pretty good time too, mister. We're adults who can do as we please. I'm just a little shocked at my behavior—hooking up in a truck like a high school kid."

He grins. "Except we never did this when we were high school kids. Kind of seems like a waste."

"Yeah," I whisper. "It does."

I don't point out that he never made a move on me in high school. Or that if he had, it might have changed the course of my whole life.

And I don't point out that attraction is just the tip of the iceberg for me. I'm uncovering feelings for this man that I forgot were there. But now is not the time to say so.

"I'm going to pluck the various parts of my dignity off the floor of this truck so we can drive home now."

"If you must." He leans in and kisses me one more time. Very slowly. "Don't overthink it," he whispers afterward. "Our time together is limited. We might as well enjoy it."

"Fine, but it's not your bra that's snarled around the brake pedal."

He laughs, and I yank the straps of my dress up over my shoulders again. Like a lady.

CHAPTER 31
LEILA

It's a hot summer day, and I've sought the solace of my father's office. The rattle of the window air conditioner is pretty loud, which is probably why I don't hear anyone approach the doorway until my visitor clears his throat.

Startled, I drop the receipts I'm cataloguing and swivel sharply to face the door.

A slow grin spreads across Matteo's face. "Everything okay in here?"

"Fine." It's an understatement. The truth is that Matteo can sneak up on me any time he wants. This thing between us started out as a simple once-a-month arrangement, but it's so much more than that now.

Whenever he steps into the room, I'm happy.

He steps forward and leans against my father's cluttered floor-to-ceiling bookshelves. "I've always loved this old room. Haven't set foot in here since I was a teenager."

"It is a spectacle," I agree. People have told my father that he should relocate the brewery to a shiny new factory, and he has never taken kindly to the suggestion. This office is his spiritual home.

I don't really blame him.

"This space should be a tasting room," Matteo says as his eyes travel the carved woodwork that covers three walls. "It's so cool."

"That would be a fun idea," I admit. "Not that my dad is the kind of guy who takes suggestions."

Matteo grins. "Did you eat lunch already?"

"Yes."

He quirks an eyebrow. "Yes…?"

I grit my teeth. "Yes, *Sir Sexy Pants*."

He cracks up, probably because it's funny every time I have to say it. We had a bet yesterday morning about the Busy Bean's weekday hours. And guess who lost?

I hate losing, so I change the subject. "Besides trolling for a lunch date, is there another reason you stopped by?"

"Sure. Two, actually. My brother asked me to pick up some samples your dad set aside for him."

"Oh! Of course." My father had mentioned something about samples for Alec in the walk-in refrigerator. I rise from the chair. "What's the other reason?"

Matteo's smile fades. "I also wanted to ask you about a beer wagon event that Skye wants to do over Labor Day weekend. She called me, but…"

My heart drops. "But you won't be here."

"Right," he says gently. "As far as I know, the wagon will close for business when I leave town. But I thought I'd check in with you, in case you wanted to do Skye's event and bank the money."

"What kind of event is it?" I ask, keeping my expression neutral. It guts me to acknowledge that Matteo is leaving in a couple weeks.

"Some kind of celebrity golf tournament."

"Wait. Real celebrities?"

"This is Vermont, so we're using that term loosely. I think it's some local TV anchor that Skye knows. And also your brother, Mitch."

"*Oh*. Does Mitch even golf?" He's a professional hockey player, and he lives two thousand miles away. I barely know the guy anymore.

"Who knows?" Matteo shrugs. "I just work here."

"Right. Sorry." I cross to the other wall of shelves and find the binder my father uses to track upcoming beer deliveries.

My mind is occupied by thoughts of Matteo leaving, and I flip through the pages with unseeing eyes.

"Can't believe your dad doesn't use a computer," Matteo says. "It's, like, 1985 in this office."

"You're not wrong." I scribble a note about a possible wagon event over the holiday weekend and then refile the binder.

Matteo moves closer. He glances toward the open door, and then pushes me up against the bookcase for a slow kiss.

This is neither the time nor place, but I grip his biceps anyway and kiss him right back.

In a few weeks he'll be gone, and I'll wish I had more of his kisses.

"Dinner later?" he whispers.

"Of course. Worthy Burger? Thai food? There's always pizza."

"No, I'll cook," he says. "I'll swing by the store on the way home. And then I get to choose the movie, right? It's only fair that the winner gets to pick."

I roll my eyes. "Sure. Milk your victory for all it's worth."

He catches my hand before I can walk away. "Oh, that comes later," he purrs into my ear. "I have a *full* evening planned for you. Very full. Just keep calling me *sir* after you take your clothes off later," he says. "I'll make it worth your while. Sir Sexy Pants has big plans for you."

"Yes, *sir*," I say in a voice so sultry that it borders on ridiculous. Then he kisses my neck, and my skin flushes hot.

"I need to win bets more often," he says under his breath before biting my earlobe.

I lean back against the bookshelf and close my eyes. *This could be your life*, a greedy little voice inside me says. I hear it a lot these days.

But that voice lies.

"Oh shit! Sorry!"

We jerk apart. That damn air conditioner is so loud that we didn't hear Livia walk in.

"Sorry," my father's assistant says again. She tosses a file folder onto my father's desk and then exits the room.

"Well, fuck," Matteo says, rubbing the back of his neck. "That was my fault. Is it gonna be a problem for you?"

"Don't worry about it." Even if she ran straight to my father to tattle on me—and why would she?—it doesn't really matter what he thinks.

Sure, I'll have to listen to his judgements. But that's just a normal Tuesday.

"What time shall I make you dinner?" he asks.

Any time at all, I'd like to answer. "Six?" I say instead.

"Six it is," he says with a sheepish smile. "Those samples for Alec are probably in the walk-in, yeah? I can find them."

"Okay. Thanks." I lean forward and give him a very quick kiss, and he smiles.

Every day I fall a little further for this man. Sometimes I roll over at night and watch him sleep, despairing over what will happen to us when he goes back to Colorado.

He said I could visit on smiley-face days. It wouldn't be easy for me to get away from work, but maybe I'll be lucky and hit a three-day weekend.

I'll still miss him all the time, though.

"Later, hot stuff," he whispers. Then he squeezes my shoulder, like he knows he has to leave but doesn't really want to.

"Later," I whisper back.

Then, after one more lingering glance, he goes.

I meander back to my father's desk and stare down at my pile of receipts like I've never seen them before. Matteo often has this effect on me. I can't remember what I was thinking about before he blew back into my life.

All I think about now is—what will happen when he goes?

I knew we wouldn't last. Our summer fling is like a hothouse flower—blooming faster and brighter than it would under normal circumstances.

Matteo likes me, sure.

He might even love me in his own way.

He doesn't *need* me, though. I can tell. It's just different with him. He's all about the fun and the sex. But he doesn't turn to me for comfort—even when he's thrashing in the night from another bad dream.

Instead, he wakes up and shakes it off. Gets a glass of water. Tells me to go back to sleep.

So I do. I'm used to having him in my bed now.

Too used to it.

"Leila?" I look up as Livia enters the office again and perches on the side of the desk. She's pretty in a fierce sort of way—with raven-black hair that tumbles in a riot of curls down her back. "Hey, I'm sorry about before. I had no idea about you and Hot Jesus."

I snort, wondering what Matteo would think of that nickname. "Not your fault. Although it would be helpful if you didn't, uh, mention this to my father."

Her hands fly up in protest. "I would *never*. Everyone is enti-tled to a secret or two. And I get it. I used to have a thing for bad boys, too."

Interesting. "Well, don't hold out on me. How did you cure it?"

Her smile is wry. "Oh, I didn't have to. Mine cured it for me—with their abusive bullshit. This is a gift from one of them." She shows me her forearm, which has a smattering of scars all over it. "He dragged me across the wood floor, through broken glass."

"Oh!" It's a struggle not to recoil. "I'm sorry."

"Long time ago," she says with a minor shrug, as if it doesn't matter. But something tells me the fear is still there. "Anyway—don't worry about me. I won't snitch. That would be a violation of the sisterhood code."

"What code?" someone bellows from the doorway.

My father has entered the chat.

"Nothing, Dad," I say. "Just getting to know Livia."

"Get to know her on your own time," he says. "Livia, shouldn't you be working on my report…"

"Here." She grabs the folder off the desk and sort of thwacks it against his chest. "I *told* you it would be done this afternoon, didn't I?"

Oh shit. People don't usually speak to my father that way. I brace myself for him to fire her right in front of me.

But he flips open the folder instead, and then grunts. "Huh. That was fast."

"I could have done this work in half the time with Excel," she says coolly. "But you be you, boo." Then she ducks around him and leaves the office.

I blink after her.

"Mouthy girl," my dad mutters. "But nobody works a calculator like she does. Did you finish the receipts?"

"Almost," I say, recovering from my shock.

"If you don't have time, just give them to Livia. She'll be taking over that job when you go back to your babysitting gig."

Babysitting gig. That's what my father thinks of early childhood education. It makes me want to choke him. But you have to pick your battles.

"Will do," I say. And then I grab the receipts off the desk and leave.

CHAPTER 32
MATTEO
AUGUST

When I was a kid, the first day of summer break was like the edge of the ocean. Time stretched out before me, unbroken. But then somehow vacation always went so fast.

The same thing is happening at age thirty-six. I'm leaving Vermont tomorrow. And I'm totally not ready.

My last day in the Green Mountain State is spent sweating in Benito's backyard. There are better ways to kill a Sunday, but at least they can say that I was helpful until the very end.

"Whose turn is it?" Alec calls. "Matteo?"

"Yeah, sure. Give it here." I hold out my hands for the posthole digger that Benito bought at Home Depot.

When Alec hands me the digger, I find the mark for the next posthole and prepare to dig.

"Hold up," Alec says. "Wait for the beep."

I roll my eyes, but I wait.

All my siblings have gathered here to help my youngest brother install a fence, and because we're us, somebody decided that it needed to be a competition. Whoever can dig the fastest posthole wins… I don't even know what.

"Is there a prize if I win?" I ask.

"Nope," Alec says. "Just the glory of being the manliest among us."

"This might be the dumbest contest you idiots have ever come

193

up with," Zara says from a deck chair, where she's holding Micah. "Toxic masculinity at its finest."

"Then why didn't you switch jobs with me when I offered?" I ask. "I'm happy to do some baby-holding."

"Then who'd keep score?" she asks with a shake of her hair. "I said it was dumb. I didn't say it wasn't entertaining."

Micah gives me a drooly smile. He is also entertained.

"Ready?" Alec says. "And…go."

His watch beeps, and I start digging. Ben's new backyard has some pretty big rocks in the soil, so this competition is based more on luck than strength. My last effort was stymied by a softball-sized rock halfway to victory.

But this time I'm lucky. I quickly dig three plugs of soil and whoop when the digger sinks into the hole at the finished height. "Did you see that? I'm winning this thing."

"Twenty-four seconds," Alec says in a grudging voice. "The new number to beat."

"Clearly you all are in this to the death, but there're only two more holes," Skye announces. "And I've just lit the grill. Let's get some panels in place so we can chow down." She claps her hands commandingly.

"Hope you don't mind holes all over the lawn," Alec says. "I'm not stopping until I reclaim my title."

"Not even for grilled kebabs?" Damien asks. "I'll have yours, then."

Benito takes the posthole digger from me and quietly digs the last two holes without comment. "Okay, done. Let's put in some fencing."

"What?" Alec yelps. "You just *handed* Matteo the title?"

"It's okay, little brother," I say, patting him on the shoulder. "You can borrow it whenever you need to impress the ladies. Just like you used to steal my Phish concert T-shirts."

Everybody laughs. Even Alec. "You know they're playing in Boston in September? If you weren't leaving, we could totally go."

"Tickets would be a fortune," Benito points out.

"Designer Jesus could afford it," Alec says with a shrug. "Rent out your sick Aspen pad for the ski season and you could buy VIP seats for the whole crew."

"Oh, I wish." They have no idea how unexcited I am to get on that plane. But it doesn't matter—I have to go. My time here is up. And it depresses me to think about it. "Aren't we here to put up a fence? Time's a wasting."

————

We put the fence together easily, and the finished product is satisfying. "You guys getting a dog?" I ask Ben as I admire our work. "Is that what this is for?"

"Maybe," he says from the grill, where he's flipping the meat. "Just thought the yard needed a fence."

"So domesticated," I tease. "All of you."

"You say that like it's a bad thing." Alec steals one of the tortilla chips off the plate I'm holding. "Just do us a favor and come home again before another fourteen years go by?"

"I swear I will."

"How about Christmas?" Zara asks.

I shake my head. "We're all booked up. That's my busy season."

I haven't mentioned my plan to come home for a booty call at the end of November. I'm trying not to make any promises I can't keep.

"You'll always have a place here," Alec says. "Hope you know that."

I look up quickly to check his face and find that it's uncharacteristically serious. "I appreciate that," I say quietly. "The summer has been great. Lots of time with you guys."

"And lots of time with Leila," my sister says, drawing out her name. "Let's put the credit where it's due."

"So?" I demand. "What's your point?"

"You seem happy. That's all." She shakes her head. "I think it's great that you have multiple reasons to come home again. Means my kids won't forget what you look like."

There's nothing I'm willing to say about Leila, but I catch Alec giving me the side eye. Last week he busted me in the act of leaving her apartment one morning. That was bound to happen, seeing that his apartment and Leila's are the only two in the building.

He's probably noticed my rental car outside, too. But he hadn't asked me about it directly until I saw him on the stairs. And that conversation went like this:

Alec: So…?

Me: *Shrug.* Not going to discuss it.

Alec: Cool.

He's solid, my brother. He was quick to get over his anger at me this spring. And he's been quick to show gratitude for all my help with the family businesses.

I have no idea what he'd think about my project with Leila, though. Hell—I barely know what to think about it myself. Right from the start, she'd said there'd be no strings attached.

But I didn't count on two things. One—that it would break my heart. When I get on that plane tomorrow, it's gonna ache.

And two—that it wouldn't work.

Our third smiley face came and went (so to speak) in July. And our final one was just a few days ago. Her job will make it difficult for her to visit me this fall. And late November seems like a long way away…

"Matteo?"

I look up to find Skye is speaking to me. "What? Sorry."

She smiles. "I asked what you wanted to drink. I'm taking orders." She points toward the house.

"Let me help," I say. "I'll bring out beers for all these hooligans."

"All right," she says. "Thanks."

I follow her into the house, where Zara is mixing a bowl of potato salad. "Matteo—can you carry this out to the table? And Skye—can you grab the deviled eggs out of the fridge?"

"Sure." Skye opens the refrigerator and retrieves a platter. She removes the foil from it and then—

I watch in confusion as her expression changes to revulsion. Then she abruptly runs from the room.

A moment later I hear the sound of retching, followed by a toilet flush. "What the…?"

When I glance at my sister, she's wearing a cat-like smile. "No *way*," she says. Then she laughs.

For a second I'm lost, because that's not a very polite reaction when someone throws up. Then she says, "Some women can't stand the scent of eggs when they're pregnant."

"Oh," I say slowly.

Oh.

I carry the offending eggs outside, along with the potato salad. When I return to the kitchen, Zara and Skye are having a whispered conversation. They step apart when they see me, and Skye gives me a startled look.

"Hey, I didn't notice anything," I say, raising my hands. "I'm a vault."

"We're keeping it quiet," she says. "For another week, anyway, until I hit the three-month mark."

"I'll just need a video of the moment you tell our mom," Zara says with a chuckle. "She'll be *so* excited."

They continue their chatter. Numbly, I remove some beers from the fridge and carry them out the back door. Outside, my youngest brother is pulling kebabs off the grill and laughing over something Damien said.

This whole day looks different to me now. The fence makes more sense. Next summer they'll have a newborn baby and not much time for yard work. And a year after that, a toddler might take her first steps in this newly fenced-off space.

And Ben looks *ecstatic*. Like a man with everything he ever wanted.

I pass out beers, which is practically an automatic reflex at this point. When I reach Ben, I touch him lightly on the shoulder blade. "Hey, man. Congrats."

He blinks at me in surprise, and then his smile drops as he glances toward the house. "Did Skye get sick again?" he asks quietly.

I nod. "Yeah, but she's okay. The deviled eggs set her off."

"Ah." He flashes me a nervous smile. "It's still early, and we

197

don't know what to expect. The whole thing was kind of a first-try situation."

I whistle quietly. "Nice job, stud."

He gives me a curious glance. "Maybe that's not something we should make into a competition? Just a thought."

First try, though.

"Mom doesn't know yet," he adds. "So if you could keep it to yourself for another week."

"Sure. Zara knows, though, so your time with this secret is limited."

He laughs and shakes his head. "I'll consider myself warned. Now get a plate. Food's ready!"

My other brothers whoop with joy.

Stepping back, I wait for Skye and Zara to come out of the house. Zara sets Micah onto a blanket in the grass and makes herself a plate to share with him. Alec teases Damien about his threadbare jeans. Damien teases Benito about his obsession for washing his car.

But I can already feel myself receding into the background again. An outsider in my own family. The next barbecue in this yard will happen without me. And the one after that.

I watch Benito put a protective arm around his wife and kiss her on the jaw. And I ask myself a question that I've never asked myself before—do I want what Benito has?

It feels like a dangerous question. Even if the answer is yes, that door isn't necessarily open to me. My life is elsewhere. Leila might not ever feel about me the way Skye feels about my brother.

Also, I haven't succeeded at getting her pregnant. She wants a baby more than anything else. I thought I was helping, but it's just dawning on me that I might be the obstacle, not the cure.

"Matteo?" Benito puts a plate in my hands. "Get involved, man, before they're ready for seconds."

"Thanks." I take the plate with the sudden certainty that he'll make a great daddy. No question in my mind.

But being a daddy might not be happening for me. This whole summer I'd been thinking that it was a choice I'd have to make— to be involved as a parent, or not.

Now I realize that I've been worrying about the wrong thing.

Numbly, I put some food on my plate. After my first bite, my phone pings with a text.

It's only the airline. *Time to check in for your flight to Denver.*

Don't I know it.

CHAPTER 33
LEILA

The light is fading in the sky outside my apartment. With the windows open, I can hear the buzzing of cicadas on the breeze.

Every teacher knows what that sound means—the end of summer break. Once the cicadas start up, you might as well break out the school clothes.

Tonight it sounds especially mournful. The fact that Matteo is leaving tomorrow has me bumping around my apartment like the last billiard ball on the pool table. I change my clothes and then wonder if the sexy red lingerie I'm wearing is too much.

I unbutton my shirt enough so that the camisole peeps out. But then I decide that looks dumb, so I button it back up again. He can find it himself. I change the sheets on the bed. Then I make home-made lemonade and set it out on the counter.

It's what I poured for Matteo that first night, when I was so nervous, but also shaking with anticipation. I wish I could rewind to that night and start all over again.

Matteo just gave me the summer of my life. It's not just the potential pregnancy, it's the *joy*. My divorce made me feel like a failure, and I guess I still do. But Matteo gave me something valuable—lemonade from lemons. Hot kisses and guiltless fun after a year that hurt us both.

But now I don't know what the future holds. That makes me nervous, which is why I find myself turning all the spices in my spice drawer so that the labels face out, and then rearranging my bookshelf.

When the knock finally comes, I jump. I run over to the door, and my first reaction is to notice how great Matteo looks with a beard. He's let his scruff grow out this summer.

But my second reaction is fear. One look in his eyes, and I know something is wrong. He doesn't smile. He leans in and slowly kisses my jaw. And then he sighs.

"Come in?" I say stupidly.

He enters, crossing to the kitchen area and seating himself on a stool.

"You look like a man with a lot on his mind," I say, even as my heart continues to plummet. I'd hoped we could have one more hot night, no tears. I'd wanted to skip the sad part.

But Matteo is throwing off a dark kind of energy. He accepts a glass of lemonade from me, then props his handsome face in one hand and studies me with those dark brown eyes. "I need to ask you a question."

My stomach tightens. "Yes?"

"You told me that a baby was the thing you want most in the world. Is that still true?"

I swallow hard, because the question confuses me. "Yes, of course. I haven't changed my mind."

His expression flattens. I have the strange feeling that I gave the wrong answer, which makes no sense. "Okay. Then I need you to do something for me," he says quietly.

"What?"

"Go back to the doctor and reconsider IVF. Or…the other one."

"IUI?"

"Yeah." He runs a hand through his long hair. "I want you to have a baby, and I haven't been able to give one to you."

My heart drops. "But I haven't given up. Sometimes it takes a year."

"I know that." He nods slowly. "But I have to go back to Colorado. I don't have a choice. And you told me that you're short on time. I don't want to be the reason you don't get your dream."

SARINA BOWEN

"You're *not*," I insist.

His eyebrows lift, as if in challenge. "It takes two, yeah? You said you're short on time. The clock is ticking."

"Well, that's true. Except…" I'm in turmoil now. He doesn't want to keep trying?

"You deserve it all, Leila. I want you to have this." He looks away and clears his throat. "Now I need to tell you a little secret, because you're going to hear it anyway, and I don't want you to be too surprised."

My stomach freefalls. "What is it?"

"Skye is pregnant," he says softly. "They haven't told anyone yet, but they will real soon."

"Oh." *Oh shit.* I can feel my eyes growing hot for some maddening reason. "Already?"

He nods slowly. "First try, apparently."

"Oh wow." I inhale carefully. I kind of knew this would happen, but I still feel the blow.

I shouldn't. But I do.

Matteo doesn't miss it, either. He sets his glass down and circles the kitchen island to pull me into his arms. I tuck my cheek against his shoulder and breathe in the sunshiny scent of him.

"I know how much you want this," he whispers. "Don't give up, okay? I couldn't live with that."

"Okay," I say. But instead of feeling grateful, I just feel sad and confused. Because the baby isn't the only thing I want anymore, is it?

"You'll get there," he whispers.

"Maybe."

"Yeah, you will."

"I wish you didn't have to go," I blurt. It's hard to know which is worse—the fact that I'm probably not pregnant. Or the fact that he's leaving.

"I wish a lot of things," he says. Then he inhales and steps back. "Leila, I need to say goodbye."

"Right now?"

He nods solemnly. "I need to swing by my mom's and hang

202

up some blinds she ordered. And I need to pack my stuff and get my head in the game."

"Okay." I gulp. It's another blow. I thought we'd at least have tonight. I'm wearing red satin underwear, damn it.

Matteo is looking at me with kind brown eyes that see right through me. "I'm going to miss you. So much. This summer has been *everything* to me. But I don't think I expected it to end so soon."

"Yeah," I say, my voice a sad scrape. This feels like a rejection. "I'll see you again, though, right?"

"You can count on it."

Can I, though? Look how that turned out last time.

He takes a step backward. I'm already losing him. "Be well, Leila. Hang in there. I'm pulling for you."

"Thank you," I say uselessly. And I do not have the willpower to stay where I am. I follow him to the door, like a lost dog.

He pauses with a hand on the doorknob. "You'll, uh, let me know if you get any good news?"

"Of course," I say quickly.

He pulls me in for a hug and looks down at me, his expression resigned. I brace myself to hear *goodbye*.

Instead, he dips his face toward mine, and I stop breathing as he kisses me gently—that silky beard tickling my chin. "Queen," is all he whispers afterward.

My throat closes up. I can't make myself say goodbye.

Neither can he, I guess. With one more long look at me, he opens the door and takes his leave. It closes behind him with a determined click.

I have the worst urge to yank it open again and chase him down the stairs.

Instead, I rest my forehead against the wood. What just happened? He asked me if a baby was still the thing I wanted most. And I'd said yes. Because that was the plan.

Except the plan got complicated. I want Matteo, too. I'm *falling* for him. That wasn't supposed to happen.

And now he's leaving, whether I want him to or not.

CHAPTER 34
MATTEO
OCTOBER

"Here you go," I say, passing the contract across the picnic table. "Oh, let me grab a pen from inside the office."

"Hey, no need." The guy I'm hiring to be our newest guide—Jeffrey—pulls a pen out of the pocket of his flannel shirt. "I'm so stoked for this. I brought my lucky pen."

He's actually grinning as he initials the bottom of the first page and then flips to the second.

I should be grinning, too. Jeffrey is a good hire. He's twenty-seven, which is the perfect age. He's old enough to have a decade's worth of big mountain experience. He's passed all the safety courses. He's proficient with avalanche risk assessment and CPR. And he just got married, so he's eager for a steady paycheck.

But he's still young enough to be "stoked" about things. Honestly, he reminds me a little of myself ten years ago. Every day a new adventure.

He signs his name with a flourish on the last page. "This is awesome. Can't wait till we get some pow pow." He actually tilts his chin skyward, as if checking for snowflakes on a sunny, fifty-degree day.

Spoiler: there aren't any.

"I'll give my notice at the gym in November," he says. "Lookin' forward to working outside all winter."

Yup. He's perfect. I reach my hand across the table to shake. "Welcome aboard, Jeffrey. Pleased to have you."

"Thank you, sir." Another grin.

Cara comes out of the office to gather up the paperwork and walk Jeffrey to his Jeep. She's friendly and animated. Her smile looks genuine.

I don't really know how she's doing it, because I can't muster the same enthusiasm.

In three months, this place will be covered with snow. The picnic table will have our insulated coffee mugs on it, along with our helmets and gloves.

Mine and Jeffrey's, I guess.

But it should be Sean and me standing here together, greeting the first customers of the season. I can't believe I have to do this without him. Every day, seven days a week, all season long.

I don't know how Cara gets up in the morning. I really don't.

She waves to Jeffrey as he backs out of his parking spot. And then she heads for the office door, stopping to give me a curious look. "You okay?"

"No," I say grumpily. "What kind of a question is that?"

She gives me a sad smile. "He's a good kid, Matty. He's going to do great. You hired a winner. And I like that guy you interviewed yesterday, too. He'll be another good addition."

"Yeah," I say without enthusiasm.

I'm right on schedule with the work. Everything is falling into place. And I feel nothing.

"Jeffrey just told me the *best* news—his new wife is pregnant."

Something goes sideways inside my chest. "Oh? Why do we care, exactly?"

She rolls her eyes. "Because he's going to stick around all season. You know how it usually is with these guys—if their buddy plans a trip to the Chugach Mountains, they vanish overnight. But not our Jeffrey. He needs the paycheck. Baby needs new shoes."

"Yeah. That's, uh, great."

"Damn right. Now have a cup of coffee and call that event

planner from the mountain lodge—she's trying to book that corporate trip in February? There's a sticky on your desk."

"All right. Sure." I follow her into the office and take my seat behind a beat-up desk.

This place isn't fancy inside, because customers rarely come in here. We spend all our investment dollars on the helicopters and the safety equipment—the stuff that really counts.

I find the note with Cara's scrawl on it and take out my phone. My first action is to check for messages from Leila. By now, it's like a tic. We text each other rarely. She has a busy life. I have a busy life.

But I miss her terribly, and I can't stop wondering how she's doing, and if she went back to the fertility specialist.

It was my sister who'd asked me—if you could snap your fingers and give Leila the life she wants, would you? And I'd said yes, without hesitation.

Doesn't make it easy to stop loving her, though.

————

When I next hear from Leila, she doesn't mention a thing about babies. I wake up one morning to find her text. ***Happy birthday!*** It's accompanied by a complicated gif of a snowboarder jumping off a layer cake.

Hell, I'd forgotten my own birthday. The date had completely slipped my mind. I'm thirty-seven, which sounds ancient. I feel older, if that's possible.

Maybe I just didn't want to think about it, because Sean and I had a birthday ritual. He'd take me out for donuts, and we'd usually hike or snowboard, depending on whether there was snow yet.

On his birthday, we did the same, but in reverse. Every year. Never missed a donut.

I get out of bed and shuffle to the kitchen, where I start the coffee brewing. It's ten o'clock on a Sunday. The family group chat already has a few entries on my behalf.

Alec got his in late last night, I see. He must have been working at the bar.

ALEC

I'm first in line to say Happy Birthday! #Winning

BENITO

Loser. It's not even his birthday yet in Colorado.

ALEC

He was born in Vermont so it counts.

BENITO

[Eyeroll emoji, followed by a cake emoji.] Happy birthday from Alec's bar. If you were here I'd let you beat me at darts.

I'm suddenly super homesick.

Birthdays are the worst. They make you broody.

There's a sudden knock on my door. So I stomp over to the entry hall and look through the peephole. And there's Lissa standing in the hallway, wearing a Colorado Cougars sweatshirt.

Uh-oh. Problem?

When I tug open the door, she shoves a box of donuts in my direction, and they're still warm. "Happy birthday, old man!"

Oh.

Oh, shit. I take the box and turn away from her, because my damn eyes are suddenly wet. "Thank you," I stammer, retreating into my pad, composing myself as I walk toward the kitchen to put the box down.

She doesn't follow me, though. I turn around again, and she's peeking into my space. "Can I come in?"

"Of fricking course," I say gruffly. "Want coffee?"

Her smile has faded as she closes the door behind her. "I just thought you might have company."

"Nah."

She crosses to the counter and studies me while I bump around getting mugs and milk out of the fridge. "Are you all right?"

207

With a sigh, I set everything on the counter and turn to her. "Yeah, baby girl. You just caught me off guard. I was thinking about your daddy when you knocked. And donuts…"

"Were your thing," she says softly. "That's why I brought them. Didn't mean to make you sad."

My eyes fill again, and I swipe at my face. "You're the best. I swear."

"Oh, Matty." She comes around and grabs me into a hard hug. "I miss him too. All the time."

"Yeah." I sigh. I kiss the top of her head and take a deep breath.

"Want to hear something weird?" she says, stepping away from me to grab a mug. "I had a dream about him, and he told me to get you the donuts."

I almost drop the coffee pot. "What?"'

"Yup." She shrugs. "He was holding his snowboard under his arm, and he said, 'Don't forget Matty's birthday. We always do donuts.' And then he walked away."

"Fuck a duck." I take the mug from her hand and pour the coffee with a shaky hand. "I have those dreams, too. He told me to make a reservation for your birthday next month. Said you like surf and turf."

Lissa gasps.

"I know."

Her startled laugh echoes in my kitchen.

"Do you dream about him a lot?"

She tips her head from side to side like she's considering the question. "Not a *lot*. But when I do, it's vivid. Like he's really there. But he always leaves before I'm ready, and I wake up mad. And yet I don't really want it to stop."

I take another deep breath. "I wake up angry at him, too. It's a mind fuck."

"My psych lady says anger is part of grieving." She rolls her eyes. "Like I couldn't figure that out myself."

I laugh, and some of the tension drains out of me. "Is guilt part of it, too?"

"Yup," she says cheerfully. "I check that box, too."

I set down the milk carton and stare at her. "Why the hell would *you* feel guilty?"

Her eyes drop to her mug. "Because he asked me if I wanted to ride with him that day. I said no."

Oh *shiiit*. I almost say it aloud but stop myself just in time.

"So he went up with you instead. And I know he would have chosen differently if I were there. We wouldn't even have been on the same peak."

"*Honey*. That is a lot to carry around. It wasn't your fault he chose that run. And even if you went somewhere else together, it could have happened a week later."

Her eyes are suddenly streaming. "I know. I know. But then we'd have another week with him."

God damn it. I don't want her to feel this way. It was never her job to stop her dad from dying.

We all know it was mine.

My heart is breaking. I wrap my arms around Lissa and hold her tightly, until she finally wiggles out of my grasp and sips her coffee. "So happy birthday. Do we know how to party, or what?"

I laugh, and my phone dings with a new text. Like the robot I've become, I grab it to see if it's possibly a text from Leila, telling me she wants to visit.

Nope. It's from my mom.

HAPPY BIRTHDAY BABY BOY.

Thirty-seven years ago, you made me a mother. I hope you're having a nice day.

"Aww," Lissa says. "Your mom is so cute. Aren't you going to reply?"

Like the dutiful son I never was, I tap out my response.

Thanks, Mom! About to have birthday donuts with Lissa.

I love that girl! Tell her hi from me. And then tell me you're coming home for Thanksgiving.

"Ooh! Your mom is smooth," Lissa says. "She just slipped that right in there. I think you have to go now." She laughs.

Fuck it. I'm homesick, and Lissa is right. I reply before I change my mind.

> I'm in for Thanksgiving.

"Good boy," she says. "You want cinnamon sugar? Or chocolate glazed?"

I peek into the box. She's brought me half a dozen. I can hit the gym later. "Both," I say. "It's my birthday. I'll get the plates."

CHAPTER 35
LEILA
NOVEMBER

Thanksgiving is a week away. This is the first one after my parents' divorce, and I can't be in two places at once. So I'm on the phone, begging my brother Nash to come up from Boston for the weekend.

"You can stay here with me, and we'll have Dad over for a meal, and then go to Mom's afterward. She wants to eat at six."

"Let me get this straight," Nash says. "I have to drive two and a half hours, sleep on your couch, and eat turkey twice in one day just to appease our parents?"

"No, you're doing it to appease *me*," I insist. "It's the first year after my divorce, too."

"Good point. We should shoot off fireworks or throw a parade, maybe."

He'd never liked Rory.

I groan. "Do you realize that every time you say that—every time you bash him—it just makes *me* feel stupid? Thanks for that."

"Hey, I'm sorry," he says quickly. "You're right. I'm being an asshole. I hate the holidays, though. If they were canceled this year, I'd be fine with that."

"They're not," I grumble. "And you're coming to help me through it. Besides, I want to see you. And I have some things to talk to you about."

"Sounds ominous," he says.

"It's not, I swear."

"Good. I don't suppose Mitch is coming home for Thanksgiving?"

"Mitch who?"

We both laugh. My other brother almost never comes home. But he has a good excuse—the NHL doesn't take Thanksgiving off, and they barely pause for Christmas. He can't just pop by for the holidays.

"Someday he'll retire," I point out. "Then he'll have to suck it up and show his face around here."

"Not likely."

"Cheer up. I'll make pumpkin pie and those corn fritters you like."

"Yeah, yeah. I can be bribed." We make a plan, and then we hang up.

When I set the phone down, it's dark outside. It's only five o'clock, but nighttime shrouds my apartment windows. I get up and turn on more lights. I stalk over to my refrigerator and peer inside.

It's too early for dinner, so I close it and pace back to the sofa.

The truth is that I'm restless, anxious and a little bit lonely. I'll probably go downstairs to the bar later, when the dinnertime crowd eases up. I'll read my book, drink a soda, and talk to Alec while he closes for the night.

Talking to him always makes me think of Matteo, though. Not that I need any help with that. I think of him constantly, especially since he texted me earlier today.

> Bought a ticket home to Vermont for Thanksgiving. Staying at Benito's Thursday through Tuesday.

> I want to see you. But if you think that's too complicated, I'll understand.

I pick up my phone again and stare at the text for the hundredth time today. I haven't replied yet.

The truth is that I can't wait to see him. I miss him like crazy.

But I can't say that. It wouldn't be fair.

Matteo and I need to have a talk, though, so I finally compose my reply.

> Can you come see me on Monday afternoon?
> How about 2? That would be the best time.

My reply sounds cold. Like I'm just fitting him into my schedule.

But I have my reasons.

CHAPTER 36
MATTEO

Late November isn't the best time to see Vermont. All the pretty foliage is gone, and there's no snow on the ground yet. When you scan the horizon, it's like someone desaturated the photo—gray-brown mountains with patches of washed-out green where the pines are thick.

We call it stick season.

But it doesn't matter. I'm having fun with my family. They waited Thanksgiving dinner until seven p.m., the earliest I could get to Otto's farm on my cheap airline ticket.

I spend the weekend watching football and hockey with my siblings. I read a book to my niece. I hang wallpaper with Benito and Skye, and I go to the movies with Alec and May. Sunday night, I even work a shift with Alec behind the bar, just for fun.

Leila doesn't come downstairs while I'm there, even though I keep watching the door for her.

When the shift ends, I don't go upstairs and knock. If she wanted that, she would have said so. She said Monday, and I'll respect that.

It's just that Monday takes a long time to arrive. By the time I'm finally climbing the stairs to her apartment door, I feel dread in my gut. And—fine—a little bit of anger.

I mean—what was she doing all weekend that kept her so busy?

God, do I even want to know?

I knock on the door, and she opens right away. Instantly, my bitterness and dread drain away. One look at her soft eyes, and I melt like butter. And she's so pretty that a man could weep.

Yet it looks like she's beat me to it. Her cheeks are tear stained. "Are you all right?" I ask softly.

She nods. Swallows. "Come in. I'm fine, I swear."

Still, she's throwing off a weird energy. I follow her to the sofa and sit down, taking her hand in mine. I stroke my thumb across her palm. "All right, sweetheart. Tell me what's up with you."

She removes her hand from mine. "There's something I need to show you. Look." She grabs an envelope off the coffee table and pulls out…

My breath catches in my throat. It's a sonogram image. With a bean-shaped baby on it. "That's…yours?"

"Yes," she whispers. "And also yours."

"Oh *shit*." I let out a strangled laugh as joy rises inside me. "Seriously?"

She nods, eyes watery. "I'm due in early May. I'm sorry I didn't tell you sooner. But I wanted to know if it would take."

Holy…

I can't stand it any longer. I lean in and scoop her onto my lap, wrapping my arms around her. "How many months are you? Three?"

"And a half," she says. "I went to the doctor on Wednesday for a whole bunch of screenings, and the results just came back today." She gives me a shaky smile. "All clear so far. This might really be happening. I heard the heartbeat."

My mind is blown. I tuck my chin onto her shoulder and try to absorb this news. "I can't believe it. We did it."

She laughs. "We did."

"And how do you feel?" I ask, my arms tightening around her.

"Tired," she admits. "I have to nap every day after I get home from school. And I'm nauseous, but not as bad as Skye."

Skye had been sick a lot. Benito could talk of nothing else for a while.

215

I'd been tuning him out to protect myself. But now my head is spinning. "I'm honestly speechless."

"But is it a happy kind of speechless? Be honest."

"God, Leila." I kiss her jaw. "I couldn't be happier for you."

Her body relaxes by several degrees. "I know this is a lot. It was theoretical before, and now it's real."

"I wish you'd told me," I blurt. "Three months is a long time."

"Yes and no," she says. "I took that first pregnancy test, and it was positive... I just didn't believe it. I didn't *feel* pregnant. So I thought I'd wait a few days. And then I started googling *pregnancy at thirty-five*, and the first thing you see are the miscarriage statistics."

"Oh," I say softly.

Oh.

"There's so much grief in your life already. I didn't want to tell you—and then *un*tell you two weeks later. So I waited. And then I had a doctor's appointment, and they explained how all the important tests aren't done until you're three months pregnant..."

"Okay," I say quietly. "I get it. And how are you feeling about this now that it's real?"

She lets out a nervous laugh. "I'm scared. I mean—I got what I wanted, but now it's all on me to do everything right." She takes a deep breath. "It's such a gift you've given me, and I don't want to mess it up."

That sounds like a lot of stress. I kiss her palm, because I don't know how else to help. "Does anyone else know yet?"

"Nash, as of yesterday." She clears her throat. "He was my trial balloon, so to speak. And I didn't name you, of course. I won't do that at all unless you decide you want to be involved."

"How did Nash take it?"

She chuckles, and I feel it in my chest. "He was weird about it. Like he couldn't believe I'd become a single mother by choice. He even said, 'Raising a child is hard.'"

We both laugh, because you have to consider the source. If you look up "playboy" in a dictionary, there's probably a photo of Nash with a beer in one hand and a woman's ass in his other. He probably doesn't even remember what a child looks like.

"He'll come around," Leila says, with a wave of her hand. "Babies just scare him."

"When are you going to tell your parents?"

"Soon. Now that these tests came back with optimistic news, and now that I've told you, I can start to share the news. I guess I'll wait until after you've left town again, though. I don't want my family jumping to conclusions."

"Smart."

She turns in my arms. "How are you, anyway? How's Colorado? How does it feel to be back at work?"

"Awful," I say, opting for the truth. "But work will get easier. Maybe once I'm back on the mountain, I'll remember why we built that business in the first place."

She takes my hand and squeezes it. "I'm sorry."

"Thanks. This isn't my favorite topic. What about your job? When would you have to take a leave of absence?"

"Not until April," she says. "I can work until my due date, if I want to. But I'll still have to warn the preschool in January or February, so they can find someone to jump in at the end of the school year. And pretty soon I'll have a bump, anyway."

Unbidden, my hand finds its way to Leila's tummy.

"It's still flat," she whispers. "For now."

"Not for long, though." I dip underneath her cotton top, my fingers on her smooth skin. Her breath catches, and my body flashes with the sudden heat of knowing that I put a baby inside her. "When did we conceive?"

"Early August." She puts her hand on top of mine.

"Do you know if it's a boy or a girl?"

She shakes her head. "Not yet. I asked them not to tell me yet. I wanted to talk to you first."

I close my eyes and picture Leila holding a little baby in her arms. A tiny Leila, or a little dude? It doesn't matter. They're both equally amazing and also equally baffling.

People call it the "miracle of life," and that always sounded like a cliché to my ears.

It doesn't anymore.

"I know I kept this from you until now. But not because I haven't been thinking about you."

"Is that right?" I stroke my thumb across her tummy and feel her shiver. "In what way have you been thinking about me, exactly?"

"Matteo," she scolds, and I laugh. My chest is light for the first time in ages.

CHAPTER 37
LEILA

With his free hand, Matteo turns my chin, so I have no choice but to look at him. Rich brown eyes are waiting for an answer.

But I feel too overcome with emotion to speak. Curled into Matteo's lap, his strong arms around me, I feel immense relief.

I was prepared for every possible emotional result when I told him my secret. But he's so happy that I feel silly now.

How exactly have you been thinking about me, was his question, but the truth wouldn't be fair to him. My thoughts are greedy, impossible things well beyond the scope of our arrangement.

It's hard to know what to say, but his gaze is so warm it's like sunshine on my face. "I was wondering what our child will look like," I say quietly. "Brown eyes, for sure."

A slow smile forms on his rugged face. "Brown hair," he whispers. "Could be wavy, like yours. Or straighter, like mine. But either way, this kid can rock the long hair."

I laugh, because I've been craving a conversation just like this one. "Will our kid have your ego?"

"*My* ego? And who used to make everyone address her as *her highness*?"

We both crack up.

Then it happens. Matteo leans in and kisses me, as if it's the most natural thing in the world.

And it is, I guess. His mouth softens onto mine, and he smells so familiar I could cry. Like flannel and soap. I part my lips, like I've done a thousand times before, and he tastes me slowly.

His beard tickles my fingers when I lift my hands to his face. I settle into our kiss, like sinking into a warm bath.

He's *home*. Finally.

After a few delicious moments, Matteo kicks his legs onto my sofa, so that we're both horizontal. I wiggle closer, and our kisses slowly blur together. Our feet tangle in the weak sunlight streaming in through the windows.

When I dream about him, it's just like this—hot, easy kisses. I dream of joining our bodies together again.

I dream of a rounded belly, his hand on it.

And I dream of us putting together a crib in the second bedroom.

It's all selfish. I want him to forget his life in Colorado and his job and all those obligations that he holds dear.

I want him to love me so much that nothing else matters.

None of that is fair. I asked him to be my sperm donor. I was crystal clear about where his obligations ended. They ended in August, when I got pregnant. And I'm a terrible human for pining for him.

Matteo, oblivious to my worries, unbuttons my shirt. His groan is full of awe when he gets a look at my bra. That's because I'm practically spilling out of it. He lowers his lips to the swell of my breast and kisses his way across my chest.

Pregnancy has made my breasts heavy and so sensitive. I slip a hand behind my back and pop the clasp of my bra.

"Mamma mia," he says, and I have to laugh.

"I know. The books all say that pregnancy makes your boobs huge, but I don't think I believed them."

His smile is both hot and sweet as he lowers his mouth to my nipple.

"They also say that pregnancy makes you horny," I say.

"Are they right about that?"

"Unfortunately."

He laughs as he switches sides, treating my other breast to the same wonders.

He started it, I remind myself as my body floods with pleasure. *His idea. I didn't jump him.*

But I wanted to. And not just because of pregnancy hormones, either.

I'm gone for him, and he can never know.

CHAPTER 38
MATTEO

We end up in bed.

Naked. Very naked.

"It's okay," she whispers when I hover above her, hesitating.

All my nerves are screaming for her. I want to join us together again. Make more magic.

But I shake my head and slide my hand between her legs instead. Sucking on her tongue, I coax her to climax until she's moaning and shuddering.

Then I curl her hand around my cock and follow her over the edge.

We end up spooned together, panting as we come down, and she gives me a curious glance. "Didn't want to risk it," I whisper. "Don't care what the books say."

Leila strokes my hair. When she eventually gets up, I watch her track across the room.

God, the view. I can't believe I have to go back to Colorado tomorrow. I just want to stay here in Leila's bed.

She returns a few minutes later, showered and carrying two mugs of hot cider. I take the mug, and we lounge against the headboard, keeping quiet company together.

"You staying the night?" she asks.

"You know I want to. But I'm supposed to hang out with my niece and nephew."

Her eyes dip. "That's my poor planning. It's been a week of waiting for those test results and trying to stay sane."

I put a hand on her knee. "Next time call me. We'll wait together. As best we can, anyway."

"Okay." She looks away. "I'm sorry, Matteo. This was all my idea, and now I don't know how to navigate it."

"It's complicated," I agree. "But I don't regret it."

"*Yet*." She gives me a shy smile.

"Hey—don't worry. What happens next for you? More tests?"

"Maybe. And more sonograms. But I'm not considered a high-risk pregnancy."

"Well, *that's* good news. Will you really stay at your job until the end, though?"

"Oh, definitely," I tell him. "The timing is great, actually. I'll have the whole summer with the baby and won't have to worry about childcare until the fall. He or she will be four months old when school starts again. Childcare is expensive, though, so I'm glad I put in all those hours at the warehouse last summer."

I feel a tickle of unease, listening to Leila sort through these issues all by herself.

"My parents will help me," she says, as if she can read my mind. "And as soon as the baby is two, I can bring them to school with me. We have a toddler program."

"That's handy," I say, squeezing her knee. "The perks of having very small colleagues."

She tucks her chin onto my chest, and we lapse into a comfortable silence.

I don't want to leave.

But I still have to.

———

As my plane lands at the Denver airport, I see fat snowflakes falling past the little window. *The flight isn't that long,* I tell myself. *Just four hours.*

It might as well be four months, though. I can't leave Colorado during ski season.

Leila's pregnancy has me questioning everything. She said it's up to me whether I'm involved or not. And she said I can take my time thinking about it. No, she *insisted* I take my time. "You need to sit with this awhile. Besides—babies don't ask questions. They accept the world that shows up to receive them."

It feels like a lot of ego to assume that their little world would be a better place with more of me in it. But Leila wouldn't have asked me if she didn't think I was the right man for the job.

My mind is so full of big thoughts that it might actually burst.

I trudge into the office the next morning. It's still snowing, and I have a lot to do and no time to brood.

Jeffrey—our new guide—comes in for a meeting about client management. We sit down on either side of my desk, and I hand him a clipboard with his first ten client invoices on it. "One of our rules is that we always have a phone call with the client four weeks before their trip. Heli skiing is expensive, so we want to offer a high-touch service. But it's also a safety issue."

"We need to know what they're expecting," he says with a nod. "Their level of experience."

"Right." I show him the first page on the stack. "That's why we have everyone in the party listed separately. Sometimes it's a family. If you talk to one person who seems to really understand everyone's skill level, then you won't have to call everyone individually. But if you don't feel confident, then go down the list."

"Should I make notes right on the page?"

"You can. But these pages don't leave this building. Alternatively, make your notes in the client record online. That's the solution for working from home."

"Got it."

"Be thorough. Always note the time and date of your call, and who you spoke to. You can assume that nobody will read your notes except you, me, or Cara. So it's okay to write down your true impressions. We've never had a client get badly injured…" My heart aches as I say this, even though it's completely true. "But you never know what will happen, and you want to have meticulous notes."

"In case they overstate their skill level."

"Right. I know you can always get people down the mountain safely, even if you have to regroup. But it's still important to cover your ass."

"Sad but true. I took this job because you guys care about the details. I've worked for a few guys who didn't."

"And we appreciate that."

"Can I ask you a question?" His young brow furrows. "Are you going to be okay up there? After last year. You know…"

"Yeah, I'll be all right," I insist. "We'll take some runs together before our first booking, yeah? You'll meet the pilots, we'll make a few turns, and work out any kinks."

His smile is quick. "Sounds great."

The door opens on Cara. "Hey, peeps!" She stomps her boots on the mat. "How's it going?"

"Great," Jeffrey says. "I'm about to make my first few calls to clients."

"Here you go," I say, passing him a pen. "You can have my desk."

"Thanks, man."

I move over to talk to Cara, who's booting up her computer. Sean's face smiles out at us from the homepage of our website. *The adventure of your life awaits!* brags the text.

Not for the first time, I wonder when we'll swap it out. It seems wrong to change that picture. Yet it also seems wrong to leave it up.

That's what happens when somebody dies—everything seems wrong.

She clears her throat. "I took his bio off our staff page last week when I added Jeffrey's."

"Oh," I say brilliantly.

Jeffrey is chatting away with a client, and Cara drops her voice. "How's our bank balance?"

"Healthier than last month," I tell her. "Lots of deposits hitting up." We charge a down payment of seven-hundred-fifty dollars per person when they book a full day, and four-hundred dollars when they book a half day.

That's what killed us last winter—refunding all those deposits after we canceled our season. Thank God our cashflow is headed in the right direction again.

She grabs a pen and taps it nervously against the desktop. "Got a call this morning. From somebody on the board of the Aspen Mountain Corp."

"Yeah? What did they want?"

"They really pissed me off." She tosses the pen onto the desk in disgust. "The guy was full of regret over Sean, and for a minute I thought they wanted to honor him in some way. But then he tells me the corporation might be looking to buy a heli-ski operation."

My blood stops circulating. "You mean *our* heli-ski operation?"

"Can you believe his nerve?" Cara whispers. "They're vultures, thinking we're in a vulnerable place, and they can just swoop in and pick up our business for pennies on the dollar."

"Did he give a price?" I hear myself ask.

"No. And I told him we'd never sell out Sean's legacy to a big corporation. That's not who we are."

My heart drops. "Of course not," I say softly.

Of course not.

CHAPTER 39
MATTEO

I'm just tightening my snowboard boots when my sister's text comes in.

ZARA

Yo. Leila was just in for breakfast.

MATTEO

She lives twenty paces from your door. How is this news?

ZARA

Her order changed! She asked for a half caf coffee and two muffins. Usually she orders a regular coffee and one muffin.

Is there something you need to tell me?

MATTEO

That's classified.

ZARA

OMG. OMG!

MATTEO

I didn't SAY anything!

ZARA

OMG.

.

MATTEO

Classified. Seriously.

Oh boy. I knew this day would come, but I expected to have a little more time before my sister caught wind of Leila's pregnancy.

I've spent the last month trying to get my own head around it. The fact of Leila's pregnancy has brought my whole life into sharper relief. The highs are higher and the lows are lower.

And I can't stop worrying about her and the baby. I sit up at night and read articles about early pregnancy. So much can go wrong. And when I'd asked her last month how she felt, she'd said she was *scared*.

I think about that a lot. And I worry.

Hence the text I'm sending her now.

Psst. Thinking about you and the baby. How are you both?

LEILA

We're good. Always hungry. I just bought a book that says I need to make every mouthful count. Super healthy. Kale smoothies and mixed nuts.

MATTEO

So you're having a lot of kale smoothies?

LEILA

Nope. Threw that book in the recycling bin. I'm eating a muffin from your sister's coffee shop. Blueberry, but I have a lemon one on reserve.

MATTEO

Warning: I just heard about this. Your breakfast order changed a little to half caf and two muffins, and now Zara is over there freaking out.

LEILA

Oh! You are sweet to warn me. I guess that was
inevitable. I just hope she can be discreet.

MATTEO

She can when she needs to be. I will make sure
she knows this is one of those times.

LEILA

No need to worry! And if eating two muffins is
wrong, I don't want to be right.

MATTEO

That's my girl.

Although she isn't really my girl. It's just that I keep
forgetting.

"Are you ready for this?" Jeffrey asks me, and I look up from
my phone.

It's eight a.m. on the day after Christmas, and we're seated at
the picnic table in our snowboarding gear. Coffee mugs steaming
in the December cold. The pilot—Paul—is performing his
preflight checks, and Cara is just inside the gear room, fitting
Lissa with a transponder and protective airbag.

The four of us are going up together for our preseason ride.
But it will be a solemn occasion. It's our first time back on the
mountain after Sean's death.

"I'm ready," I lie to Jeffrey.

The office door opens, and Cara emerges. She holds the door
for Lissa, who carries a small packet of folded tissue paper against
her chest.

I rise from the picnic table and prepare myself for Sean's last
big ride. We're about to scatter his ashes on our flight.

Solemnly, we all approach the bird, where the pilot is waiting.
Cara takes the front seat next to the pilot. Lissa gets the seat
behind him, and Jeffrey and I climb in beside her.

"Got your gloves?" I ask, inspecting her gear as I clip her seatbelt into place.

"In my pockets," she says, cradling her father's ashes. She flashes me a quick smile.

"All right, girlie. Here you go." I slide the headphones over her ears and put on my own.

It's a beautiful day to fly. The sky is a deep blue, and the peaks around us are blanketed in white. They're nearly blinding in the sun.

Usually, these moments are for predictions and smack talk. But nobody speaks as Paul turns to the west and climbs.

After all these years, the snow-covered wilderness below us should be a familiar sight. But as we glide through the blue, I'm mesmerized all over again.

I chose this life for a reason. It's spellbinding. Most men my age are sitting at a computer in an office. But this is my day job. It's humbling.

Sean chose this life, too. He didn't plan on leaving so soon. But he wasn't the kind of man to have regrets.

I'm sorry, buddy. I wish you were here with me. I'd give anything for it.

Paul says, "Vents are all set, Lissa. Go ahead when you're ready."

Cara turns in her seat to watch her daughter. Lissa carefully slots the wrapped packet of ashes into the air vent on her door—the only one that's open right now. Then she nudges it all the way out of the helicopter.

Paul holds us steady, and we all watch the packet hover in midair for a split second. Then the wind unwraps the packet, and the ashes form a sudden cloud. It's a quick white *poof* before our eyes.

Lissa gasps, and it comes out like a sob. "Daddy is…like a *firework*."

Cara wipes her eyes, and mine prickle, too. *Goodbye old friend.*

Paul flies us in a slow circle, but Sean is already gone.

———

A few minutes later, we climb out of the bird on a favorite peak we've ridden dozens of times before.

I hand Jeffrey the shovel and ask him to do the snowpack check. It's no surprise that he does a thorough job.

"Jeffrey gets first tracks in honor of his first day," I announce.

Our new guide turns to us and grins. "Thank you all. It's an honor to be up here with you today."

"Have a good run," Cara says, her smile bittersweet.

Jeffrey clips in, scans the slope to choose his descent, and then drops in with a whoop. We all watch as he makes a few expert turns, tracking the snow with a Z-shape as he goes.

"Ready, kid?" I ask Lissa.

"You know it," she says, clipping on her helmet. Her tears are already dry.

"We'll go together?" Cara asks her daughter.

"You know it," she repeats.

"Hold still, ladies," I say. "We always start the season with a photo."

They turn to me, and Cara puts an arm around her daughter. They both don brave smiles.

I point my phone and take a picture of the two of them against the blue sky. "All right. Let's see you fly."

Lissa takes a deep breath, sets her shoulders, and drops in first. Her mother follows a moment later.

Tucking my phone away, I wait for them to clear the slope beneath me. I'll be bringing up the rear today, in case of trouble.

There won't be any, though. This is a very safe spot. Alone on the peak now, I watch Lissa slice her way down the slope like the little pro that she is.

"She's so amazing, Sean." I say it out loud, hoping he can hear me. "We miss the shit out of you. But I think we're going to be okay. Cara is hanging in there. The business is stable again."

The whistle of the wind is the only response I get.

"And me? Well…" The sky is so blue it almost hurts my eyes. "Funny story. I got Leila pregnant. Yeah, *that* Leila. Before you blame me, you should know that she asked me to. So next year I might get to meet a future snowboarder of my own."

SARINA BOWEN

Below me, Lissa pops a jump off a gentle rise, while the sun sparkles overhead.

"Never thought anyone should call me *daddy*. Still not sure that makes any sense. But it's real now. I have to decide what to do. If you want to weigh in, you know where to find me."

I clip in and hop to the edge. "This one's for you, man."

Looking down, I take a deep breath, and then I fly after my friends.

CHAPTER 40
LEILA
JANUARY

It's the deepest part of winter, and I'm struggling on several levels. I'm tired all the time. It's frigid. The temperature is minus ten this morning. And it's still gloomy outside as I stumble around my lonely apartment getting ready for work.

I miss coffee. *Real* coffee, full of caffeine. I'm hungry all the time, too.

In the kitchen, I pack my shoulder bag for the school day. I add my water bottle and then a snack, courtesy of Matteo. After I'd told him what the pregnancy books say about nutrition, he'd sent me a case of kale chips and mixed nuts.

That was unexpected, and a little pushy. But it turns out that kale chips taste better than they sound, so I'm not too annoyed.

We talk occasionally, and I try to keep things light. I give him updates about the baby's development. But I don't pry into his feelings, because I want him to take his time deciding on how involved he is. I don't want to push.

He always conveys an undercurrent of worry about me and the baby, though. When I happened to mention that I'd lost a winter glove, the UPS guy showed up two days later with a new pair.

It was sweet, but it made me wonder if Matteo thinks I made it to age thirty-five without knowing how to take care of myself.

The irony! Last month he sent me a selfie from the top of a

mountain, and I've never seen a more frightening photo in my life. He was standing on a peak so high that I almost got a nose-bleed looking at it.

Matteo has a dangerous job. I don't think I realized it before he told me all about his friend's death. Recently I did some googling and learned that forty people die every year in skiing and snow-boarding accidents.

And it's literally his job to tackle the wooliest slopes in Colorado.

It's terrifying. I'm not sleeping well.

Although my pregnancy might be to blame for that. I'm past the midpoint, but there's still a long way to go. And I'm showing now, so I get a lot of questions from well-meaning acquaintances.

This past Sunday, an elderly man at church said, "I didn't realize you'd remarried."

I never know what to say to comments like that. "I didn't," was all I managed to come up with. It was awkward.

Even people I know well are a mixed bag. A high school friend assumed I'd had a one-night stand with my ex. "That's a thing people do," she'd said, as if I wanted her blessing.

The worst reaction, though, came from my father. When I told him I was pregnant, he went ballistic, demanding to know who "did this to me."

Honestly, it was unexpected. I knew my father had certain backwards viewpoints, but I hadn't realized how bad they could be. He hadn't believed that the pregnancy had been my choice.

But he'll come around eventually. I'm his favorite child. And anger is his default reaction to everything. "It's how he shows love," I'd joked to Nash.

"He must love me a lot, then," Nash had quipped.

If it weren't for repeated sunny updates from the obstetrician and a trove of new sonogram pictures on my fridge, I'd probably be depressed about it.

At seven o'clock, I put on my boots, my coat, and my new gloves. (Thank you, Matteo.) I head for the coffee shop, but pause at the door to see who's behind the counter. I'm avoiding Zara, because I know she has an inkling that this is Matteo's baby under my ill-fitting coat. And I'm not ready to discuss that with her.

It's Roddy at the counter, though, so I go inside for my muffin and half caf.

He serves it up with a smile and says, "Take care in the parking lot, okay? I put down some salt this morning, but it might still be icy."

"Thanks, but these boots have a really good tread," I tell him. I'm secretly wondering if he's giving everyone this same advice, or if he's reserved it just for the disheveled pregnant lady. He gives me a friendly wave, and I head back outside into the gloom.

I pull up short as I approach my car. There's a strange man leaning over the open hood.

"Excuse me?" I sputter. "That's my car!"

He turns around, and I notice he's wearing a coverall that says *Marker Motors*, and he's holding a screwdriver. "I'll just be a minute, ma'am. Would you mind unlocking the car so I can make sure this bulb is good to go?"

"Wait." It's hard to make sense of what's happening. "My headlight went out yesterday. And you just… fixed it?"

He frowns at me. "The work order said it was a yellow Wrangler. There's only one in the lot, ma'am."

"Whose work order?" I demand.

He plucks a piece of paper out of his pocket. "Mr. Matteo Rossi. Front passenger's side headlamp."

My mouth falls open. I'd mentioned the burned-out headlight to Matteo offhandedly—when I was trying not to blurt out how much I miss him.

I miss him a little less right now, though. What the heck is he doing?

"Ma'am, if we can test the light, you could be on your way."

"Right," I grumble. Then I stomp over to the Jeep and get in.

When I hit the lights, they both work brilliantly.

CHAPTER 41
MATTEO
MARCH

My phone rings while I'm standing in my kitchen watching my dinner revolve slowly in the microwave.

Instead of answering it, I look away. I'm exhausted from another long day on the mountain. Seven days a week—weather permitting—I spend six to eight hours riding some of the best terrain in the world. It's a dream job. But I might as well work in a sweatshop for all the joy I take from it now.

I know my lack of gratitude is a problem. I just don't know how to solve it.

On the fridge is a photo I took about two years ago. It's Sean and Cara and Lissa standing together. I found the picture on my phone, and I had a print made at the drugstore. Seeing it reminds me of why I get up every day and go back to the mountain.

They look so happy, and it helps me to see that. It really does.

The microwave dings, and I slide the cooked meal onto a tray and carry it to the sofa. I bring my phone along. I notice that my caller—Rory—left a voicemail.

I sit down, eyeing the phone. Not hitting Play.

Instead, I pluck my laptop off the coffee table and open it up. The browser window is where I left it on Leila's baby registry. I start to scroll.

I wouldn't have thought to look for this if it weren't for our new employee, Jeffrey. He and his wife welcomed their baby last month, and Cara had directed me to their baby registry so that we could pick out a gift together.

After that, I googled Leila's name and found her wishlist, too. Now it's my main form of entertainment. Even if I'm two thousand miles away, it's a small sliver of insight into her excitement. I peruse the sleepers and the baby bottles and wonder how she's doing.

She's a little frustrated with me. After I had her car fixed, she made a point to tell me that if she needed my help, she'd ask for it. And it gutted me. I can feel the distance growing between us like a gaping wound.

I can admit that hiring a mechanic without asking makes me seem overbearing. But when I saw Leila in November, she'd said she was *scared*. I can't stand the thought of her all alone and feeling nervous. Swapping out a headlight seemed like a simple way to ease her stress.

At least when I scroll the baby registry, she can't accuse me of overstepping. You don't make a registry if you don't want anyone to peruse these things, right?

Although some of the items on the list are inscrutable. While I wait for my dinner to cool, I read the product description for a fleece swaddle with a velcro closure. Given the photos, I'm pretty sure you're supposed to wrap the baby into it—the same way you'd wrap a burrito.

But I'm not exactly sure why. And the product listing doesn't say. It's moments like this when I wonder if there's some daddy gene I'm missing. Maybe other men look at the burrito thing and understand.

I take a bite of chicken cordon bleu and move on to the next item on the registry. It's the same kind of frontpack that Zara has for Micah. It comes in three colors. Leila needs the navy blue one. She also needs a set of glass bottles in various sizes, plus a bottle sterilizer.

I picture her feeding a baby in her arms, the same way she did with my nephew on the sofa. And I feel a little calmer than I did a few minutes ago.

The new voicemail on my phone nags at me. I might as well

get it over with. Like ripping off a Band-Aid.

I hit Play, and right away I can tell that Rory is drunk and emotional. He's probably brooding in his living room the same way I am right now.

Matteo. God. Leila did it. She went and did it. She's pregnant.

I'm thinking you probably already know this. She probably told you herself. Thanks for the fucking warning. I had to hear it last week from Andy down at the barbershop. He heard it from his aunt who heard it at her book club.

Nobody knows who the father is. She won't say. It's not me, in case you're wondering. I always told her I wasn't ready for kids. It's not a good time. Next year will be better. I said that a lot.

I kept putting it off. Maybe you'll think I'm an idiot. But it's true—it was never a good time. I let her think that money was the problem, but it wasn't really. Fuck. I never had a dad. No idea how to be one.

You know, right? You had a shitty dad, too.

God. I thought that if I put it off, it might seem easier. Like, at some point I wouldn't feel like such a loser. I'd know what to say to my own kid if I had one.

He takes a ragged breath.

Well that never happened. And Leila started to hate me for it. So you know what I did? Maybe she told you already—I cheated. One night after we had a fight, I picked up some woman in a bar and went home with her.

Leila left me two weeks later. I think I knew she would. Maybe that's why I did it.

"You idiot," I whisper. And for one shining minute I feel superior to Rory. He cheated? I'm gobsmacked.

But then he keeps talking.

There has never been a single day when I thought I'd be any fucking good at being a daddy. So I let her go, even if I did it in a shitty way.

Still hurts, though. Like a knife to the heart. She got pregnant with some other guy.

Lotta people are saying maybe it's you.

I stop breathing.

You'll hate me for saying this. Go ahead and hate me. But the only comfort I got is knowing it wasn't you. Nah. Not a fucking chance, right? Because you're smarter than I ever was. And if you got Leila pregnant, you wouldn't be in fucking Colorado.

So that's how I know. If it was you, then you'd be here by her side.

No question.

The recording ends.

I push my dinner away and set my head in my hands.

CHAPTER 42
LEILA

I study the schematic again, trying to figure out how I'm going to attach the short side of the crib to the long side.

The first few steps went fine, but now I've hit a snag—I don't have enough hands to brace the long side while I screw the short side onto it. And I'm afraid to prop it up against the wall, because it might scratch the paint job that my mother and I did last week. It's a mural—a mountain landscape, with the moon in gold.

This is so frustrating. And I can't ask my mom for help again, because she's playing bridge today. It's a big tournament, and she's trying to defend her title.

In these moments, my traitorous brain always offers up an impossible scenario—a mental picture of Matteo screwing the bed together while I hold the sections steady.

Thanks, brain. I feel guilty every time I wish he was here. But the more I try not to think about him, the worse it seems to get.

As a cure for guilty yearnings, I've tried to dial back my contact with him. When we do speak, I try to keep things simple. I give him updates on the pregnancy. *The doctor tells me the baby is the size of a grapefruit. My blood-sugar test was normal.*

He seems a little gruff with me lately. He worries about me, and that's not healthy, either. I'm pretty sure Matteo thinks I'm in over my head. Like, I'm going to drive around in a broken Jeep, or that I don't make enough money to feed this child we created.

Why else would he do so much online shopping? The man has systematically purchased nearly everything I've added to my baby registry. The crib? Purchased by Matteo. The mattress? Matteo. The sheets I picked out? Matteo.

See also: the bottles, the baby carrier, and the nursing pillow. Plus, a case of diapers and a white-noise machine.

Last week my college roommate complained that there was nothing left on the registry but a bottle sterilizer. "And that's no fun, so I'm sending you a cute baby outfit instead."

I don't want to sound ungrateful. Matteo's generosity is lovely. But I don't want him to go broke on baby gear just because he's having regrets about my pregnancy.

The worst part is that I still ache for him. I miss his face. I miss sleeping in his arms. I miss the way he teases me. I miss everything about him.

But our intimacy seems to have vanished. We were so easy with each other this summer. So effortless. It makes me feel a little crazy—like maybe I dreamt the whole thing.

Maybe I did. My attachment was probably one-sided, and I was just so gone for him that I couldn't see it.

Frustrated with myself—and with the crib—I set down my tools. A glance at my watch tells me it's a quarter to four. The Busy Bean closes in fifteen minutes, and I need a break. I scurry toward the front door and step into my tumbled leather boots with the fuzzy tops.

It's a challenge to be fashionable when you're super pregnant. I haven't wanted to spend money on maternity clothes, so I've been relying on a steady rotation of black leggings under long tunics. I miss my tight jeans. Hell, I miss painting my own toenails. But here we are.

I smear on some lip-gloss and shrug on my coat—although it no longer zips—before trotting down the stairs.

Outside, it's wet and muddy. I cross the parking lot and hesitate at the door to the coffee shop. Maybe it makes me a coward, but I'm still avoiding Zara. I can tell she's deeply curious about my pregnancy, and I don't feel ready to speak freely about Matteo's part in it.

Plus, I'm afraid of what I'll say if she asks me how I feel about him.

I don't see anyone behind the counter. What I *can* see is a lone pumpkin whoopie pie in the pastry case, so I decide to risk it. I open the door, and the bells on the push bar jingle to announce my presence.

Zara steps out of the kitchen. *Whoops!*

"Hey! I knew it would be you," she says. "Right on time before closing."

"That is *not* a compliment."

She laughs. "I didn't mean it like that." She removes the whoopie pie from the case before I even point at it and sets it on a china plate.

"I'll take it to go if you're trying to get out of here."

"Nah." She shakes her head. "Sit with me a minute. I need a break, too."

"Okay, sure," I say, because it would be rude to decline.

"Want some decaf?" she asks. "I was just about to pour it out, anyway."

I guess I'm not getting out of here quickly. "Love some."

Zara makes two mugs, doctors both with a splash of milk, and carries them over to a table.

I try not to fall on the whoopie pie like a hungry lion. I'm only partly successful.

"How are you feeling?" Zara asks, sipping her coffee and eyeing me over the mug's rim.

"Pretty good. You know how it is. I'm large. I'm clumsy. I am always hungry. I need three pillows supporting various parts of my body just to fall asleep. But none of that really matters, does it?"

She considers the question. "Eventually, no. But it can be pretty uncomfortable while you're going through it."

I shrug, because there's no point in complaining. I chose this. I want this baby. Badly.

"Are you having a baby shower?" she asks.

"Not exactly," I admit. "My college friends are all out of state. But my mother and my aunts are having a tea for me in a few weeks. And, uh, I don't need much." *Thanks to your brother.* "I'm actually assembling the crib today."

Zara frowns. "By yourself? I tried that, and it didn't work. I couldn't figure out how to attach the panels together."

"Well, yeah." I hide behind my coffee mug. "It's an issue."

"Finish that coffee," she says crisply. "Then we'll put the crib together. RODDY!" she hollers toward the kitchen.

"Yeah?" the baker calls back.

"Can you make the bank deposit? I gotta help Leila with something."

"Sure," he says.

"You don't have to—"

"Too late," she says, rising from her chair. "We're putting the damn crib together. If Matteo were less of an idiot, he'd be here to do it for you."

I gulp, because I can't believe she went there.

"Come on," she says. "The crib won't assemble itself."

———

Five minutes later, we're heading across the parking lot. The UPS man beats us to my door. "Hey, Leila! Got another delivery for you." He hands me a box from Target.

"Thanks, Mickey!" He and I are quite close, seeing as he brings me boxes practically every day.

"Ooh! What's this?" Zara asks, taking it from my hands. "Looks like a bottle sterilizer. And it's from Matteo!"

I sigh and open the outer door.

"What's the matter?"

"He's bought everything on the registry. Like, literally everything."

Zara laughs. "That idiot."

"I didn't even *want* a baby registry. It felt crass to make a list of things people could buy me, but my mother insisted. And then it backfired, because Matteo keeps buying all the stuff on it."

Still laughing, Zara bounces up the stairs at a pace that I

SARINA BOWEN

haven't matched since December. Not with this belly. "That's hilarious. He probably doesn't even know what half the stuff *is*."

———

It isn't even fifteen minutes later when the crib is fully assembled. I can't resist unwrapping the mattress and hoisting it inside. The sheets have already been washed, so I put those on, too.

The result is adorable. My nursery is really coming together.

"What a lovely room," Zara says. "Turn around for a second? Look at me."

The moment I turn, I hear the sound of a photo being taken. "Hey! What was that for?"

"For my stupid brother." She squints at the screen. "You look super cute with your big belly. But I caught you looking confused. Smile for me?" She holds up the phone again.

"Zara," I protest. "I haven't been sending him photos of me. It would seem like I'm pressuring him."

"Did he say that?" she asks.

"No, but…"

"Cheese!" she demands.

I smile as a reflex, and she takes a photo. "Hey! If I'm making an awkward face, do NOT send that."

I hear the whoosh of an outgoing text.

"Zara!"

"He needs to see what he's missing," she says.

"No! That's emotional blackmail. He hasn't even decided yet if he wants to be involved. And I told him he could take his time."

Zara shakes her head. "But Matteo needs to understand that time is precious. And I'm worried about him."

"Why?" I can't quite keep the panic out of my voice. "Is something wrong?"

"Not exactly," she says slowly. "But I think he feels stuck, and it's making him sad."

Well, that *is* sad. If it's true.

"He's the oldest, and in the habit of taking on too much responsibility. You probably understand, right? That's you, too."

"That does sound familiar," I admit.

Zara sits down on the fluffy rug and leans against the crib we just built. "I bet Matteo would like to be right here with you. And you want that too, right?"

I sink down beside her, leaning against the toy chest that Matteo sent me last week. "If I answer that question honestly, are you going to tell him?"

She claps a hand over her heart. "I solemnly swear to keep this conversation private. The girl code is hereby in force."

"Nothing would make me happier," I say quietly, "than to have Matteo involved. With me. With the baby. But I can't tell him that."

"Why not?" she asks, her brown eyes widening. "Doesn't he deserve to hear it?"

"No way," I insist. "When I asked him to be my sperm donor, I was very clear that I wasn't expecting him to be my partner, or my co-parent. I can't change the rules. You said it yourself—he's a responsible oldest child. I'd be guilting him into a relationship he doesn't want—with me or the baby, or both."

"Unless it's just the opposite. You might be making all his dreams come true." She shrugs. "You could say, 'Look, my feelings changed. I love you. I want you in my life. But if that's not what you want, I'll accept that. It's your call.'"

She makes it sound so simple. But I know what would happen —Matteo would feel even more stuck than he already feels. He'd feel obligated to take care of Sean's family and also mine.

Now that the baby registry has been picked clean, he'll probably move on to the kid's college fund. Out of obligation, though, more than love.

And that's the real problem. I don't want him here because he feels guilty. I want him here because he's crazy about me.

"You're not in the habit of asking for what you want," Zara says. "Are you? I mean—you didn't even want to make a baby registry!"

"Well, no. But it doesn't matter. There's no boyfriend registry. You can't just ask for the partner of your dreams, in the model of your choice, delivered to your door."

"But I've seen the way he looks at you," Zara argues. "If there was a girlfriend registry, he'd pick you first."

"That's nice to hear," I say quietly. "But attraction and commitment aren't the same thing. Matteo has never needed me like Rory did. He's just not built that way."

"Whoa." Zara picks up an Allen wrench off the rug and points it at me. "Do *not* compare my brother to your ex."

"Okay, sorry."

"Rory is a boy who didn't know how to grow up. Matteo is the opposite. He was the man of the house even when he was a boy. He's never allowed himself to need *anyone*."

I swallow hard, because that sounds like him. "But I still don't know what to do. It seems wrong to burden him with my feelings. I don't want to be another problem he has to solve. He's already working so hard."

"That's exactly my point. He needs to do something for himself for a change."

"But *Zara*." I throw my arms out wide. "Isn't it up to *him* to decide what that is?"

"Okay. Probably." Zara sighs and climbs to her feet. "I tried. Now I should go home and rescue my husband from playing tea party."

"Um, could you help hoist me off the floor? Otherwise, I'm calling a tow truck."

She laughs and extends a hand. "Yeah, been there."

I'm back on my feet when my phone starts ringing. I scoop it off the toy chest and see LIVIA CALLING.

Okay, that's weird. My dad's assistant doesn't usually phone me. "Hello?"

"Leila? This is Livia. I'm sorry to say that your father collapsed in the brew house. I called an ambulance, and they just took him to the hospital in Montpelier."

"He collapsed?" I repeat stupidly.

Zara freezes on her way to the door and then turns white. "Matteo?" she whispers.

I shake my head violently. "Thank you so much. I'm on my way."

CHAPTER 43
MATTEO

It's an overcast day on the mountain, but not too cold. A steel-gray sky hangs over Colorado, and the distant mountains in the direction of Denver are obscured by clouds.

I'm carving easy turns behind the Simmonds family of Palo Alto. Mom and Dad are on skis, their two teens on snowboards. It's the last run of the day, but I'm still watching like a hawk for trouble. That's my job.

The heli touches down in the distance, and Mr. and Mrs. Simmonds ski towards it. I pick up my pace and follow their kids a little more closely. It's time to go home.

"Man, that last one was sweet!" says Cody, their youngest. He's seventeen.

"One more?" asks Minnie, their daughter.

"Sorry," I say. "That's not in the plan." An extra run for four costs six hundred dollars, and Jack—Mr. Simmonds—didn't book that option.

"Next year," he says.

We stash our boards, climb into the bird, and Paul lifts off. In my headset, I can hear the family exclaiming at the scenery. But I close my eyes, exhausted by the pace of my job and all the questions weighing on my mind.

———

After we land at the office, I go through the motions of our usual sendoff—collecting transponders and handshakes, urging the Simmonds family to return next year.

Before they go, Jack presses some bills into my hand. "For you and Paul," he says.

"Thank you, sir. It's always a pleasure riding with you."

He gives me a backslap. "Same."

After they drive away, I find the pilot in the hanger and hand him two hundred dollars—half the tip.

Then I head into the office and put one of the other bills in a zippered pocket of my backpack. Every couple of days I deposit this special stash in a savings account I started for Lissa.

She'll be in college in another year and a half. She'll need it.

The last bill goes into my baby-gear fund.

"How was the day?" Cara asks.

"No problem," I say. "They're regulars."

"Cool. Want to go for a beer? Oh wait—I'm supposed to remind you to call your sister on Facetime. Do that first."

I put my headphones on and prop my phone up on my desk. Then I start a video call to Zara.

It rings for a minute, and then I see the ceiling of Zara's home. And then the rug. And then the ceiling again. And finally Nicole's round little face. "Uncle Matteo!" she crows. "Whatcha doing?"

"Just came inside. I was snowboarding."

"But it's raining," she says, her nose wrinkling. "We didn't go out for recess today at school."

This makes me think of Leila, of course. Although everything does. "It's not raining here. How are you? How's your cousin?"

Benito and Skye had a baby six weeks ago—a little boy. Justin. I sent them a gift off their registry, too.

And now our family group chat is eighty percent baby pics. I keep finding myself staring at them. Justin learned to smile at about the one-month mark—a gaping, toothless grin that sears me in a way I don't think I've felt before.

Nicole, though, is not so impressed. "He still can't do *anything*. Not even crawl."

"No? What a slacker."

She giggles. "He sleeps all. The. Time."

"I'm sure Skye *wishes* that were true," Zara says somewhere in the background.

"How was school today?" I ask, even if it's a shameless ploy to hear about Leila.

"Not good," Nicole says. "Miss Mary forgot about the bread in the oven! It burned."

"Oh no!" I exclaim. "I bet Miss Leila had another snack for you, though."

"Miss Mary gave us sun butter on crackers. Miss Leila isn't at school anymore."

"Wait, what?" My stomach drops. "Why not?"

Nicole spreads her hands, as if to say *how would I know?* "She had to go. Her daddy needed her."

"Her daddy…" That doesn't make much sense.

Nicole tells me a story about doing a puzzle at school and playing a game. And I nod and smile in all the right places. When she finishes, I tell her I love her, and then I ask to speak to her mama.

Zara appears a minute later holding Micah. My nephew still has a baby's round face, but he isn't tiny anymore. He's a big lunk and currently shoving a slice of apple in his mouth. "Hi," Zara says, peering into the camera. "You rang?"

"What's this about Leila leaving the preschool?" I demand.

Zara blinks. "I assumed she told you."

"Told me what?"

"You two. I swear to God…" She sighs. "Last week Lyle Giltmaker had a massive heart attack and nearly died."

"Christ."

"As of yesterday, Leila took a leave of absence from the preschool. They'd already found someone to take over for her during her maternity leave, so it worked out for her to step away."

"So she could take care of her father?" *While eight months pregnant?* My head is about to explode.

"I think he's still in the hospital? But Alec says she's coordinating his care and trying to keep the brewery stable. They have a big product launch every spring."

"Oh, shit."

Zara puts her hands over Micah's ears. "Watch the language?"

"Sorry." But I'm struggling. "That can't be easy for Leila."

"Probably not," Zara agrees. "Maybe if you called her more often, you'd know for sure. Just a thought. You two will probably figure yourselves out eventually. But it's hard to watch from the sidelines."

"I don't even know what that means." Besides, I don't know if Leila wants to hear from me. Last week I'd done some reading about the best kinds of baby food. I sent Leila a case of it, but her thank you text was a little terse.

"Just *call* her," Zara says tiredly.

"Okay. Fine. I will."

We hang up, and I drop my head in my hands and growl. It was already killing me to be so far away. Now it's worse.

"Everything okay?" Cara calls.

I laugh, because it's really not.

"I mean—aside from the fact that you haven't had a day off in months, and you're doing two guided trips tomorrow, plus a business dinner?"

"A dinner?" I yelp.

"It's on your calendar. We're taking a group of concierges out and pitching them on the airport expansion idea."

"Right, right." I'd put that out of my mind. Just the thought of expanding our off-season services makes me tired. "Cara, what can I send a very pregnant woman to make her life easier?"

"Oh, I know this one! A certificate for a day at the spa. Prenatal massage and a pedicure, because she probably can't reach her own feet."

"Cool idea," I admit. But I wonder if Leila has time to go to a spa.

"Who's the pregnant woman? I thought your sister-in-law already had the baby?"

I rub my temples and consider the question. Sooner or later Cara is going to hear the truth. After the snow melts, I'm not going to be able to resist another trip to Vermont. "Would you believe that it's Leila?"

She gapes at me. "*Your* Leila? Oh *God*. Who's the father?"

"Um…" I rub my chin. "I am."

Her jaw unhinges. "Get out of town."

"No, it's true."

She stands up from her desk. "No, I meant that literally. Get out of town! What are you *doing* here if the love of your life is carrying your child?"

"I'm *working!*" I holler. "*That's* what I'm doing here! Seven days a week. Is that really not enough?"

The minute the words come out of my mouth, I feel terrible. Cara looks stricken. She sits back down in her desk chair and drops her gaze to her hands.

"Cara, I'm *sorry*," I say immediately. "That was uncalled for. God, seriously. I'm so sorry."

"I know," she says softly. "It's okay."

"No, it's really not." I stand up and put my phone in my pocket. "Look, I need to get out of here. I need to call Leila. Please forgive me for shouting. I'm so sorry."

She nods, but she looks so troubled that I want to slap myself.

I grab my jacket and head outside.

CHAPTER 44
LEILA

There is no second chair in my father's hospital room, so I'm standing against the windows, rubbing my belly, and counting the minutes until my dad's meeting with the social worker will be over.

My back hurts today. My feet are swollen. My stomach is off kilter. I haven't been taking the best care of myself, but there's nothing to be done about it. Since the moment I got that frightening call from Livia, I've spent all my time shuttling back and forth from the hospital to the brewery and back again.

"Your physical therapy sessions will increase to three times a week at the nursing home," the social worker says to my father.

I brace myself for his reaction, and he doesn't disappoint. "I'm not going to a goddamned nursing home!"

"Rehabilitation facility," I say through clenched teeth.

"Rehabilitation facility," the social worker echoes.

But the damage is done. My father is shooting laser eyes at the nice young woman whose job it is to guide his recovery.

Tomorrow, when my father is transferred to the new facility, I'm betting that the hospital staff will throw a party to celebrate. Dad spent his first forty-eight hours here unconscious and barely alive. It hadn't taken even two hours after he regained consciousness before a nurse said, "Your father is a horrible patient."

"This is my surprised face," had been my response.

Since then, he's mistreated everyone from the cardiologist to the young man who brings in his meal tray.

There are moments, though, when I see the fear and remorse in his eyes. A triple bypass gives a man a good look at his own vulnerability, and I don't think my father likes what he sees.

The social worker is probably used to surly, scared people. She's brisk as she wraps up her business with my dad. "You have my number," she says, rising from the chair.

"Thank you for your help," I say, because he won't.

She gives me a fleeting smile before escaping.

I sink down on the glorious plastic chair and hold in my groan.

"Can't wait to get out of this goddamn place," my father says for the millionth time. "Nobody listens to me."

Who could help but listen to you when you are shouting all the time? Out loud, I say, "I still need that list of things you want from home."

"Save yourself the trouble. I just want to *go* home."

We've had this conversation many times already. "Dad, you need round-the-clock care. Do you really want me helping you into the shower?" It's a ridiculous question, because I can barely reach past my belly these days. And we both know my father would rather chew off an arm than get any help from me.

But that doesn't stop him from saying ridiculous things and demanding to be sent home. At one point he even said, "This whole thing is your mother's fault." As if their divorce had led directly to the ninety-six percent blockage in his artery.

He stares at the ceiling and sighs.

"Either you give me a list now, or you're going to arrive at the new facility with nothing. I have ten more minutes here before I have to go talk to your graphics guy about your new Facebook campaigns."

He lifts his head off the pillow. "Somebody has to *monitor* those campaigns. Every click costs me money."

His rant continues as my phone rings. It could be anyone. I owe so many people calls.

The caller is Matteo, and even though it hurts me, I decline the call. "All right. What's on your list? Do you want your bathrobe?"

253

"No. Bring me some real clothes."

"Fine. Toiletries?"

"Whatever you find in the bathroom," he says grudgingly.

We go on like this for five more minutes. I make a cursory list, and then I tell him I'll see him tomorrow.

At no point does he thank me.

When I finally step out of his hospital room, the social worker is lurking nearby, ready to buttonhole me.

"Sorry about his attitude," I say. I've said that a lot this week.

She just shakes her head. "Listen, he has a long recovery coming and he doesn't seem to acknowledge that."

"I noticed."

She smiles. "Is there anyone in your father's life that he would listen to?"

I actually laugh. "No, and there never has been."

Her gaze softens. "I'm sorry. You have a lot on your plate right now. And it looks like you're going to have even more in very short order." She eyes my belly.

"True. But it will all work out," I tell her. What other choice is there? "Now if you'll excuse me, I have to run to a meeting."

———

I'd lied to my dad about one thing. That meeting with the graphic designer? I'd postponed it. My real meeting is with Nash.

My brother and I sit in Dad's office. I've got my feet up on a stack of accounting ledgers, but I'm still achy and uncomfortable.

I haven't been sleeping well, either.

"How did he get this sick?" Nash wants to know. "Grandpa died of a heart attack at seventy-nine. But Dad is only sixty-five."

"Apparently, he'd been having symptoms for months. Pain in his chest and neck."

Nash makes a noise of disgust. "Are we even surprised? He probably thought he could bully his heart into cooperating."

I'm guilty of similar thoughts. And when I'd overheard his sheepish confession to the cardiologist, I'd wanted to scream. "Regardless, we need to discuss the future. He's looking at several months until he's fully recovered. And I've got maybe three weeks left to be his full-time whipping boy. I really need your help here at the brewery."

My brother's eyes widen. "Are you joking? Dad wouldn't want me to *touch* his precious ales."

"He doesn't have a choice! He needs you. *I* need you. And I'm asking for your help."

"Leila, Jesus." My brother gets out of his chair and—hands on his head—does a quick circuit of the big room. "I'm really sorry, but I don't see how I can help. I have a demanding job and a life of my own. I left Vermont for a *reason*. And that reason is lying in the hospital, probably shouting at all the nurses."

I flinch at this uncomfortably accurate assumption. "Nobody is saying that you made the wrong choice. But the facts still stand— this business is valuable, and it's not small. It's also your family's legacy, whether you wanted it that way or not. If Giltmaker stumbles, that's a disaster for both Dad *and* Mom. Furthermore, you're the only one who's qualified to step in. He runs a one-man show here."

"That's because he's an idiot!" Nash explodes. "A brewery of this size should have a CEO, a brewmaster, and a marketing executive. Not just a single grumpy asshole who thinks he knows everything."

My phone rings for the tenth time today. I pull it out to see who's calling. Matteo again. So I have to decline it.

"Who called?" My brother asks.

"A friend."

His eyebrows shoot up. "Which friend?"

"Don't change the subject. What if you asked your company for a leave of absence? You could take over for six weeks."

"Six?" He practically chokes on the word. "God, Leila. Six weeks is a lifetime. And I can't think of a more thankless job. If any little thing goes wrong, I'll never hear the end of it. And even if it doesn't, he'd only accuse me of industrial espionage."

He isn't wrong. But I still press my case. "So you won't be the bigger man? That's what I'm asking of you. If this business tanks —that's our parents' retirement."

Nash spreads his arms. "Leila, go have your baby. Let his ship sink if it's going to sink."

"Nash! You don't mean that," I insist. "Some small part of you cares what happens to this crazy thing Dad built from nothing but stubborn grit and big dreams."

He wilts a little. "The company is incredible. But dad is not. And you're asking me to sacrifice myself for a man who wouldn't do the same for us."

That's accurate. And now my argument has run out of gas.

So have I. I rub my back and pray for a break, or a nap, or a sandwich.

"Shit." Nash drops his head. "I don't think anyone at BrewCo has ever asked for a leave of absence."

"You can have first tracks, then."

He snorts.

"Six weeks of utter pain," he grumbles. "That's what you want from me. And he'll never say thank you."

"But I will," I point out. "And think of all the new ink you could get while you're up here. If there's still room somewhere on your body."

He gives me a rueful grin.

We lapse into silence, and I rub my swollen stomach. Nash watches me, curiosity in his eyes. "I can't believe you're really having a baby."

"Well, it's not a beach ball under here."

"And you still don't know if it's a boy or a girl?"

I shake my head. "Too superstitious."

His smile softens. "Other than six weeks of my life, what do you want for a baby gift? Do you have one of those registries?"

"Honestly, it's all taken care of."

"Really?"

"Trust me. You're off the hook for baby gifts."

"Look, have you had lunch?"

I shake my head.

"I'm going to go get us something to eat. I need to clear my head. Want a Thai wrap from the deli?"

"You know I do."

My brother leaves the office, and I will myself to get up and check in with the guys in the canning room. But before I do, the phone on my father's desk rings. I answer it. Big mistake. It's the hospital's billing department calling, and it turns out they've got last year's version of his insurance card. "He has a new group number," the caller insists. "We can't bill his insurance until we get this straight."

"But I don't know where to find the new one, and I don't have his old details memorized. You *took* his insurance card—with the 800 number on the back—and didn't return it."

"I'm sorry, ma'am, we can't move ahead with his transfer until we have the correct billing information."

I just want to cry. But my phone is ringing again. *Matteo*. I silence it, but he calls *right* back.

"Could you hold a moment, please?" I say to the billing guy. He won't go anywhere if he wants his money. Then I answer my cell phone. "Matteo, I'm sorry, this isn't a good time."

"But I've been calling all day!" he argues. "I just heard about your dad, and how you left your job—"

"Yessir. Which means I'm on the phone with the hospital."

"All *day?*"

"Feels like it. And when I'm not on the phone, I'm running around trying to figure out how my father's company works."

"Leila—should you be on your feet like that?"

And I see red. It's like he found my last nerve and yanked it. "Are you questioning my judgement from two thousand miles away? When I'm doing the best I can?"

"Umm…I'm just *worried*, here. You shouldn't have to run the world right now."

"It's not going to run itself," I say through gritted teeth.

He sighs, the way you would at a misbehaving child. And that makes me even angrier. "When I was waiting for you to call me back—or at least text me to say you're okay—I was trying to think of some way I could help…"

"You can't," I say flatly.

"Uh…how about a spa day?"

That's when I kind of lose my mind. "A SPA DAY?"

"Hey—I know it's—"

"You *don't* know. You don't have a *clue* what's going on here! You are two thousand miles away, dangling off mountain tops, working through your own shit, and that is fine. Just stay out of my shit. Don't question my judgement. And don't try to help me. Because the help that I need is not the kind you can provide."

For a long beat after I deliver this awful little rant, there's nothing but silence on his end of the line. "Okay," he says eventually. "I see."

I feel terrible now. "Matteo—"

"No, you're right. My apologies. Take care, Leila."

Then he actually hangs up, and I'm left here with a phone to my head and a pounding, anxious heart.

CHAPTER 45
MATTEO
APRIL

Sean holds the shovel, wearing nothing but a T-shirt with his snow bibs. The sun is hot overhead.

And he's standing *way* too close to the edge of the cliff.

"Spring skiing was always my favorite," he says as he extracts a shovelful of snow for inspection.

"How's it look?" I ask.

"Doesn't matter, right?" He drops the shovel and the snow without showing me.

"Of course it matters!" I'm angry now.

"Not anymore." He shakes his head. And then the jerk actually smiles at me, the sun reflecting off his mirrored sunglasses. "I'm going now, okay?"

"Wait!" It always goes like this, and I'm already panicking. "Just hang on. It's not safe."

He shakes his head. "No, I mean it. I'm going. Don't follow me anymore. I'm not the one who needs you."

"Sean—"

"You know it's true," he says. "Stop following me. You're chasing the wrong person. Take a step back."

"Jesus." I take a step forward instead. I could almost grab his bibs from here.

"*Hey.*" He sidesteps me. "You're not listening."

"I'll listen. Talk."

But he's shimmering now. Melting in the sunlight. "It's okay now. Be well, Matteo. Go on home."

I'm trying to yell, but no sound comes out. Then I hear a pounding noise in the distance.

I finally wake up, springing to a seated position. I'm sweating like a beast.

Then I notice all the sunlight streaming into my room. It's late. *Shit!*

And that pounding noise? It's at my front door. "Matteo!"

I roll out of bed and stumble toward the living room. "Coming," I say thickly.

When I yank open the door, Lissa is standing out there, arms crossed. "You look like hell."

"Thanks? What time is it? I'm supposed to be—"

"Mom took your tour. You can show up for the noon one." She gently pushes me aside and heads for my kitchen. I watch, still half asleep as she fills the coffee pot with water and grinds the beans.

Eventually I remember to close the door. "Shouldn't you be in school?"

"It's *Saturday*, wise guy."

"Oh." I squint at the clock on the microwave. Nine thirty. "I can't believe I slept in." In all my years as a guide, that's never happened. Not once.

Lissa just shrugs. "You haven't had a day off since December. Not sure why it doesn't happen more often."

"Your dad showed up in my dream again."

She lifts her chin. "Yeah? Did he tell you to buy me a new set of ear buds? The cool ones, with active noise canceling?"

"What?" I chuckle. "No."

"Worth a try," she says, smiling as she presses the button to start the machine. "What did he want?"

Stop following me. Go on home. You're not listening. "It's hazy now," I lie. In the kitchen, I find the mugs and the milk. I need this cup of coffee more than I need my next breath.

And I know I can't go on like this.

Sean told me what to do.

260

It's time to do it.

———

I pull into the parking lot of our helipad at eleven thirty. The bird is back from the morning session, which is perfect. I need to talk to Cara before I take my afternoon ride.

First, I'll apologize for sleeping in. Then we're going to have a come-to-Jesus conversation. Which has nothing to do with my hairstyle.

But Cara is on the phone. When I enter the office, she holds up a hand to silence me. "Okay, yes. Tuesday it is. Thank you, Roger. I'll be there."

I try to wait patiently for Cara to end her call, but I'm so fidgety that I find myself spinning around in my office chair.

It's nerve-wracking to change your life.

Finally, she hangs up and turns to me. We both try to speak first. And then we both stop and wait. But when the other doesn't speak, we both jump in again.

Cara laughs. "Okay, fine. You go first."

"Yeah, I really need to, okay? I'm sorry I slept in. I know you're not supposed to run tours right now."

She shrugs. "It was fine."

"Still. We run a tight ship, and it won't happen again. But I need to make a change, honey. I don't feel right staying in Colorado after this season."

Her eyes widen. "Did you and Leila have a talk?"

"Well, no." I clear my throat. "Not a good one, anyway. We're not in a good place, and I'm going to have to do something drastic to fix it. If I don't, I'll regret it for the rest of my life."

If I'd been expecting Cara to panic, I'd be disappointed. Because she smiles. "That's the smartest thing I've heard you say in a long time."

"Really? I've peaked?"

She gets up from her chair, crosses the room, and swats me on the arm. "I can't believe you waited so long to tell me that you're having a baby together. You let me work you like a carthorse all season, when she's so far away?"

"That was our arrangement."

"But now you realize it's the dumbest arrangement ever made?"

"When you put it that way…"

She laughs. "Matty, go home. I mean it."

"I will, but we need a plan first. I'll finish the season. And we'll figure out where to go from there."

She points at the phone on her desk. "That that call I just made? It was to the Aspen Mountain Corporation. I asked them if they're still interested in buying us out."

I stare. "What? You hated that idea."

She sighs. "Yeah, but I hate a lot of things. Like being a widow at forty-four and letting Sean go. But I also hate watching you sacrifice yourself. Trying to fill a hole that can never be filled."

"It's not *that* dire. And Sean would do the same for me."

She spins a chair around and sits down in front of me. "Maybe that's true, but hear me out. Yes, Sean would have stepped up if something happened to you. He would have made sure your family didn't suffer if he could help it. But think about it—I'm Leila in this scenario. Would you want Sean to cast me aside out of a misplaced sense of duty?"

"I haven't cast Leila aside."

"Really?" She shrugs. "I think Sean would kick your ass right now."

That lands. After all, Dream-Sean had a few choice words for me. "So you want to sell?"

"Yeah, I do." Her smile is sad. "I can pay off my house. Send my girl to college. And who knows? I can probably still work here for a while, too. Why not, right? Who runs this place better than us?"

I sit with this for a moment. I try to picture this business under new management. "They'll erase him, though," I say quietly. "His photos. His desk…"

Both our gazes travel to the empty desk in the corner, where his favorite coffee cup still sits—featuring a Yeti on a board.

"They *can't* erase him," Cara says. Her eyes are red, but she powers through. "He built this place from the ground up. We all did. He left a valuable business behind, and his family will forever benefit. That's what he'd want more than anything."

My throat is thick, but I know she's right. "So what do we do?"

"We finish the season. We get our books and records ship-shape. And we find a buyer."

"No—*two* buyers," I insist. "Let them fight over us. It will drive the price up. Our land is valuable. So is our customer database. And our reputation."

She takes a deep breath. "When is this baby going to be born?"

"Next month."

"So let's get to work."

CHAPTER 46
MATTEO

The next several days are a whirlwind. Cara and I talk to the people at the Corporation and to several other outdoor-touring companies.

And I break the news of my departure to Lissa, who takes it like a champ. "Oh my God. A baby? Oh my GOD! I have to meet this baby. You can only move away if I can come and visit you."

"I'll need you to," I say. "Next winter. We can ride the highest peaks of Vermont, and you can pretend to be impressed."

She gives me a squealing, teenage-girl hug and tells me she's happy for me.

Still, I'm filled with nervous energy and a little bit of anxiety. What if Leila wasn't banking on me moving back to town?

If she's not into it, we might not have a chance as a real couple.

But it's a chance I'm willing to take. And I've stayed away from Colebury for too long. It's my town, too. I don't want to live my life at a distance, just because I was afraid to try.

One afternoon, while I'm walking the streets of Aspen, a photo lands on my phone. It's a candid pic of Leila in the coffee shop. She's wearing a big fluffy sweater that's stretched over her belly. And she's smiling.

The sender is Zara. So I call her.

"What's up?" my sister asks when she answers the phone. "Any baby news?"

"Nope. But thanks for that sneaky shot of Leila in the coffee shop."

Zara chuckles. "She looks so round. It's adorable. And I'm trying to get you to come to your senses."

"What if I already have? I'm calling to tell you that I'm moving back. There's a realtor showing my condo to her clients right now."

Zara squeals. "Thank you, Jesus. Leila must be excited."

"She doesn't know yet."

She gasps. "Why not? And what is *wrong* with you two?"

"Nothing! God. I just want to tell her in person. She's so busy right now that if I call her up, it's just one more call to deal with."

"Hmm. I suppose that's a fair point. And now you can make a big entrance. With a diamond ring and the whole nine yards. You can declare your love in the middle of the Gin Mill."

"Whoa. Let's not get carried away." It's going to be hard enough already to tell Leila how I really feel. "I'm not going to put her under any pressure. Does she come into the coffee shop every day, though? It would be fun to surprise her."

"Like clockwork!" Zara hoots. "Do it! This is going to be amazing. You can just be chilling at a table when she comes in. I can play 'Layla' by Clapton and tell her that there's a special baked good of the day!"

"Am I the, uh, baked good in this scenario?"

"You know it!"

I laugh in spite of how ridiculous this idea really is. "Okay. Fine."

"When are you coming?"

"Soon? I don't have a date yet. I'm busy trying to sell the business. Sell my apartment. Plan my life…"

"Well, hurry up," my sister insists. "And please consider the diamond ring. I bet she'd rather have that, and not another bottle sterilizer."

I have no idea if that's true, and I'm not going to be swayed by Zara's antics.

Besides, I have another gift for Leila.

And it's finally time to give it to her.

CHAPTER 47
LEILA

Being very pregnant is kind of like being a bowling ball. I'm round and heavy and I bump into a lot of things.

It's somehow worse this morning. I feel awful when I wake up. My head is full of static. I feel a little nauseated and a little dizzy. Plus, my ankles are swollen.

Must be the salty dinner I ate last night.

Oops.

And—this is new this week—I'm having Braxton Hicks contractions. They come and go. The books say not to worry about it. But I do anyway.

I'm too tired to wash my hair this morning, so I pin it up on top of my head. I get dressed in my one pair of black maternity pants and a tent-sized top that I'm so tired of I could cry.

Then I eye my jewelry with a cool disdain. I'm too tired to properly accessorize, so I grab the nearest pair of earrings and put them on.

It will have to do. I'm late to meet Nash at the brew house. It took me a couple of weeks of begging, but I've finally convinced my brother to take that leave of absence and help the Giltmaker Brewery.

The hard part was convincing my father of this plan. "Unless you want your entire business to crash and burn while you recuperate, you have no other choice."

He'd cursed the heavens. He'd bellowed. He'd moaned. But then he'd grudgingly admitted that I was right. "I guess there's no other choice," he'd said.

Today will be Nash's first day. I need it to go smoothly.

I grab a jacket and my bag. No snacks today, because I feel kind of queasy. When I walk downstairs, exhaustion follows me, and so I hesitate outside my door. Can I stomach a cup of coffee right now? Because coffee fixes everything.

Yes, I suppose I can.

The trek across the parking lot feels extra-long. I'm practically panting when I pull open the door. The bells jingle, as usual, but it sounds sort of far away.

Zara is behind the counter, smiling at me. "Listen!" she says, and then she points at the ceiling.

Clapton's "Layla" is playing on the stereo. That's nice and all, but I just need to make it to the counter. The room is suddenly too bright and jittery.

"Leila?" Zara says.

"*Layla!*" Clapton sings.

"Leila?" another voice asks. "Are you okay?"

I grasp the counter with a white-knuckled grip, and I try to take inventory.

"Leila," a sexy voice says beside me. "Honey. *Hey.*"

I try to turn towards that gorgeous voice. But it's harder work than it should be, and I lose my grip on the counter and pitch towards Matteo.

Matteo?

Suddenly the floor rushes up at me, but strong arms catch me before it hits.

———

When I come to, I'm riding in a car. My eyes flicker, showing me the backseat of my own Jeep. Zara is up front, at the wheel.

And Matteo is whispering in my ear. "Wake up, baby. That's it. Look at me. I'll do anything if you will just show me those brown eyes again. Come on, queen."

Maybe I'm dreaming. "*Matteo?*"

"Yeah, honey."

He comes into focus. I'm basically lying on him as he braces me in his arms. "Hi. I'm so happy to see you."

Zara snorts.

But Matteo's eyes are worried. "Tell me what's wrong. Are you sick?"

"I feel…" It's so hard to describe. "Woozy. It's hard to be vertical."

"Okay," he says gently, his hand rubbing my round belly. "We're going to the ER. They'll sort you out."

Matteo will fix this. The relief I feel at that idea makes my eyelids feel heavy again. But I fight it, because I'm too busy sneaking looks at Matteo's scruffy, handsome face. In his flannel shirt, he looks like a western hipster.

Honestly, I wish I'd taken a little more care with my appearance today. But I really like his hand on my belly. "Why are you here?" I demand.

"Because he's back!" Zara says as she cuts someone off in traffic. "We were trying to surprise you."

"I'm surprised," I murmur, and Matteo flashes me a cautious smile. In the back of my mind, I know I'm causing everyone to worry. But I'm too dizzy to care.

"Stay with me." Matteo pats my cheek. "I have a present for you. If you can stay awake until we get to the hospital, I'll give it to you."

"Another present?" I ask sleepily. "For the baby?"

"No, this one's for you."

"I'm just so glad you're here," I say sloppily. "How long can you stay?"

"As long as you need me," he says softly. "How long do you think that will be?"

"Uh…" It's hard to answer questions when you're woozy. "I miss you so much, but I'm not supposed to answer that."

His face breaks into a smile. "How come?"

"It's breaking the rules." I sigh against his flannel shirt. "You can't ask your sperm donor to be your man. Everyone knows that."

"Do they, now?" He strokes my hair. "We'll just see about that."

———

By the time we arrive at the hospital, I feel less dizzy and more lucid. Zara pulls up near the door to the ER and sprints inside to get a wheelchair.

Matteo sets me into it with a comical, exaggerated grunt of effort.

I'm so happy to see him that I don't even mind this little joke at my expense.

Then he pushes me inside, buttonholes a nurse, and says, "This one fainted, and she needs to be seen immediately."

The woman blinks at him for a long moment, as if distracted by how handsome he is. *Girl, I know the feeling.* Eventually she shifts her gaze to me. Specifically, my belly. "How many weeks?"

"Thirty-seven," Matteo and I say at exactly the same time.

I didn't even know he knew that.

The nurse gives me a clipboard full of forms to fill out, and Matteo takes it and begins the work for me. If that's not love, I'm not sure what is.

They call my name fairly quickly. It's hard to say whether that's due to my pregnant belly, my pale face, or the fact that Matteo keeps approaching the triage desk, insisting that I need attention.

In the exam room, the doctor says I'm not in labor. "Those contractions you're having aren't serious," she says. "But I don't like your blood pressure."

"It's been a stressful couple of weeks," I supply.

She shakes her head and launches into an explanation of several scary things that could happen if my blood pressure goes haywire. "We're going to do a blood draw, a urine test, and give you a blood-pressure drug. And admit you for observation."

"I need to call my brother," I realize. "He's waiting for me."

"Let me handle it," Matteo says soothingly. "You just relax."

He kisses my cheekbone, and I grip his hand tightly. "You're not leaving, right?"

"Not a chance," he whispers. "The farthest I'm going is the parking lot. Give me your phone and let me call Nash. You just rest."

They find me a room on the labor and delivery ward and hook me up to an IV and a fetal monitor.

"Just sit tight, honey," the nurse says to me, checking my wrist and then tucking my hand back under the blanket. "Try to relax, maybe close your eyes. I'll be in and out to check on you."

"Thank you."

She hurries out of the room, and I'm left alone for a moment. Matteo is walking his sister back to my Jeep, so she can go back to work.

I'm still not sure why Matteo is suddenly back in Vermont, but I'm not going to question it. The nurse said that if they can't get my blood pressure down, then I'm going to have to deliver early.

That's terrifying. I'm trying not to panic.

Except I'm totally panicked. I'm not mentally ready for the birth. The fetal monitor beside me is showing a wavy line of my baby's heartbeat. I can't tell if it's normal or not. The doctor had used a lot of scary words, like "C-section" and "possible signs of preeclampsia."

I'm scared.

A head suddenly pops around the door frame, and I jump. Another monitor—the one that measures my blood pressure—beeps loudly.

But then I realize that head belongs to Nash. "Is it okay?" he asks. "Can I come in?"

"Yes, of course. I'm sorry I stood you up."

He strides into the room and leans over to hug me. I grip him like a drowning woman grips a life preserver. "Leila, buddy?" he asks softly. "What mess have you gotten us into this

time? I thought the baby was supposed to stay put a little longer."

"It still might. And that would be helpful."

He releases me with a smirk. "Just promise me you won't have the baby while I'm standing here, okay? Blood is not my jam, and I don't want to accidentally see something gross."

"Nash!" I swat him, and he laughs.

"Honestly, this wasn't in my temporary contract," Nash says, eyeing all the monitors I'm hooked up to. "I'm gonna need to renegotiate."

"Aren't you hilarious," I grumble, holding the halves of my hospital robe together with both hands. But I'm happy Nash is here and joking around with me. I'm completely unnerved.

"How are you feeling now?" my brother wants to know. "Matteo said you fainted."

Terrified. "A little more stable."

"Are you still dizzy?"

"It's less, but I'm sitting down now."

"Matteo, huh?" He glances toward the hallway. "I did wonder about you two."

I sigh. "It's complicated. Mostly because I made it that way."

"Hey—no judgement from me." He shrugs. "I've always liked that guy better than what's-his-name."

"Nash…"

"I know, I know. It's really none of my business."

"It's really not. Now let's talk about the brewery. There's so much to discuss. I'm sorry we aren't having our tour this morning. You'll have to get the lay of the land from Livia—Dad's assistant. She's a little sharp-tongued, but she's good at her job."

Nash's face darkens instantly. "Not her. Nope."

"What do you mean *not her*. Have you even *met* Livia?"

"Met her this morning," he says. "And I'm not a fan. I'll work with anyone except her."

"Nash! So long as I'm stuck in here, she's all you've got. She's the only one who knows how that place works."

He scowls. "She's only been there, what, a few months? How useful could she really be? I don't think we can work together."

Oh, God. A machine beside me starts beeping. Loudly.

A nurse rushes in. "That's your blood pressure spiking," she says. "Is everything okay?"

Nash puts his head in his hands. "I'm sorry, Leila. I'll do whatever you say."

The beeping stops. The nurse adjusts something on my IV, pats my hand, and walks out again.

"Look," I tell my brother. "You're going to have to set all your assumptions aside for a minute and just strap in. You don't have to like Dad, or Livia. But for the next six weeks, you're at the helm of the most decorated brewery on the Eastern seaboard."

"Got it," he says quietly. "Don't worry about me. Don't worry about *anything.*"

"I'll try."

"Be well, Leila." He gets up, kisses the top of my head, and then leaves the room.

Alone again, I listen to the machines beep. I look at the fetal monitor and wish I could understand what it's telling me.

I put both hands on my belly and close my eyes. *Listen, baby. We've come this far. If we pull together here, I think we can go the distance. I'm really eager to meet you, but if you could stay put for two or three more weeks, that would be great. Think it over.*

"Leila, honey? You okay?"

I open my eyes to see Matteo smiling at me from the doorway. "Yup. Just, uh, having a word with the baby." I slide my hands off my belly in an attempt at dignity.

He skips the chair and parks on the bed's edge, as near to me as he can manage since the bed rails are in his way. "And how is the baby doing?"

"Fine, as far as I can tell."

He takes my hand in his, stroking his thumb across my palm. "Glad to hear that. But I'm glad they admitted you for observation. I don't like seeing you faint."

"Nice catch, by the way. But we didn't think this through—now you're stuck here with me."

His brown eyes become serious. "Leila, there's nowhere else I want to be right now."

"Except visiting with your family, right? And there's no baby yet."

"Leila, I'm here for *you*, not just the baby. If you let me. That's what I wanted to tell you this morning at the coffee shop. If I'd gotten a chance."

"Oh." My stomach does a somersault. "Really?"

He lifts my hand to his mouth and kisses it, his whiskers tickling my palm. "I know I was supposed to have a limited role in this production. And I'll take what I can get. But I'd like to apply for a more meaningful position on the team."

My heart lifts. "Is that right?"

He traps my hand against his chest. "I've missed you so much I ache. I flew home to say that. And also this—I love you, and I have for a long time."

"*Oh*." Later I'll blame the pregnancy hormones. But suddenly there are tears rolling down my face. "I love you too. It's been hard work holding that in."

"So let's put it all out on the table. I'll start. What we had together last summer was so good. I want more."

"Me too, except you have to know that it can't be the same," I point out. "Having a baby changes everything."

He shrugs. "It doesn't change how I feel about you. You're it for me. Big belly and all." He cups my face and gives me a very gentle kiss.

I feel myself truly relax for the first time in months.

CHAPTER 48
MATTEO

Leila makes a soft sound when I kiss her. So I do it once again before I force myself to pull back.

She's red-faced and wearing a blue hospital gown. Her hair is a mess. And I've never seen anyone more beautiful in my whole life.

Everything I've done these past two weeks is for her. Every new complication. Every life-changing plan. And I'd do it all over again, a thousand times with no guarantees, so long as she and the baby come through this safely.

"Baby," I say. "About that present I brought you…"

Her eyes sparkle. "Oh yeah. You said something about that. What is it?"

"It comes with a story." I chuckle awkwardly, because I can't believe I'm about to admit this. "It's about a young guy who didn't think he was good enough for you."

Leila leans back against the pillow. "Then it can't be a story about you. You're the best man I know."

"That's incredible to hear. But I'm going to let you in on a little secret—young men aren't very smart sometimes."

"Ah." She smiles.

"Remember when you asked me why I never came home for Christmas that year before you graduated from college?"

She nods, her face solemn again.

"Yeah, well I *did* come home. I'd brought you a gift. Kept it in my pocket all the way from Colorado. And the minute I got here, I borrowed my brother's car and drove to your house. I wanted to see you so bad."

Her eyes widen. "You're joking."

"Dead serious." I close my eyes for a moment, picturing that winter night. "Your house was all decked out for Christmas. There were lights strung across the porch, and a half-decorated tree in the picture window. And I was gathering my courage to knock on the front door. When I was growing up, your house was the nicest one I'd been to. I'd spent a lot of time trying to figure out how a guy like me could deserve a girl from the nicest part of town."

"But I didn't care about things like that," she whispers.

"I know that now." I give her a sad smile. "But I didn't know it then. I thought I had to prove myself to the world, and earn enough money to buy you presents. But I lost you instead. See, I walked up the drive that night, and I saw you and Rory in the window."

"*Oh.*" Understanding blossoms in her eyes. "Together."

"Yeah, obviously together. And I realized I had missed my chance. I'd stayed away too long. So I doubled down by staying away even longer."

Her face drops. "Oh. News flash—young women aren't always smart, either. I knew Rory and I weren't soulmates, but I stayed with him anyway. I probably derailed his life just as badly as I derailed mine."

"What if we stopped blaming ourselves for being dumb?" I suggest. "Let's stop wasting time."

She squeezes my hand. "Okay. I will if you will."

"Good. And at least I was smart enough to save this." I have to stand up for a moment so I can reach into my pocket and pull out the tiny cardboard box. "It's the gift I'd brought home all those years ago. You probably forgot all about it, but that's okay."

I hand her the little box. It says *Alpine Arts* in silver letters.

Surprise registers on her face as she tugs the lid off the box. And then she gasps when she sees the snowflakes necklace inside. "Omigod! It's from the shop in Beaver Creek!"

The smile on her face makes my heart beat faster. "Yeah. Took me a few years to go back and buy it, but I never forgot."

She looks up at me again as she unclips the chain, and drapes it around her neck. "I can't believe you kept it this long."

"You still like it?" I ask with a chuckle. "Tastes change." I reach up to help her with the clasp.

"I still *love* it," she insists, fingers pressing the pendant to her collarbone. "My tastes don't change that much over time, I guess. On that trip, I realized how much I missed you. I just didn't call my feelings by their real name."

"Love you, honey," I whisper. "I sold my business and my condo and flew all the way home to tell you that."

She blinks. "Really? You're leaving Colorado for good?"

"Oh yeah." I smile at the look of shock on her face.

"I didn't know you could do that right now."

I laugh. "I didn't either. But here I am anyway." I find a position where I can wrap my arms around her properly. "My tastes don't change, either. You have no idea how much I care about you."

And then I hold her tightly to prove just how much.

———

Leila's obstetrician—a gray-haired woman named Dr. Constance —turns up later to examine her. Leila seems relieved to see a familiar face.

Dr. Constance clucks over her and checks all the monitors and charts. "The blood pressure medication has improved you," she says.

"Oh good! Does that mean I can go home?"

The good doctor shakes her head. "It's improved, but not enough. And your lab work suggests that we should go ahead and induce you." She places her hands on Leila's belly and uses her fingers to palpate the baby.

"Shit," Leila says, blowing out a breath. "I really wanted to make it to full term."

"At thirty-seven, almost thirty-eight weeks, your baby is going to do just fine. I'm just happy you didn't have this complication earlier in your pregnancy. It happens, and it's a lot more difficult to navigate."

"Okay. What do we do next?"

The doctor explains that her IV will deliver a new drug that will induce labor contractions. But it will take hours.

"She hasn't eaten today," I point out. "Can I bring her some food?"

The doctor okays this, gives Leila a few more details, and then goes off to order the new IV meds.

I rise from the bed, but Leila grabs my hand. "You're coming back, right?"

"Always, honey. But the labor book says that labor is like running a marathon, and I don't want you starving. Can I find you a sandwich?"

"You read the book?"

"I needed a new hobby after the baby registry was finished, so…" I shrug.

She smiles but there are tears in her eyes. "I don't deserve you."

"Not true. Now let go of me so I can feed you."

She releases her grip, but her eyes are scared. "I know this was all my idea. But I'm in over my head." She puts her hands on her belly. "Your sister said I'm not good at asking for what I want, and she's right. But I asked the universe for something precious, and I'm terrified I won't stick the landing."

"Hey." I lean over and hold her again. "I got you. Think of it like a new trick on the half pipe—seems impossible the first time but then it gets easier."

"You really think we're doing this *again* someday?" Her eyes fly up to mine.

And I have to laugh. "That will be your call, queen."

She gives me a little shove and a sheepish smile. And I go off to buy the lady a sandwich.

CHAPTER 49
LEILA

The next twenty-four hours are a painful blur. Matteo doesn't leave my side, but neither of us gets much rest. At first, it's because we have so much to say to one another. But then my contractions kick in, and the pain is a distraction.

That labor book had said I wouldn't remember the pain. I've got a feeling that's a lie. By the time the contractions really get going, I'm a miserable, panting mess. And when my water breaks in the wee hours, the pain doubles.

I don't want to ask for an epidural, because it seems like there are already so many drugs in my body. But, wow, this is intense.

"Breathe," Matteo says as I push my shoulder into his body, like a lineman in a football game.

When the contraction passes, he hands me a cool cloth for my forehead and waits patiently for the next onslaught.

We both look a little worse for wear. His hair has been pulled back into a ponytail, and his flannel shirt has been shed in favor of a tee.

But he's still the best-looking sight I've ever seen in my life. His brown eyes make a quick assessment of me, and then he offers me the cup of ice chips.

I just hug him instead. "I don't know if I could do this without you."

He sets the cup down and clucks into my hair. "You're doing fine."

Leddy, my labor nurse, enters the room again. "Let's check your progress."

I flop back against the pillow and put my feet into the stirrups. This has already become routine. By this point, I would let anyone look at my vag if I thought it would make the birth progress.

"Nine centimeters! It's almost time to push."

"Nine?" I cry. "We'll be here until Christmas."

Leddy chuckles. "Nah. Halloween, maybe." Then she leaves the room.

I close my eyes and grab for Matteo's hand. "I've just made a decision—one kid will be plenty for us."

"One it is, then," he says smoothly.

"Maybe I need an epidural," I whimper.

He starts to pull away. "You want me to go find the doctor?"

I cling to him. "Don't go anywhere. What time is it?"

"About six a.m."

"God." We've been here for almost twenty-two hours.

He squeezes my hand. "How about this—if you have the baby by noon, I'll have to call you queen for a month."

"And if I can't?"

"Hmm. Sir Hunksalot has a nice ring to it, yeah?"

I snort without opening my eyes. "It's a deal."

"Cool. Six hours to go before my victory dance."

"No way," I argue. "I got this."

When the next contraction hits, I'm less sure. Each one is like a cresting wave, sucking me under. I can barely catch my breath.

But every time I look up, Matteo is there. He's holding my hand or wiping my brow. He's my rock. If you ever need to know how a man performs during a crisis, I recommend labor.

Actually, I don't recommend it. By the time they ask me to push, I'm exhausted and practically speaking in tongues.

"It's ten thirty," he says as I pant. "You can still make the deadline."

"There's no deadline," the nurse admonishes. But he gives me a saucy wink.

"Oh, I'm making the deadline," I insist with far more bravado than I feel.

The nurse issues a lot of instructions. "Relax your face. Find a gaze point and focus. Let's make some progress on this next push."

None of that helps half as much as when Matteo whispers "*Sir Hunksalot*" right before I bear down.

I open my mouth and roar. The pain sears me.

"Your baby is crowning," the doctor says. "Good job! On the next push, you can deliver the head."

But I'm so tired. When the next contraction comes, Matteo lifts my leg and grins at me, and somehow I find the strength to push. There's pain, but also progress as my body urges me on.

"Hello, baby!" the nurse says. "One more good one."

I sag against the sheet. "I'm winning this thing."

"You are," the nurse encourages.

Matteo laughs. "Yes, queen."

CHAPTER 50
MATTEO

The labor book says that men can experience feelings of helplessness in the delivery room.

But I don't get that at all. Right now, I'm exactly where I'm supposed to be. It doesn't matter that I've been up for over twenty-four hours or that I don't know a thing about babies.

All that matters is being present for Leila. My job is to be right here, every time she looks my way. It took me half a lifetime to realize it, but I'm not going to forget now.

Leila takes a sharp breath as the next contraction begins. I brace her leg with one arm and her shoulders with the other. And she roars.

"Baby girl!" the doctor says. "Time of birth, ten forty-eight."

I forget to breathe as the doctor scoops the baby into a blanket and wipes off a face so tiny that I can't see it properly.

The doctor cuts the umbilical cord and places her on a scale. "Six pounds, twelve ounces."

Then I hear it—a high-pitched little cry.

My eyes are instantly wet. The doctor turns around and nudges me. "Steady hands?"

"The steadiest," I promise. Then she places my daughter into my arms, and I finally get a look at her shocked little eyes. My voice is an awe-filled scrape. "Tiny queen."

Leila sobs. "Can I…"

I lean close to the bed, and together we look down into our baby's angry red face.

"Good job, little girl," I say, gathering her close. "Thanks for joining the party."

She stares up at us and howls.

I'm taking it as a compliment.

———

Later that afternoon, our families descend on the hospital. I'm groggy from catching a couple hours sleep on the reclining chair in Leila's hospital room. Leila is exhausted, too, but she's so happy, and the baby is nursing well.

She's currently sleeping in a little plexiglass bassinet beside Leila's bed, while her grandmother coos over her.

Mrs. Giltmaker seemed completely unsurprised when I turned up yesterday, suddenly placing myself in charge of Leila's care and notifying her family that the baby was on her way.

And that's cool. Apparently, Leila and I weren't as discreet as we'd imagined ourselves to be. This morning I posted a picture of Baby Giltmaker-Rossi on the Rossi family group chat. No surprise on that front, either.

My mother was the first to reply.

MAMA

She's gorgeous! I'm so glad I can stop pretending not to know that I had another grandchild on the way. I'm on my way to the yarn shop for supplies to make her a baby blanket.

BENITO

Nice baby. You copycat.

DAMIEN

Good job, Jesus.

ALEC

Wait, you're in Vermont? Want to work a shift tonight?

ZARA

I'm in charge of the sibling baby gift. You all owe
me $100.

"My grandchild needs a name," Helen Giltmaker says. "Unless you're sticking with 'baby girl Giltmaker-Rossi,' which is kind of a mouthful." She winks.

Leila and I turn toward each other with matching sheepish smiles. "I didn't choose names," she says. "I mean—I have a few ideas. But I didn't know if I was having a boy or a girl. And I kind of wondered if you'd want to help me choose."

"All right," I say, kissing the top of her head. "Let's brainstorm."

"And I'll go find us some lunch," Helen says. "Can't wait to see what you come up with. But I'd like to point out that Helen is a solid choice. Or even Helena."

"Noted," Leila says with an eye roll.

Cackling, my future mother-in-law lets herself out.

"Okay, what's on your list," I say, rubbing my hands together.

"Pass me my phone? Now that I've seen her sweet face, I need another look at my list of names." She glances lovingly down at the bassinet.

I hand Leila her phone, and then I take mine out, too. Baby names are not part of my repertoire, but I do have one idea. So I perform a web search.

"Okay," Leila says. "I like flower names, like Iris and Daisy. And I also like Heaven and Amelia. But…" She hesitates.

"But what?"

"We didn't discuss her *last* name," Leila says shyly.

"Oh." I'm so tired that this hadn't even occurred to me. "Giltmaker-Rossi has a nice ring to it, no?"

I expect a playful punch for this suggestion, because our names don't hyphenate well. They just don't.

But Leila looks thoughtful. "What if her *middle* name was Giltmaker and her last name was Rossi? Then she'd belong to both of us, but still might learn to write her name on kindergarten paintings?"

I wrap my arms around her and hold tight. "I'd just kind of assumed you'd use your own last name, since I've spent the last decade or so being too stupid to marry you. But I would be honored to give her my name."

She laughs in my arms. "All right. We need a first name that sounds good with Rossi, then. From my list, I think only Iris works. What do you think? Any other ideas?"

"Yeah, I got one." I wake up my phone and hand it to her.

The screen says: *Reina*: *meaning queen.*

Leila inhales sharply. "Seriously? I kind of love it. Reina Rossi." She glances at our sleeping daughter.

"Reina Giltmaker Rossi," I correct. "And it has the same vowel sounds as your name. Leila and Reina."

"You are kind of a genius," she whispers.

"Nah. Thinking about you is the easiest thing there is. I just love you, queen."

And then the most tired and happy new dad in Vermont gives his queen a kiss.

CHAPTER 51
MATTEO
SEVEN WEEKS LATER

It's a warm June day. I know from experience that Reina is not a fan of air conditioning, so I've put her in a little cotton sleeper for our big trip to the grocery store. I carry her in the front-pack for extra snuggles.

Leila is at her follow-up visit to the obstetrician, so it's just the two of us on this shopping trip. We're out of everything, so we're going to be here a while.

After I clear the produce department, Reina starts to look impatient. By the time I make it to the cheese counter, I'm singing Bob Marley's "Three Little Birds." And by the time I'm waiting in line at the butcher's counter, I've moved on to Three Dog Night's "Joy to the World."

This wins me a lot of strange looks. And by "strange" I mean strangely lustful. "Your baby is sooooo cute!" one woman says with hearts in her eyes.

"Thanks! She gets that from me," I joke.

"Oh *definitely*," she growls.

Huh. People act differently around babies.

Finally, it's my turn, and I load up on a couple of steaks and some burger meat. I've installed a gas grill on Leila's balcony, and I'm eager to use it.

These have been the best seven weeks of my life. Before we left the hospital, the nurse told Leila, "Your only job for the next few weeks is feeding the baby and taking care of yourself. Everything else comes second."

So that makes me the family chef and tour director. I've cooked some excellent meals. I've puttered around the apartment, doing small projects as needed. I've taken my little family on some nice walks with our new stroller, and a sunset rowboat ride on the river.

I've held the baby as often as I can, giving Leila a break between feedings. And whenever my family tries to ask me to do anything I don't feel like doing, I say, "Sorry, I can't. The baby isn't sleeping very well yet, and I have to be there for Leila."

My life is bound to get busier in the future, but I'll never regret spending this time cocooned with my new family.

When the butcher is finally done with my order, I put the packages into the cart, spin around and… nearly run into Rory.

Oh shit.

He looks from me to the baby and back to me. "Hey."

"Hey," I say stupidly. "How've you been?"

The corners of his mouth twitch. "All right. You? Keeping busy?"

"Uh, yeah."

A smirk. "I hear congratulations are in order. I got a teddy bear all wrapped up at home, but I haven't found the balls to bring it over."

"Thank you," I manage. I'm so uncomfortable right now, even though I've done nothing wrong.

He rubs the back of his neck. "You musta loved that voicemail I left you."

The truth is that I'd forgotten all about it. "I've heard worse."

He actually laughs. "It was a bad night. But I don't have as many of those as I used to."

"That's good to hear."

His eyes drop to the baby again. "Can I, um, see her?" He steps closer, so he can see past the padded, protective shell of the baby carrier. He clears his throat. "Hey there, princess."

Reina regards him with wide eyes.

"She doesn't say much, unless she's really pissed off."

Rory laughs. "Man, I don't know a thing about babies."

"Join the club." Although that's not really true of me anymore. I've discovered that learning about babies isn't so hard —when you spend enough time with them, they're easier to understand.

"She's cute," he says, tilting his head for a better look. "She wears her hair shorter than yours."

"Yeah, yeah."

He grins and steps back. "Don't fuck this up, okay? Don't be like me."

"I'll do my best," I say quietly.

"Hey!" A woman with shiny brown hair cascading down her tan shoulders arrives next to Rory. "Did you get the meat?"

"Working on it." Rory clears his throat. "This is my friend Matteo. And his baby daughter. Matteo, this is Jess."

As I watch, she tries to bury her surprise. "Nice to meet you, Matteo."

"Likewise," I say. "You two have a nice weekend."

Rory takes her hand, and then the two of them step toward the meat counter. Rory must sense that I'm still watching them, because he looks over his shoulder.

I mouth, *Don't fuck this up.*

He smiles.

And then I pay for all my groceries before Reina gets sick and tired of watching the grownups make awkward conversation.

It's a short drive, but Reina starts howling before I make it home. My brother Alec—on his way into the bar to open the place—ends up helping me carry the groceries upstairs so that I can quickly heat up her bottle.

"Thanks, man. I really appreciate it."

"No problem," he says. "I guess I can't pressure you to work for me, huh? Not if you're busy feeding the baby."

"*Very* busy," I say, relaxing on the couch and watching Reina take hungry pulls of the bottle.

"Let me know when you feel like making some extra cash," he says. "I'm here for you."

"Uh-huh. Thanks." We both know that *here for you* also means *shorthanded at the bar*.

"Had to ask!" he says cheerfully. "Come down for a beer before close?"

"Could happen!"

He goes, and I focus my attention on my daughter again. "Want to have a drink with Uncle Alec later? My treat."

Reina is too busy gulping milk to weigh in.

CHAPTER 52
LEILA

When I return home from my doctor's appointment, Matteo is carrying Reina around the kitchen, putting the groceries away one-handed. I stop on the threshold for a moment, just taking them in.

Seven weeks ago, on the day I was released from the hospital, I asked Matteo if he wanted to stay with me here.

"There's nowhere else I'd rather be," he'd said.

And that was that. After more than twenty years of friendship —and a secret, scorching, sexual relationship—we skipped a few steps and crash-landed into a whole new phase of life.

I'm sure everyone with a newborn probably feels as though a meteor hit them. I don't even remember what a full night's sleep is like. But it's not so bad when there's a hunk in your bed who brings you coffee every morning and takes the baby when she gets fussy.

I could have managed as a single mom. I could have done it. But it's really nice that I don't have to.

"Look, Reina," Matteo says. "Your mommy is home."

My baby girl lifts both her short arms in greeting, and my heart melts a little bit.

"Hi, peeps!" I circle the counter to kiss them both. "Want me to take her?"

"Don't you have to pump?" he asks.

SARINA BOWEN

"Well, yeah."

"Go ahead," he says. "We're fine."

So I kiss Reina's fat little cheek again and then go milk myself with that strange contraption known as a breast pump.

When I return twenty minutes later, Matteo is walking a sleepy baby around the living room. He's speaking to her in a low, calm voice. "It's okay to take your nap, tiny queen. We'll have more fun later."

I detour to the kitchen, because I don't want to interrupt. But the sight of her little body tucked against his broad chest makes my ovaries dance a jig.

After another few minutes of his soothing, her eyes go half-mast. Matteo heads slowly towards the bedroom. I follow at a safe distance, peering around the door frame as he lays her gently down in the crib. "That's a girl," he whispers. "See you in an hour."

She wiggles on the mattress for a heart-stopping moment and then settles.

Matteo gives me a sly, victorious smile. Then he eases out of the room, closing the door behind him.

"Did you see that perfect dismount?" he whispers.

"You are so hot to me right now."

He grabs me around the waist and steers me toward the kitchen. "Tell me everything. How'd the doctor's visit go? You were gone a while, so I got worried."

"Oh! Everything is fine. They're just slow." I open the refrigerator and survey the new groceries. "Steaks? Weren't we having burgers?"

"The steaks looked good. And I'm making that salad you like with gorgonzola and pecans."

My mouth waters. Even so, I think I'll volunteer to do the grocery shopping next time. Matteo spends more than I would.

I pour us each a glass of iced tea, and then notice the grocery receipt, which is still on the counter. He's bought all sorts of things I like, including a bottle of wine.

But the total makes my eyes water. "Ouch," I whisper.

"Ouch?" he says, taking a sip of tea. "What's the matter?"

I hesitate, because I don't want to criticize him for feeding me. But I'm a little worried about our lifestyle. Two people who aren't currently employed shouldn't be buying imported cheese.

"Leila, what's wrong? Did I forget something we needed?"

I shake my head. "I'm really indebted to you for all the cooking you're doing. But I think we should spend a little less until I pay off my health-plan deductible."

Giving birth costs a fortune, and my insurance isn't that great.

His brown eyes widen. "You're worried about money?"

"Not worried," I backpedal, because this is an unfortunately familiar conversation. I spent years trying not to fight about money with Rory. "Just cautious."

"It's covered, baby." He taps the receipt. "This is on me."

"But I want to pay my share," I say carefully. "I'm really enjoying all the help at home. I'd rather eat burgers than end up in a spot where one of us is suddenly looking for extra work."

"You're worried because I don't have a job," he says flatly.

Now I'm really on shaky ground. "Well, it must be expensive to uproot your life, pay off your mortgage, and all that stuff."

He puts his elbows on the counter and looks up at me. "Honey, you should know that I'll clear a chunk of money selling my condo. And even more on the business. I'll have more than a million in the bank when those transactions close."

"A… *million?*"

He circles the counter and puts his hands on my shoulders. "Please understand—I would not be buying steaks if I couldn't afford to. That's not how I roll."

"Wow," I say softly. "I just had no idea your business was worth that much."

"You know how I got all that money?"

"Hard work?" I guess.

"Nah." He chuckles. "Lucky real estate choices. The business that Sean and Cara and I built was hard work, and I'm proud of it. But the value of our helipad and our permits were the bulk of the profit. Same story with my apartment. Mostly luck and timing, plus a few good decisions."

"Oh. Wow."

He kisses me on the forehead. "Don't be too impressed. My timing with *you* was pretty terrible. Poor communication. Sketchy decisions…"

"Until now," I argue.

"Until now," he agrees. "But if you see me enjoying my free time with you and the baby, that's intentional. I don't want to miss out." He kisses my eyebrow. "I'll go back to work pretty soon. My family—or yours—will suck me back in, yeah?"

"Yeah, true." I chuckle. Between the Rossis and the Giltmakers, there's practically a new business plan every day before lunchtime.

"So let me have this time with you and Reina."

"Absolutely," I say, feeling relieved already.

"You should know that I paid the rent for next month, too."

"You *did?*"

"Sure. I was chatting with Benito about the apartment, and he told me how much he's been charging you. He said he hopes we stay a long time because he doesn't want the hassle of selling it. Then I cut him a check."

"Why?" I demand.

"Because I want to pay my share. Didn't you just say the same thing a minute ago?"

Huh. I guess I did.

"It's my bad, though—I should have discussed all this with you before," he says thoughtfully. "But you've been so tired I didn't want to bother you with money crap. That was a mistake, I guess. We're supposed to talk about this stuff, so you won't worry for nothing."

"You're right, we need to get better at discussing things. I'll work on it. But maybe not this second, because…" I lean into him and wrap my arms around his waist. "The baby is sleeping right now."

"Yeah, because of my skills," he says, stroking my back. "But what does that have to do with it?"

"You have *other* skills, too," I point out. "And my doctor just cleared me for takeoff."

His hands go still on my back. "Does that mean what I think it means?"

"We are good to go. Unless you're too tired…"

I don't even get the sentence out. He lifts me up off the floor and carries me toward the bedroom, snagging the baby monitor off the counter on his way.

I wrap my arms around him and laugh.

"Stay focused," he says. "We're on a tight timeline." He drops the monitor on the bedside table and sets me down on the bed. "You look cute in that sundress. But it's in my way. Take it off."

"Yes *sir*," I say, and his eyes go feral.

God, I've missed that look. Cuddling him in my bed for the last seven weeks was nice. But this is even better. I toss off my dress but then cup my hands in front of my breasts. "You can't play with these. I might spring a leak."

"But you just pumped," he says, unfastening my bra. "I'll be careful. Just don't hide the big mama tatas."

"You've been warned," I say as he yanks his shirt over his head and then pops the button on his jeans.

Wow. *Hello sir*. Matteo is looking as fine as ever, partly because he's joined the same gym that his siblings belong to. "I get a morning workout, and I get to hang out with the guys at the same time," he'd said.

That's all well and good, except I'm yanking back the bedclothes now and diving under the sheet. It's broad daylight, and this body had a baby *very* recently. I'm still fifteen pounds heavier than I was a year ago, according to my doctor's scale.

"Whoa, whoa," Matteo says, lifting the sheet again. "Don't hide the goodies."

"I'm hiding the stretch marks," I grumble. "Maybe I should have waited until nightfall to suggest we get naked."

"Fuck no. No waiting," Matteo says, crawling over me and looking down into my sheepish gaze. "We did not rearrange our entire lives to let a little thing like stretch marks get in our way."

I reach up and push his long hair out of his face. "That's an easier thing to say if you don't have any stretch marks."

He frowns. "Listen up. I've only had a couple of months to show you how much I love you. Maybe it will take some time for you to understand how deep this goes. But pay attention, baby. There is not one ounce of you that I don't love. And someday when I get old and gray, I'd expect you to feel the same about my wrinkles."

"Of *course,* I will."

Matteo's smile is like a satisfied cat's. "It works both ways, queen. So you have nothing to worry about, yeah?" He punctuates this thought by leaning down to kiss my neck.

I decide to believe him, because his touch is doing magical things to my body. I've missed this so much. His beard tickles my jaw as his muscular bulk settles onto my skin.

"God." He kisses his way down to my breasts and groans. "I don't know if I can go slow. This might be a lightning round."

In answer, I lift my hips and trap the firm length of him between my legs. Then I shiver from anticipation.

"Oh, it's *on.*" He slides a hand down my body and then *right* into my panties. "I want you so bad. Always have, and I always will."

That's all the convincing I need to kick the sheets away and reach for him again.

And I can hardly believe how lucky I really am.

EPILOGUE

ONE YEAR LATER

MATTEO

As I hike up the trail, Reina seems excited to be riding on my back. I can't see her, but I can feel her wiggling back and forth in the pack as she looks out at the forest. And when the ravens in the treetops call out their warnings, she babbles back at them.

Leila is walking ahead of us on the trail, her phone in her hand. This is only a three-mile hike, but it's going to take hours if she keeps stopping to take photos of us.

I don't mind at all, though. After a long week with my work crew, this is exactly how Saturdays are meant to be spent. I have big plans for this evening, too.

Big, romantic plans.

"Wave, baby!" Leila says, and I'm not sure if she means me or the actual baby.

I wave anyway.

She grins. "That's a cute one."

Again, I'm not sure which one of us she means, but it doesn't really matter. It's a beautiful June day in Vermont, and I've got everything I need right here. My family, and my future.

After taking a few more photos, Leila doubles back and takes my hand. The trail I've built up this slope is just wide enough that we can walk side by side.

We don't speak for a few minutes. It's so peaceful here, and everyone knows that if you want to see wildlife, you can't make much noise. Even the baby seems to understand, because she quiets down.

"The trail looks great," Leila whispers, squeezing my hand. "Nice work."

"Thanks, queen." I cleared every fallen log myself, and it's really shaping up. It's just one of about a million things I've done in pursuit of my new business plan for this hilltop property a few miles outside of Colebury. "Wait until you see the house."

Instead of answering, Leila gives my hand a sudden tug. I stop walking and lift my gaze.

A red fox stands on the trail ahead, giving us a stern glare.

"Reina, look!" I whisper.

The baby squeals. I expect the fox to bolt, but she simply gives us an arch look before trotting off.

"If a red fox crosses your path, that's good luck, right?" Leila says playfully. "I'm sure that's a thing." She reaches over to pat my ass. "Now let's pick up the pace. I'm dying to see the house."

"There's still no furniture in most of the rooms," I warn her. "I'm getting a big delivery next week."

She gives me a saucy glance. "Is there a hot shower and a bed?"

"You know it."

"Then we'll be fine," she says with a smile.

"Noted." I rub her palm with my thumb and think happy thoughts. Not every hour of the last year has been perfect. We'd had some long nights and tense moments when we were tired and strung out from the new-parent routine.

But those moments hadn't lasted too long. That's because Leila and I have chosen each other with fierce determination. We want this to work, and we've both decided it will.

That goes a long way on the hard days. When the sun sets, we're always curled up together somewhere, grateful for loving each other.

"There are sheets on the bed?" Leila asks.

"Of course." I laugh. "I'm capable of making a bed, you realize. There's also food. Funny how you didn't ask about that."

She shrugs. "You look edible today. Very *mountain man*." She reaches over and runs her knuckles against my scruff. "Food is the last thing on my mind."

Encouraged, I pick up my pace.

———

Half an hour later, we come to the final bend in the trail, and I'm really starting to get excited.

Here goes nothing.

"This is it, right?" Leila says, practically bounding now.

"Yeah, baby. Brace yourself."

She darts forward ten paces or so into the meadow and laughs with excitement.

I follow her to the tree line and lift my eyes up the grassy slope, where my crew and I have constructed an oversized, off-the-grid, luxurious getaway that sleeps sixteen people. There's a lodge-like contemporary building with a stone foundation, solar panels, and cedar-shake siding. There's a recreation hall behind it designed as a barn. You can't see them from where we're standing, but there are also outbuildings for storage and sports equipment. And space for the tennis court and swimming pool I plan to add in the future.

This is not, however, a home for the three of us to inhabit every day. It's too big for that, and we're happy with our apartment in town.

This place is an investment property. The main lodge has four bedroom suites, a bunkroom for eight people, a chef's kitchen, and a great room with a dining table that seats twenty. The recreation hall has a wood-fired hot tub, a ping pong table, and a movie screen.

We're going to have a million big family moments here. And when we're not using the place, deep-pocketed tourists are going to pay a small fortune to spend time with their families here, too.

"Wow," Leila says, her voice full of glee. "It looks *amazing*. That paint color for the barn worked out great, right?"

"Yes, queen," I admit. She chose that shade of green, but I hadn't let her see the final product until now.

In fact, Leila helped me with a lot of the details. The whole project was her idea. I'd been working odd jobs for the family and trying to figure out what to do next. Our families had lots of opinions, and I've put in my fair share of hours for Alec, Otto, and also the Giltmakers.

But I wanted a project that was just mine.

And then one night I was searching the internet for a family compound to rent, brainstorming a Rossi family getaway out of state. Frustratingly, there were very few properties large enough to accommodate a family reunion.

Leila had said, "You should build a place in Vermont and rent it out to other families when we're not using it."

"Oh *damn*," I'd said. "You're a genius."

I'd written up a business proposal—not for investors, but for my own planning. I'd laid out the costs of land and construction, and I thought I could make it work.

Turns out I was right. Recently, I'd posted a listing on a rental site, including photos of the property and the not-yet-furnished house, and the response had been immediate. The place is booked solid from July through October, with people willing to pay two thousand dollars a night with a four-night minimum.

I expect to do a good business during ski season as well. The house will be snug all winter, with a generous fireplace and skiing and skating nearby.

I'm calling it the Colebury Family Compound. It's the business opportunity I never knew I needed. Maybe it's not as flashy as my heli-skiing outfit, but I feel great about making a place where families can be together.

"I want to see the hot tub," Leila demands. "And you said there's food in the kitchen?"

"There is." Earlier today, I'd delivered groceries and bedding. I'd made a thorough sweep of the house, picking up any stray construction detritus. Reina is walking now, so the place needs to be toddler proof.

The three of us will be the first ones to stay here. It's ours, even if it's not our every-day home. I'm saving one primetime week a year for the Rossis, so my growing family can have a proper getaway together. And I'll save another one for the Giltmakers, too.

That family is full of drama lately, so it's going to make for some interesting gatherings.

"What's for dinner?" Leila asks, grabbing my hand as we walk toward the house.

"Steaks, of course. And roasted broccoli, for little miss bossypants."

Leila peeks into the backpack. "She's not looking so bossy right now."

"What do you mean?"

"She's out cold."

"Really?"

Leila raises her phone again and takes another picture of us. Then she shows me the result.

Yup. My baby girl is passed out, her head parked against the back of my T-shirt, her eyes screwed shut.

I laugh, because my daughter's ability to sleep anywhere never ceases to amaze me. "So much for appreciating the new place."

"She's appreciating it in her own way."

That might be true, but now there's a kink in my plans. I had this big idea…

It can wait, though.

"Come on. Let's go inside," she says. "You can put Reina in the new crib. And then I want a tour of our bedroom."

"That I can do."

———

LEILA

"I approve of the new bed," I say, my chin on Matteo's bare chest, my skin cooling in the breeze from the open window.

He gives me a slow, sexually satisfied grin. "We broke it in."

"Christened the place."

He laughs. "Is it weird to think that strangers are going to break in all the other beds?"

"A little." I run a finger down his abs. The ripple still gets me every time. "But not as thoroughly as we can. We're in a category all by ourselves."

I'd meant it as a joke, but his face gets serious. "We are, baby. I love you a little more every day. And I hope this place makes lots of happy memories for years to come."

"It will. I know it."

"Hey, did you just hear…?"

Even before he finishes the sentence, I hear Reina babble into the baby monitor. She'd slept through the transfer from the backpack to the crib. And then she'd stayed asleep long enough for Matteo and me to jump each other.

"I'll get her," Matteo says. "Just let me put on my pants." He slides out from under me, locates his boxers, and hops into them.

Feeling a little dazed, I cast around for my clothes. This is the perfect Saturday. "We should find Reina a bottle and then go outside for a while."

"Good plan," Matteo says, leaving the room.

I hear him through the baby monitor as he lifts her from the crib. "Hey, baby girl. How was your nap?"

She babbles a response.

I'm crossing the room to turn off the receiver when I hear Matteo tell her, "Look, I got a job for you. Can you give Mommy a present for me?"

I freeze. It had occurred to me that maybe Matteo might take this opportunity to ask me if…

Okay, stop it. I quickly shut off the monitor. I'm being ridiculous. This day is perfect, and I don't want to ruin it with weird expectations.

I head for the kitchen to pour some milk for my baby.

————

We head outside a half hour later. The sun is bright, and the air is warm and breezy enough to keep the bugs away. I love the sound the meadow grasses make when they rustle. The lupine is still in bloom, so there are purple flowers everywhere.

The grass closest to the house has been mowed, and I spread a blanket on the ground and set Reina in the middle of it. She doesn't want to be contained, though. She pushes her chubby hands against the ground and rises to her unsteady feet.

"That's it, baby girl," Matteo says. "You can go exploring."

She toddles to the edge of the blanket, and then hesitates. The first few times we set her in the grass, she didn't enjoy the sensation on her toes.

But this time—after a couple of cautious steps—she decides to chance it. She picks up her pace, toddling toward the meadow grasses where white moths flutter above the wildflowers.

"You go girl," Matteo calls encouragingly. "It's a big world out there."

"Aw. Look." We both grin as she lets out an excited little shriek. Luckily for the moths, she's not agile enough to catch them.

"Can you watch her for a sec?" Matteo asks. "I forgot something in the house."

My heart gives a weird kick, wondering what he's left inside. "Of course I can."

"Right back." He disappears inside, and I laze on the blanket, watching our child playing.

When he reappears about five minutes later, he's carrying a generously sized tray, which he sets onto the blanket. There's a bowl of strawberries, a bottle of French champagne, two flutes, and two wrapped gifts stacked on top of one another. They're about the size of a book, but squarer.

"Aren't you fancy. Champagne?" I say.

He gives me a slow smile. "I felt like celebrating."

I nudge his bare foot with my own. "Didn't we just do that?"

"Well, yeah. But there's always more celebrating to be done." He calls to Reina. "Baby girl! Daddy's got presents and straw-berries."

Daddy. My heart swells.

This year has been an amazing gift. In my heart, I don't really care what's in that oddly shaped box. I've got everything I need already.

Reina abandons the moths and toddles in our direction. Matteo gets up to meet her, taking the wrapped presents with him. "Can you give these to Mama, just like we talked about?"

My baby takes the gifts in two hands.

"Good girl. Give them to Mama so she can open them. There's something for each of you."

Reina looks up at me, thinks for a minute, and then toddles in my direction. But walking is tricky, so she trips on the edge of the blanket, and I have to catch her.

"Good save, Mama!" Matteo hoots.

I set Reina in my lap and tug on the ribbon that holds the two gifts together. The top one—the slightly smaller box—says *Reina* on the tag, and I open it first.

Inside, nestled in tissue paper, is a cute little tiara. "Daddy is taking this queen thing kind of far," I tease. But then I put it on her head, and it looks adorable.

Matteo is ready with his phone, taking pictures of us.

"Okay, you next!" he says.

I pick up the second, similar box and give it a little shake. Do I feel another tiara sliding around in there? "You didn't."

"Oh, I totally did!" he says gleefully. "Let's see it." He holds his phone ready. "And hurry, before Reina tosses hers down."

"Sure. I'll look good in a crown, anyway."

He laughs as I open the box and brush the tissue paper aside.

"Wow." My tiara is surprisingly weighty. It's not a plastic toy —it's made of silver, with a few rose quartz "jewels" dotting the metalwork.

That's a lot of effort for a joke, but I always knew Matteo was a good time. Quickly, so he can get his shot, I slide it on top of my head and smile at him. Reina hasn't shaken hers off yet, so this picture might be a keeper.

"Perfect!" He returns to the blanket and kneels down with us. Reina flings herself at him, because Daddy is her hero. He catches her automatically, hoisting her up against his chest, as if he'd been holding babies his whole life. "Hey, it looks like there's a loose part on yours. What's that?" He points at my tiara.

"Really? Where?" I lift it off my head, careful not to catch my hair. I examine the crown. Maybe I *should* add crowns to my accessory repertoire, because it's honestly pretty. But there's a metal loop dangling from…

It's not a loop. A jeweled ring is hanging precariously from one of the tiara's elaborate designs.

I gasp. It's a diamond solitaire.

"Baby," Matteo says with a husky voice. Still holding the baby, he kneels on one knee. "You told me two years ago that you wouldn't get married again. But I thought I'd ask anyway. Will you make me the happiest man in Vermont?"

"*Yes*," I say on another gasp. "I sure will." I carefully slip the ring onto my finger. "It even fits."

"I'm sneaky like that." He comes closer and folds me into a hug. And since he's got Reina, it's a group hug. "Logically, you realize, if we're married, you'll have to call me king now."

"Worth it," I choke out.

And he laughs.

★ THE END ★

ACKNOWLEDGMENTS

A special thank you to medical professionals Lindsey Waters and Caroline Moore, who advised me on Leila's delivery. All mistakes are my own!

Thank you to Melissa Frain for the brainstorming sessions! Working with you makes this job less lonely.

Printed in Great Britain
by Amazon

24646662R00179